The

Roger A. Price

Copyright © Roger A. Price 2024.

The right of Roger A. Price to be identified as the author of this work has been asserted by him in accordance with the Copyright, Designs and Patents Act, 1988.

First published in 2024 by Sharpe Books.

For David, this one is for you, son.

THE CABAL

Prologue

Sally came from a loving home and had attended a respectable school where she had done well. That was before she'd become entangled in this horror. Prior to meeting the boyfriend from hell. She no longer saw Danny - at her parents' insistence - but the damage was done. She'd *had* good friends; but now only had bad ones. If she could even call them friends. She knew her parents were worried sick, but never really stopped to think what it was doing to them. They had pleaded with her to seek treatment, but she'd reused. She was an adult now. It was her decision. But in truth she was too ashamed. She thought she could manage things herself. She couldn't.

It was not that she didn't care for her folks; she loved them dearly. It was just that whilst not of herself; *it* didn't allow her to care. *It* didn't care about anything other than *it*self. *It* was a self-serving, all-consuming evil.

It was Heroin. It knew no boundaries. It failed to respect any social divides. It tortured the body and crushed the spirit of those it controlled, until *it* was sated. And even when replete, the peace which drifted in was never allowed to replace its callous calling for long.

Sally was eighteen and weighed six stone. Her front teeth were starting to rot, and her breath bore the foul fetid fish aroma that heroin gave when smoked. Just because it could. It had made her heave at first, but now she didn't notice it. What she had noticed was the time lag between smoking the vapours and the effect. The pain involved in withdrawal - or the rattle, as it was called - was horrendous. It only ever grew worse until more heroin took it away. It used to be a buzz, a pleasure, a high, but now there was no joy to be had. All that heroin did was to remove the pain of withdrawal, so it could create greater suffering. It was the cruellest of mistresses.

Her dealer, the brute with the twisted face, had suggested that she inject instead of inhale. He said that the rush would be instant. It would hit the brain in a millisecond; take all the pain away before the needle left the arm. The beast with the perverted visage had even showed her how to do it. He gave her a syringe to use. She noted that it wasn't new, or clean, but she didn't care. Even Danny had warned her never to inject, knowing how impulsive she was. But he wasn't around anymore.

After twisted face left the squat, she rushed into the main room where other addicts were smoking their gear. She quickly removed her belt to use as a tourniquet. The others turned on her, hissed abuse at her. Even in this rat-infested hovel with others at the depths of depravity, a protocol existed; you never cranked up in company. Smoking the wicked substance was social, injecting it was not.

She muttered an apology and headed into the rear of the dilapidated terraced house, into what had once been a family kitchen in what Sally hoped had been a happy home. She prepared herself as quickly as she could, and as she did so, she saw a torn and forlorn looking teddy discarded in the corner. It reminded her of her childhood, of happier times. She scooped it up and laid it down next to her and then finished readying her syringe. She sat on the floor with her back up against a wall and stuck the needle into her arm. She depressed the plunger and felt a heady response immediately as the pain in her bones disappeared. She pulled the needle out and put the syringe down; she'd keep it to use again.

She picked up the tatty teddy bear as her eyelids took on weight. The toy reminded her of one her aunt and uncle had given her as a child. My God, she thought, what would her uncle make of her now if he knew she'd fallen backwards. The family shame. Her parents had told few of her addiction, even after she'd broken a thousand promises to them.

None of that mattered now as she held the teddy bear close to her, and the noxious potion gave her the temporary freedom which was only ever *its* gift to give. She smiled at the bear as her eyes closed fully, unable to hold their growing weight a moment longer.

It was the last thought she ever had.

THE CABAL

Chapter One

SEVERAL DAYS AGO.

Lancashire Chief Constable George Dawson stood by the window of his vacuous office looking out over his fiefdom. Today was a day of mixed emotions; good and bad. He tilted the window shade to keep the sun from blinding him as he stared out from the front of police headquarters. It was situated at Hutton on the outskirts of Preston which was one of England's newest cities and oldest towns. The headquarters was spacious, as was the training school in the distance. Built in 1973 just before the line dancers got busy with their pens and cut the Lancashire force by two thirds to create the new ones of Greater Manchester and Merseyside. Nevertheless, in the 2020s it was still one of the best forces in the land. A force he had had the privilege of serving for over thirty years. The last ten as its chief constable.

He looked at the lounge suit he was wearing and wondered if he should have put his uniform on; the opportunities to do so were now limited and he looked good in it. For a fifty-five-year-old he was as fit as he could be, and kept his weight to fifteen stone; about right for his 6-foot 3-inch frame. He could hardly chastise his officers over fitness if he were overweight. He turned back to face his huge mahogany desk, with its conference table jutting from it like a mini wedding reception set up. Beyond that were four Chesterfield armchairs around an occasional table. He'd miss his workplace and its grandeur that came with high office. As a youth he'd lived in flats that weren't a lot bigger.

Back at his desk, he ended his procrastinating and turned back to his half-written email. He re-read it to get back in its vibe before he continued:

Dear Mayor,

I write to you today in your position as Police and Crime Commissioner, and do so with a heavy heart. Having enjoyed working with you over recent years in our service of the great people of Lancashire, I must give you notice of my termination of service…

Dawson baulked at his use of the word termination and rewrote it to read: *I must give you notice of my intention to retire.*

He stopped as he mused over his words. *Heavy heart:* he decided to leave it. The Mayor would just assume his sadness at leaving was a normal reaction. But Dawson knew it was more than that. He had achieved many great things during his time and had had few regrets until recently. Two things bothered him: one was the career criminal Johnny Piper. He had spent years avoiding the police. And when they had managed to bring him to trial, he had always found a way to be acquitted. Not as an innocent man rightly freed, but through corrupt means.

Piper now stood charged with several serious crimes, and one might wonder if Dawson should stay around to see him convicted this time. But therein lay the route of his second botheration; Dawson was not convinced he was guilty this time. He knew others didn't care; Piper deserved all that was coming his way. Natural justice, some might say. But it concerned Dawson. 'If we bend the rules too far, we are in danger of becoming that which we despise,' was an adage he had often used. But the cause of Dawson's deeper disquiet was the fact that he had failed to stop it. He had tried unsuccessfully to hold those responsible to account. He knew who their leader was, and suspected what he was up to, but had failed to find a shred of evidence. This is why his heart was so heavy.

Well, one reason.

Some may think if they knew his concerns, that he was a quitter. Normally he was not, but the added complication of recent news had changed everything. He opened the top right drawer of his desk and looked down at the letter therein. He picked it up and read it again, not sure why, he knew it off by heart. 'Bastard,' he shouted as he put the missive back in its place and slammed the drawer shut.

The Cabal had won.

His door opened with a knock, and he knew it was his staff officer before he saw her. Chief Inspector Shirley Lancaster was the only one, apart from his deputy, who would enter without permission - and the dep was out of force today. She was bright and sharp, and only forty. A future chief if ever there was one. Chief Constable Lancaster of Lancashire! He smiled as he looked up and waved at her to confirm her entry.

'Who is a so and so, sir?' Shirley asked.

'No one, just cursing my typing skills,' he lied.

'Are you free for ten minutes?'

Dawson looked at his unfinished email and welcomed the distraction, 'Sure, what is it?'

'Detective Superintendent Peter Bartholomew is outside and wants a word.'

Another bastard, Dawson thought. His earlier use of the word had been quite prophetic. Bartholomew was the head of the force's Serious and Organised Crime Dept., and as far as Dawson was concerned, he was also the head of The Cabal. 'Show him in,' he said without inflection in his voice.

Bartholomew must have been listening at the door as he immediately entered. Dawson waved to one of the hard chairs around his conference table, rather than invite the man to sit in a Chesterfield. Shirley left as he took his seat and when the office door clicked shut, he asked Bartholomew what he wanted.

'Just to make sure that you are aware we have CPS permission to proceed against Piper on the conspiracy charges.'

Dawson already knew this so wondered what the real reason for the visit was. He nodded and asked, 'Anything else?'

'I thought you'd be more pleased, sir, if you don't mind me saying so.'

Impertinent tosser, Dawson thought. 'I am, anything that lawfully brings an end to Piper's reign will be a blessing for the communities of Lancashire. I'd be the first to congratulate you. But there is a big difference between being charged and being convicted.'

Bartholomew pulled a sideways smug expression in reply, as if it were a moot point he disagreed with. 'Are you confident, that there are no legal loopholes this time?'

Ignoring Dawson's question, Bartholomew asked his own, 'Interesting choice of words, chief constable?'

'Pardon?'

'You initially said "anything that *lawfully* brings an end to Piper's reign" as if we do things unlawfully over at Serious Crime.'

'I meant if we drop a legal clanger at court and he gets off, then its unlawful, or not a lawful conviction,' Dawson said, immediately cursing himself for his cravenness. He'd meant nothing of the sort, but it would serve no purpose to put Bartholomew on notice.

Bartholomew stood to leave, and then hesitated. Here comes the real reason for the visit.

'A little bird tells me that you are thinking of retiring?'

This took Dawson by surprise; he'd discussed this with no one other than Shirley. He searched his memory in that instance to try and recall where they had been at the time. The canteen, he remembered now. They must have been overheard. He decided to use the obvious surprise on his face to his advantage. 'You must know something that I or the Mayor do not.'

Bartholomew gave that smug smirk again and walked to the door. Dawson watched the small-framed man as he went and wondered if he'd carried that heavy chip on his shoulders for all his fifty years. At the door, Bartholomew turned and said, 'You could still join us, stay and be a force for good?'

This did stun Dawson, it was tantamount to an admission, but of course the remark was cleverly vague enough. Bartholomew hadn't said what he was suggesting he join, or indeed what being 'A force for good' meant. He decided to keep the man guessing, and replied, 'I'll think about it.'

Bartholomew nodded and left. Dawson was unsure if the man had believed him, but he knew the man's offer, even if genuine, was never an option. Not for him. He returned to his resignation email with renewed vigour, and five minutes later he speed-read it before pressing the 'send' button.

He sat back in his chair and felt a great pressure lift from him as he stretched and felt his neck crack. He still had a heavy heart, but a little bit of peace had now edged its way in.

THE CABAL

Chapter Two

Peter Bartholomew walked from the headquarters buildings towards the force's training school where his office was located. It was in a substantial new build where a cricket pavilion once stood, hence its nickname The Pavilion. Outside his office, Detective Superintendent Don Merson was waiting. Of similar age to Bartholomew with an even whiter complexion, but that's where the similarities ended. He was built like a rugby prop forward, with wild black bushy hair, and as head of the Covert Policing Dept. he was usually dressed casually. Today was no different. 'I see your suit is still at the cleaners,' Bartholomew joked as he neared.

'Not heard that one before.'

'You're keen.'

'Just give,' Merson said as he followed Bartholomew into his office.

'Take a seat while we wait for the others.'

'Sounds interesting.'

'I wouldn't get too excited.'

Merson looked as if he were about to reply when the door swung open and in walked Detective Superintendent Carol Winstanley, but before anyone could speak, she put her hand up to silence them as the phone in her hand started to ring. She listened and then said, 'Be there in five,' before ending the call. She turned to face Merson and Bartholomew, 'Four became three, and now it's just you two. I've been summonsed, I'll bell you later,' she said, and with that, Winstanley turned on her high heels and left.

Bartholomew watched her go; Carol was in her mid-forties but looked ten years younger, slim, and attractive, and single, which always surprised him. Merson broke his reverie before he started to have improper thoughts.

'Well, is it true, is the risk-averse tosser going?'

'He wouldn't confirm it, in fact he claimed I knew more than him.'

'So, he didn't actually deny it.'

'No, and I took a punt.'

'What do you mean?'

Bartholomew took a deep breath and told him what he'd said to the chief.

'You should have discussed that with us all beforehand.'

'I know.'

'What did he say?'

'Said he'd consider it.'

'Believe him?'

'Probably not.'

'Let's hope he is going after all.'

'It's a win, win,' Bartholomew said. 'If he stays and takes up our offer, we can control him. If he stays but doesn't, we can still control him now we've seen his private mail. And if he does go, we can run things as we see fit.'

'That would be a win, win, win, not just a win, win.'

'Always the joker. Anyway, no point in discussing it further until we've heard from the other two.'

'Granted, but what about Piper?'

'We'll do that together later, somewhere well away from here.'

***

Shirley Lancaster popped her head around Dawson's door and said, 'The deputy head of professional standards is here, sir.'

Dawson looked up from his desk and smiled, 'Send her in.'

The deputy head of professional standards oversaw all internal corruption investigations, whether covert, or overt. She was the effective SIO - senior investigating officer - of all such enquiries. Her DIs ran the jobs, but she was the strategic lead. She provided direction and decided which jobs they did and which they did not. Shirley held the door open, and Dawson could hear the deputy head's trademark heels before he saw her. He left his desk and headed towards the Chesterfields as Detective Superintendent Carol Winstanley entered the room.

'Take a seat, Carol,' he said, as he plonked himself down on one of the easy chairs.

THE CABAL

Winstanley sat opposite, and said, 'How can I help, sir?'

'It's sensitive.'

'Sure, all my work is.'

Dawson smiled, and said, 'I'd like you to revisit the investigation you did into Peter Bartholomew. I'm more convinced than ever that he is running an off-the-books corrupt agenda.'

Winstanley half-smiled awkwardly, and said, 'Have you any new evidence, because we couldn't find any last time.'

'I know that, and no, I haven't any new proof.'

'So, what makes you think he is actually corrupt?'

'Because half an hour ago he asked me to join him.'

Dawson could see the look of genuine shock on Winstanley's face, so he iterated the conversation he'd had with Bartholomew.

Winstanley didn't answer straight away, but after a few moments said, 'That question is vague and open to various interpretation.'

'I know that,' Dawson said, a little more firmly than he had intended. He added, more softly, 'But it is an indication, is it not? One that means your investigation into him is worth a revisit, to make sure we have not missed any investigative opportunities.'

'I suppose, yeah, I can do that.'

'That's all I ask.'

'What answer did you give him?'

'I said I'd think about it, to play along with him.'

'So, you wouldn't say yes?'

Dawson was surprised, had Winstanley, a woman he trusted utterly just asked him that.

'What I meant is, you could say yes to see what he would say next,' Winstanley quickly added.

He saw where she was coming from now. 'I hadn't thought of that, I could do, what do you recommend?'

'Just ask him what he meant, and let him answer you, but be careful not to incite him, just ask openly for him to explain exactly what he meant.'

'OK, you're the expert.'

'One other thing, do you have any idea who else is working with him?'

'Unfortunately, not, but I just know he can't be operating alone.'

'Fair enough, just give me half an hour and use the internal telephone system so we can monitor it without any legal hassles.'

'OK, and if he is prepared to openly invite me to join his little bent Cabal, what should I say?'

'Tell him that you are very interested, but need more time to consider it, after all, it's a big decision for you to make.'

Dawson nodded a reply and glanced at his watch, it was 10.30 a.m., 'Thirty minutes, at eleven?' he finished with.

'That's fine,' Winstanley said, before rising quickly and hurrying out of his office.

***

Bartholomew was in his office having just said goodbye to Merson a few minutes earlier, when his mobile phone rang, it was Carol Winstanley.

'You stupid tit,' she started with as he accepted the call.

'What?'

'Offering the chief to come on board.'

'It hasn't taken Merson long to bubble me.'

'Not Merson; the chief.'

'Is that what he wanted you for?'

'As well as asking me to reinvestigate you.'

'Just as well we have you on the team,' Bartholomew said, regaining some of his natural confidence.

'Don't get too cocky, you're still a tit.'

'Look, Carol, it was a spur of the moment thing, a punt, that's all.'

'A punt that has firmly arisen suspicions again.'

'Suspicions that can't be proved.'

'Thanks to me; but suspicions needlessly elevated, nonetheless. Just because he's a risk-shy tosser, as you like to point out, doesn't mean you have to be a risk-taking one.'

'Point taken,' he conceded. He'd buy her a drink or two later when they all met for a 'board meeting'.

'Anyway, I haven't got time to argue with you now, and nor have you.'

'What do you mean?' Bartholomew asked, and instinctively glanced at the clock on his office wall. It said ten forty-five.

'In fifteen minutes, our beloved chief constable is going to ring you and ask you what you meant by your earlier comment. And I'm going to tell you exactly what you are going to say.'

'OK, thanks.'

'And no deviations whatsoever. You could put us all in danger, and I'll know if you do.'

'OK, OK stay calm, but what do you mean, "I'll know if you do"?'

'Because I'll be listening in.'

Chapter Three

Peter Bartholomew was the first to arrive at The Higher Lock pub. As its name alluded to, it was situated by a canal at the end of a series of locks - which allowed the Leeds to Liverpool canal to continue its rural journey along the flatlands of West Lancashire. The pub was at a quiet hamlet near Ormskirk. The place was always half empty, if not more, which made it a perfect place to meet. That said, they always met around 7 o'clock and were usually away before eight. It probably filled up with locals after that. He knew what the others usually drank so took the liberty of ordering for them. He had just sat down at their usual table in a conservatory extension, when Merson wandered in.

He picked up his pint of real ale, a dark stout called The Naughty Witch, and thanked Bartholomew, who nodded as he sipped his pint of lager. He didn't get the real ale thing and found the array of stupid names that brewers gave them tedious. But Merson and Winstanley were fans. A minute later, Carol Winstanley joined them, and Bartholomew pointed at two pints of Naughty Witch.

'Two pints?' she asked.

'Bought you an extra one to apologise for earlier.'

'It's strong ale, not like that poncy lager you drink, and we are all driving,' she said.

'Who the hell is going to stop any of us to check if we've been drinking? Well, not in Lancashire, anyway.'

'If you had an accident, they'd have to bag you then,' Merson joined in with.

'Well don't have an accident, then. Or is your driving as bad as your dress sense,' Bartholomew said.

'Will you two stop comparing dicks,' Winstanley said, as they were then joined by the fourth member of their group. Chief Inspector Shirley Lancaster, the chief's staff officer.

Lancaster sat down and picked up her G&T. 'Sorry I'm late, the chief kept me behind again banging on about his final decision to go; he thinks everyone gives a toss.'

THE CABAL

A chorus of exclamation went up from Bartholomew and the other two. 'So, it is true?' he added.

'He's just told me that he's emailed the Mayor with his notice,' Lancaster said. 'And then he added his stupid joke, "one day you'll be Chief Constable Lancaster of Lancashire" for the hundredth time.'

'I once knew a sergeant Sargent,' Merson said.

'Shut up,' Winstanley said.

'Anyway, what did you tell him when he rang?' Merson asked Bartholomew.

'As per Carol's script, I said that I was thinking about setting up a crime reduction initiative, made it sound like it was a legit thing with our strategic partners, such as the County Council.'

'What did he say?' Merson asked.

'He said he knew exactly what I meant and that it wasn't that, said I was part of some "underground corrupt Cabal".'

'The very thought,' Merson said as the others laughed.

'It might have pushed him into going,' Lancaster added.

'Anyway, the king is dead, and we'll deal with the new king when we must. Whoever it is will be clueless as to what's going on.'

'We just need to keep it that way,' Lancaster said. 'And don't be a misogynist.'

'What?'

'Might be a queen,' she said.

'I'm not, it's just an expression.' Lancaster just raised her eyebrows at him. 'Back to the here and now,' Bartholomew continued with, and then gave the other three an update into the investigation of Johnny Piper. They all knew Piper by reputation, but only he and Merson had first-hand knowledge.

Bartholomew, because he oversaw the investigations into him, and Merson, because he managed surveillance, undercover and informants used as part of the investigations. Although only surveillance had proved fruitful. No undercover officer or snout had been able to get anywhere near Piper. He ran his gangster organisation like a Mafia; no outsiders involved, ever. This was always part of the problem using normal investigative techniques.

The other two knew that one of Piper's premises had been raided when surveillance had followed him there, and that the resultant search had uncovered a kilo of heroin in his desk drawer which had Piper's fingerprints and DNA on the handle.

'Pity we couldn't get his dabs on the drugs too,' Winstanley said.

'Christ, you don't want much,' Merson added.

'Just saying,' she answered.

'Well, we managed the next best thing: no one's prints or DNA.'

'As if the packaging had been wiped?' Lancaster said.

'Exactly,' Bartholomew said, 'which is totally believable. But we need more.'

'What have you got in mind?' Winstanley asked.

Bartholomew told them. As head of Serious Crime, he was in charge of the Drugs Profit Confiscation Fund - which was an account where monies awarded by the courts seized from drug dealers went. It was then spent on fighting drug-related crime. It really wound the villains up to see their dosh and assets used by the Police. He remembered as a young DS on the Drugs Squad; a court had ordered a drug dealer's car be given to them. So, they re-registered it and used it as a general enquiry vehicle. What fun they had, ensuring a daily drive past the drug dealer's house with a pomp on the horn and a cheery wave from them. Then Lancaster interrupted his memory blast.

'But I thought that The Proceeds of Crime Act superseded seizures made under the old Drugs Act?' she asked.

'It pretty much does,' Bartholomew said. And explained that the newer approach was to have an assets hearing after conviction to work out how much a drug dealer had benefitted from his crimes. The court then gave a timescale for the money to be paid back or the dealer would face added prison time. 'But it doesn't stop seizures under the old act, when the circumstances are right, and seizures that way come direct to police rather than the government.'

'So that got us thinking,' Merson joined in with. 'This often-forgotten fund is just sitting there, so we drew out some money on the pretence of buying new computers and kit for both Serious Crime and my dept.'

'We just need access to the exhibits, as in the recovered drugs, which is where you come in, Carol,' Bartholomew said.

'In what way?' Winstanley asked.

'The money is clean, having been drawn from the bank. We need you to sprinkle some particles from the recovered drugs over it.'

'And how do I do that?'

'Put the money in a large colander and then sprinkle some of the heroin over it. Catch the drugs and put them back in the evidence bag.'

'And then what?' Lancaster asked.

'Then we take the cash with us when we search Piper's home address and "find" it in his bedroom, suitcase or wherever,' Bartholomew said.

'And when the lab tests it, they will find the same drugs on the notes as we have already seized from his other premises,' Merson added.

'Brilliant,' Winstanley said.

'Love it,' Lancaster added. 'How much dosh is there?'

'Ten grand,' Bartholomew said.

'Wow,' Winstanley said. 'That's a lot of computers.'

'No one will ever know, especially as I run the fund,' Bartholomew added.

'That should bang his sentence right up,' Merson said.

All four burst out laughing, and then Lancaster asked, 'Where did the drugs actually come from?'

'I switched some out of the post-trial drugs store for brick dust; looks just the same,' Bartholomew said.

'Won't someone eventually notice?' Lancaster asked.

'It was an after-conviction exhibit on its way to the hospital to be incinerated. It's long gone,' Merson added.

All four laughed again.

'What do you want me to do?' Lancaster asked Bartholomew.

'Just keep a close eye on the chief.'

Chapter Four

Somebody once told Daniel Wright that it took a few months to get used to *not* being a copper. He thought it rubbish at the time but knew different now. It was like leaving a family you had been a part of for most of your adult life. He'd been gone three months and was still going through a transition. One minute you're a DI in charge of the Force Intelligence Unit, working God knows how many hours a week, making difficult and often no-win decisions. Then you are not. You are stuck at home doing nothing. It was like running full pelt into a wall. The first few weeks were great, like being on an extended holiday, but after that the dynamics started to change. Daniel was in his mid-fifties, average height, and weight and relatively fit. He was starting to need a purpose again. He was sat in the conservatory at home with the newspaper on his lap. He'd read the same paragraph several times and still had no idea what it said.

His wife Sue worked for the County Council and since the Covid-19 pandemic had worked from home. She thought she would be recalled into County Hall after life got back to normal, but had been given the option to continue homeworking. He didn't blame her, but it made being at home a little more difficult. The door opened, Sue walked in, and Daniel knew it was lunchtime without looking at his watch. He looked up and smiled, 'Busy morning?'

'Not too bad. What have you been up to?'

'The usual.'

'"It'll change our lives," you said.'

Daniel looked at her as she passed him to look out the window into the rear garden. 'What?'

'"Get a greenhouse and change our lives", you said.'

'You know how I exaggerate everything.'

'You bored with it already?'

He wasn't, and said so, it had been surprisingly good fun, and with little experience in growing anything but weeds, he was enjoying the whole 'Good Life' experience. But you can only watch tomatoes grow for so long before wondering what have you been reduced to, and what happens next?

'Get a hobby, or a job,' Sue suggested.

'I had a job, one I loved.'

'OK, don't go off on one again,' Sue said, and offered to make him a sandwich.

He thanked her and she left the room. Quick exit, but he couldn't blame her. He'd played that song too many times already. But it left him brooding once more. He hadn't known exactly when he had planned to retire from the force, but had known that he wasn't ready, until that fateful day four months ago.

He was head of the Lancashire Headquarters Force Intelligence Unit, and oversaw the creation of the serious crime intelligence packages. Detective Superintendent Bartholomew's team would investigate and turn them into prosecutions. He had great staff working with him - and across the Covert Policing Department - of which his unit was one leg. He also had a great working relationship with the DIs in charge of the other legs. The Surveillance Unit, The Dedicated Source Unit - which ran all the informants - and particularly with Jill James who ran Special Ops. - which was the undercover operatives' unit. Then one day he was sat at a senior managers' meeting and realised that all his contemporaries were either gone, or going. He suddenly grasped that he was the last person standing. But that said, he was still not ready to follow them, and felt he should give their replacements a chance. Even if they all seemed more interested in scoring points from each other in their attempts to impress the departmental superintendent the most. And there lay another problem. Detective Superintendent Don Merson was a weapons-grade tit. He thought he was a natural comic and insisted on dressing casual like the field operatives, in some vain attempt to be down with the kids.

Then the call came from the chief's office. He'd no problems with George Dawson per se, the man was a bit black and white, but honest with it. And Daniel knew he cared about the good folk of Lancashire. He wasn't too sure about his bat woman, though,

Shirley Lancaster; she was obsessively ambitious and not someone he would want to cross. The conversation had not been a long one. The chief was cutting two DIs from the department to reduce costs. Special Ops and the DSU were merging and one of the two new DIs - who replaced Jill - would run the amalgamated unit. The Surveillance Unit and Daniel's Intelligence Unit were also to merge, and become The Intelligence and Surveillance Unit. Whoever came up with these names should work in TV advertising.

But then came the real shock, the new DI at surveillance was to head up the new joint unit. The chief offered to find Daniel a uniform inspector's job working shifts at Preston. How kind of him. Now there is nothing wrong with being a uniform inspector, a particularly important job, Daniel knew. And if he was one, then Preston would be a top place to work, he was sure of that. But he wasn't one. Having spent his entire service as a detective, it was like asking a plumber of thirty years' experience to suddenly become a joiner. He could feel his anger rising as he replayed the scene in his mind. How he had sat in stunned silence looking into the sheepish eyes of the chief as he took in the double whammy facing him. Then in that instant he made the decision he knew they were after. 'After all these years of loyal service, you have stuck your fingers right up me,' he recalled saying.

'Now just a minute,' the chief had started to reply.

'No, you wait just a minute; this is ageism pure and simple. Plus, the new - younger - DI will cost a lot less. But what of loyalty, experience, and reward for great service. I can see it means nothing to you. Well, you've got what you wanted, I quit. And I will work my notice, just because I can. It will give me a month of pleasure in getting on your wick as often as possible.'

The chief didn't answer. He was speechless. Daniel reckoned no DI had ever spoken to him like that before. It was wrong and totally unprofessional, but out of the pain of having to retire at a time not of his choosing, he also felt a great release. For the next four weeks he could pretty much do and say as he pleased, to whom he pleased, and there was nothing they could do about it. As long as he kept it legal.

He stormed out of the chief's office without a further word being spoken, and knew where he was headed next. The office of his departmental head, Detective Superintendent Merson, the spineless coward whose decision it would have been to axe him. Done so that he could keep his young brown noser replacement, irrespective of ability. He hadn't even the courage or good grace to fire the bullet himself, but had pushed it upstairs for the chief to do. In the bitter horror of the moment, Daniel was at least going to enjoy the next ten minutes.

Then he returned to the here and now. He had to stop reliving this in his head. He had to start letting it go. Sue was right, he needed something to do, something to occupy his mind. The trouble was, what? He was only any good at what he'd spent the last thirty years doing. He'd have to start giving it some serious thought before he drove himself mad. But for now, he'd better go and water the tomatoes.

Chapter Five

Johnny Piper was known to some as The Fish, he had recently turned forty and yet the police had never convicted him. He'd been put on trial twice, and twice he'd been acquitted as the cases were little more than circumstantial and based on innuendo. At the second trial, the judge had ruled after the prosecution had laid their case, that the defendant had no case to answer. He hadn't even had to put his defence case forward before he'd walked free.

The judge made two significant comments afterwards; one, that circumstantial evidence was rarely of any value unless it had hard evidence to cling to, which was not the case here. And secondly, that this was the second time the defendant had been tried in Preston Crown Court in such weak circumstances. He even went as far as to add, that should the defendant seek civil redress for wilful prosecution, he would expect the defendant to have a high chance of success. He was to write to the Lancashire Chief Constable and warn him that reputation alone - rightly or wrongly - attributed, was not sufficient grounds to put an individual's liberty at peril. And that any further attempts to prosecute Mr Piper had better be on firmer grounds with a solid case to answer. He would also be writing to the North West's Senior Crown Prosecutor in a similar vein.

Piper had been ecstatic and if he hadn't known better, he would have thought that the judge had been bought, which of course he hadn't. No one had ever bought a judge. Not in the UK, not that he'd ever heard of. He headed straight from court on that day 18 months ago to a celebration at his office in the haulage company he headed up. The company was legit, but its cargo often was not. The second acquittal had firmly established his nickname.

The Fish. Head of Lancashire's most successful crime syndicate: except he wasn't.

Johnny Piper lived a lie, a very well-paid lie, but a lie, nonetheless. He ran the haulage side of things, but was only the figurehead. He was a large imposing figure but a jellybean at

THE CABAL

heart, he just didn't look it. This of course was part of his persona. His half-brother, Tommy Johnson on the other hand was the exact opposite. A small weasel of a man with no morals and no off switch, who was capable of sickening violence. He kept himself under the radar, but ran everything. It was a unique relationship, but one which paid great dividends. The thick cops kept trying to find evidence to prosecute Piper, while the real head stayed in the shadows. The police didn't even know that Johnson existed. Everything was going well - and after Piper's last acquittal and the resultant comments by the trial judge - everything was even easier.

That was until Piper had been arrested at work with a kilo of heroin in his office desk drawer; that hadn't been there thirty minutes before the police arrived. He'd been locked up, charged, and was stuck on remand in Preston Prison. He'd never been remanded before and was struggling to keep up his hard man persona. On the surface, every other con gave him a wide berth showing him undeserved respect, but inwardly, he was really struggling.

He walked towards the wing phone to call Tommy, but there was a queue which snaked double along the narrow corridor. Everyone turned to look as he approached; everyone abandoned the queue. The poor chap who was on the phone slammed the receiver down without saying goodbye to whomever he was talking. 'Sorry, boss, it's all yours,' he said as he scurried away. Piper rang Johnson's mobile which was picked up on the second ring. 'It's me,' he started with.

'Listen bro, just keep it sweet, don't forget the screws will be listening,' Johnson said.

'I know but look, you've got to get me out of this hellhole.'

'Man, it's only been 24 hours, chill a bit.'

'Tommy, I'm not you.'

'No one will touch Johnny Piper in there.'

'I know that, but it's just unbearable.'

'Careful what you say next, don't want to spoil your image.'

Piper took a breath to calm himself, and Johnson continued, 'Anyway, I have good news, the brief's done good. You have a bail app tomorrow at Preston Crown, and the brief is assured the case with come up before your saviour judge from last time.'

Piper felt the tension lift straightaway, 'How the hell did you manage that?'

'Just pot luck I guess, as you know, no one can control the court's listing,' Johnson said before bursting out laughing.

'Of course, pot luck.'

'With the huge surety we have to offer and your previous good record, the brief is confident he can get you bail. You may have to hand in your passport and sign in at the pig shop once a week, but by this time tomorrow we can have a face-to-face and work out what happened here. Though I have my suspicions. Just sit tight, it'll soon be over, bro,' Johnson said and then ended the call.

Piper put the receiver down and headed back to his cell. As he rounded the corner onto the wing, a throng of cons who had been waiting rushed past him toward the phone. As he reached his cell, he saw a prison officer waiting outside.

'Been looking for you, Piper. You've got a bail app in the morning, have yourself ready for 8 a.m.' the prison officer said.

'Will do, boss,' Piper answered with the fake respect that all cons used.

He walked into his cell and his cellmate, a guy called Dan said, 'Do you want me to do one?'

'No, you're alright, it'll be all yours from tomorrow,' he replied, before jumping onto his bunk. The sooner he got to sleep, the sooner the morning would come, but he knew that would be a tall order in this place. There was always someone shouting, yelling, crying, or calling for their mum, whatever the time of night. He lay back on his bunk and tried to relax. He mused over what Tommy had said about their impending 'face-to-face.' What *had* gone wrong? This was not supposed to happen. He knew the drugs could only have arrived in his desk drawer by one of two ways.

THE CABAL

Chapter Six

Daniel Wright was early to the coffee shop and chose a table by the window; force of habit. When he had been a police officer, coffee shops were a great place for clandestine meets with criminals who would always want a window seat so they could monitor outside. Being seen breaking bread with the filth could be bad for your health. But today's meet was with another retired DI, Jill James. She used to run the Special Operations Unit, and had herself been an undercover officer years ago. She had left covert policing a few months before Daniel, and he had missed her sage counsel. They often bounced off each other when faced with a ball-acher. He heard the door chime ring and looked up from the menu to see Jill stride in. She was a stunningly attractive woman in her fifties who didn't look a day over forty. She always reminded Daniel of the singer/songwriter Alexandra Burke; and had often told her so. She usually shrugged off his comparison; she never seemed to deal too well with compliments. Daniel stood to greet her and they pecked each other on the cheek before sitting down.

They usually met one a month if they could, and now having left the police, it was a meet he very much looked forward to. He knew Jill also had too much spare time, though she spent a fair amount of it caring for, and riding her horse. Sue was right, Daniel did need a hobby. 'Maybe I should learn to ride?' he said as Jill made herself comfortable and started to check out the chalk board opposite advertising the daily specials.

'You on a horse, Daniel, now I'd pay to see that.'

'Why so funny?'

'I don't know; you just don't look like a horsey person.'

'I used to ride a motorbike.'

'Horses only have one horsepower, you'd get bored.'

'I meant I'd have some balance, must help.'

'Look, if you are still serious when we meet next, I'll introduce you to Saffron, but only if I can video it,' she answered before laughing.

Daniel raised his eyebrows in mock defeat and then picked up the menu.

'Don't tell me, you'll be on tomato soup and a beef sandwich on brown?' Jill said.

'God, am I that predictable?'

'Yup.'

Jill ordered a Tuna wrap and a coffee, and Daniel did the same just to prove her wrong. Though he had been looking forward to tomato soup all morning; they made their own here and it was excellent, nice, and peppery.

The next half an hour flew by as they both chattered. Firstly, about how mundane their new lives were, and then about the job. The conversation always ended up about the job. It would start off light-hearted, full of anecdotes of cockups and funny instances from yesteryear, and then end up with how the force had gone downhill. Daniel tried not to. He didn't want to become a grizzled ex-cop who always thought anything new was bad, and that the old days were the best. He used to pity such people when he'd been a younger officer. And notwithstanding the circumstances of his leaving, he was determined not to fall into that trap. He decided to turn the conversation spotlight away from himself, and asked Jill, 'What made you decide it was time for you to go? I never did ask you.'

'Not too sure really, although I'd achieved pretty much all I had wanted to. Plus, running undercover operations was always a 24/7 job, and as much as I loved the buzz, it was becoming a bit of a drag sometimes.'

Daniel just nodded an understanding in reply.

'But if I had to put a finger on it, I was getting tired of all the managerial politics. And not wanting to set you off on a rant, it was more than just that. Perhaps a feeling that it was my time.'

'Time to do something else with your life?'

'You could say that. Just haven't worked out what exactly.'

'Makes two of us.'

Then the waiter appeared with the bill and Jill excused herself to go and powder her nose.

After checking the bill for a minute or two, Daniel beckoned the waiter back and gave it to him with a debit card, it would be his treat.

'It's OK, sir, the lady has already paid at the till,' the waiter said before moving off.

THE CABAL

The bugger, 'just off to powder my nose' indeed. He'd get her back next time. While he awaited Jill's return, Daniel busied himself watching the world outside drift by. The coffee shop was in the small village of Longton, about five miles out of Preston and only a couple of miles from both Jill's and his home, which made it ideal. It was on a quiet side road which was the entrance to a large residential area. A quiet location where not much happened.

Then Daniel saw a large red Transit van drive into the estate. He didn't see the driver, but something about the van rang dormant alarm bells. He tried to see the registered number, but all he got was that it had a K suffix. The van didn't look right in this environment. It jarred with his copper's sixth sense.

He heard Jill return before he saw her.

'What are you staring at?'

'Probably nothing,' he said, and then explained.

'Probably, just a tradesman, on a job on the estate,' she offered.

'Too shabby for that, looked like the sort of van those old bent roofers used to use, but without the ladders.'

'Dodgy tarmacers?'

'Could have been, and it was driving slowly.'

'Looking for a house number?'

'Possibly. Anyway, you did a sneaky one paying the bill.'

'This means, you also tried to pay it.'

'True, but I'm sure it was my turn.'

'Who's counting; you can pay next time.'

'Deal.' Then Daniel saw Jill look intently out of the window. He instinctively followed her gaze expecting to see the red van, but there was no traffic. Just a bloke in his thirties, casually dressed, walking past on the opposite side of the road. 'What's caught your attention?'

'See that geezer?' Jill asked whilst still staring out the window.

'Yeah.'

'I'm sure that's one of Johnny Piper's underlings.'

Now Daniel was interested and stared at the man, too. If he was one of Johnny Piper's gang, then he was well out of place in Longton. Daniel heard a diesel engine, just before he saw the red van pull up on its wrong side of the road. It covered where the underling was, and as he didn't appear beyond the van, he must have stopped. Daniel couldn't see the driver from this side and at this angle, but did note that the passenger side was empty. 'Come on, let's go and have a nosy, Daniel said and quickly pulled a fiver from his wallet and left it on the table. Jill was up and at the door before he'd put his tip down.

They were both outside in seconds, and every synapse in Daniel's ex-cop brain was now back online as adrenalin-fuelled awareness raced through his system. He could see by Jill's dour demeanour that she was also fully alert.

'Something's going down,' she said.

But before Daniel could answer, he heard raised voices from across the street. The van was about twenty metres away at a slight forward angle. 'Let's go have a look?' he said. Jill nodded and they both started to cross the road, but had to stop in the middle and wait as a single decker bus passed. As the bus cleared, Daniel could hear that the voices were raised further and animated. He struggled to decipher what was being said, apart from the many expletives which rang out loud and clear. He glanced at Jill as a tacit understanding passed between them and they both picked up their pace.

Daniel heard a side door on the van being slammed shut, and a second later the vehicle moved off at speed. Its diesel engine revving far higher than it needed to. There was no sign of the underling. The van reached a T junction with Liverpool Road in seconds, and didn't stop or slow as it slewed around the corner causing a car on the major road to hit the brakes. The van sped off in the direction of Preston and out of view. Daniel realised that his cop senses were not quite what they were; he had failed to look at the number plate. 'I didn't get the number, did you?'

'I looked, but the plate was caked in mud, all I got was KK at the end.'

'Fair enough, we'd better call this in quickly,' Daniel said as he reached in his pocket for his mobile phone.

THE CABAL

Chapter Seven

The underling's name was Billy Wellard, and his name had been the butt of many jokes throughout his life. He was well built and six feet tall, but was no match for Tommy Johnson, even though he dwarfed him physically. Johnson was 'officially' Johnny Piper's right hand man, but he realised that many - including Billy - knew that he was the true head of The North End Crew. Tommy or Toe Jo as he liked to be called, knew he was considered fierce and feared. He also knew he had to try and keep on the right side of losing it now. But that would depend on what Billy said next.

The North End Crew had started twenty years ago, born out of a bunch of street punks who loved robbing folk. They were all ardent Preston North End football club fans, and emanated from the Deepdale area of the city. Johnson and his half-brother Piper had been founder members. The gang was now involved in criminality on many levels and ran Central Lancashire. They owned a haulage firm that exported and imported goods to the EU; some legit, most not. It was how Billy had ended up working for them; he was a heavy goods vehicle driver.

They were currently in the gang's haulage warehouse, and Johnson had Billy tied up with his arms above his head, fixed to a steel beam. His feet were touching the floor, just. He looked very frightened, which was good. Johnson had given him a few slaps to warm him up, and when Billy had pleaded to know what was wrong, Johnson had not answered him. That had been half an hour ago.

Johnson re-entered the vacuous main hall of the depot with two of his men following on closely; it was they who had lifted Billy off the street in Longton. It was the last place Johnson would have thought to look for him. But one of his men had heard him bragging that he was giving a bored housewife one on the Franklands estate, there. He approached Billy who was sweating even though he could see his breath.

'What is it, Tommy? What have I supposed to have done? If you tell me, we can sort this out, I'm sure. It'll be a misunderstanding, a mistake,' Billy said.

Johnson noted he had called him Tommy, a good start; he'd already slapped him for calling him Toe Jo; only his friends and allies were allowed to use that moniker. 'This should be easy then,' Johnson said.

Billy didn't answer.

'Now's not the time to go all coy on me.'

'Sorry, I just don't understand.'

'Your tongue was pretty mobile when you were bragging to everyone about that posh totty you were shagging; no doubt she loved your active tongue.'

Again, Billy didn't answer.

Johnson pulled a flick knife from his pocket and extended the blade from its handle. He saw Billy's eyes widen in terror. 'You won't be so popular with her without a tongue, will you?'

Now Billy started to wriggle in a vain hope of loosening his restraints. Johnson retracted his knife's blade and put the weapon back in his pocket. He then spent the next few minutes pummelling Billy with his best jabs from the left and straight arm punches from the right. If only he'd kept up boxing when he'd been a kid, he'd no doubt be world champ by now; but a life of crime had got in the way.

When he'd finished, he stood back to catch his breath and admire his handiwork as Billy slumped forward; his face looked like a blood orange.

'That was just for starters, you'd be amazed how much worse it hurts once we elevate you off the ground. And use a baseball bat, which helps, too. And if that doesn't work, I'll get the knife back out. I half hope you hold out; it's been a while since I've shivved anyone.'

Billy spat bloodied phlegm out and spoke through gasps, 'I truly don't know what I've done... please, please just tell me... I beg you.'

'I usually like it to come from you, that way I know it's right. But I'll give you a couple of clues just in case you've shafted us more than once. And before you bleat, I'm not talking about skimming a bit off the top, although normally that too would be a hanging offence.' Johnson paused for effect and then added, 'you remember a couple of days ago, when Johnny got nicked?'

Billy nodded enthusiastically, which Johnson knew was a good sign; compliance was kicking in. 'And he was in his office when the filth arrived.'

More nods.

'Who had been in his office a short time earlier?'

'Me, yes, me. Johnny wanted to talk about an urgent run to Belgium, and could I do it.'

'Good we are making progress. And did Johnny leave you alone in his office?'

'No.'

Johnson took a step forward.

'I mean, yes.'

Johnson stood still.

'But he only went for a wee.'

'And where were you when the filth arrived?'

'I'd just left,' Billy said, and then a look of absolute horror ran across his face as he quickly added, 'Oh my God, you think I called them in. Look Tommy, I'm no grass, I never knew Johnny had gear in his desk, honest, you must believe me—'

Johnson silenced him with a wave of his hand. 'This isn't just about ratting Johnny out, as there was no gear in his drawer to rat on. Well, not put there by him. Unless?'

A silent impasse was quickly followed by a further look of terrified realisation on Billy's face. Johnson studied him intently, reading him.

'Dear Lord, you think I put it in the drawer, and then told the police. No, no way, Tommy, I'm not a drug dealer, where would I get heroin from, and why? I love working for Johnny.'

'Maybe one of our rivals got to you, made you do it? I could understand it if they threatened your family,' Johnson said, dropping his tone to as friendly a one as he could muster. 'Look, if they kidnapped your wife or something, then you're off the hook - literally - so long as you tell us who, and tell us now. I'll give you five minutes. But that's it, this is a onetime offer, never to be repeated,' Johnson said, and then turned on his heel without waiting for a reply. He walked to the other side of the hall where the site office was, and entered, closely followed by Goon One and Goon Two. He turned to face them, as they formed a triangle.

'If he 'fesses up, you're not going to let him get away with it, are you boss?' Goon One asked.

'Am I hell. We'll need to send a message. You two can have a go if you want, just make sure he can never be found.'

Both goons grinned and nodded.

Then Johnson's phone vibrated in his pocket. He pulled it out and smiled when his saw 'Bro Calling' on the screen. The bail app must have gone sweet; he pressed the green icon to accept the call.

THE CABAL

Chapter Eight

'You're late back, it must have been a good catch up with Jill,' Sue said, as Daniel arrived home.

'You won't believe what Jill and I witnessed,' Daniel said, still feeling some of the post incident rush as his adrenalin levels eased back. He had forgotten what that buzz felt like. And not just since leaving the job; truth be known, as head of an intelligence unit, he rarely got out operationally. But today was like being a street cop, or an operational detective all over again. He quickly told Sue what had happened, and how Jill and he had made written statements back in the café while it was all still fresh in their memories. As they'd finished, the attending detective from serious crime said that the van had seemingly disappeared into thin air. That meant that it hadn't gone too far. Probably in a lock-up somewhere. Jill had then been shown a bunch of digital photos of the known members of The North End Crew and had picked out a driver called Billy Wellard. He was an associate, not believed to be an actual member of the gang, but he was one of the haulage company's drivers. At least they now knew who they were looking for. The name didn't chime with Daniel. As far as he could remember, Billy Wellard had not been on the list of nominals in the original intelligence package. But that was before it had left his old unit and gone across to serious crime to carry out their investigations.

'Sounds like Jill did a great job,' Sue said.

'A lot better than me.'

'But you did clock it first; the whole thing could have passed unnoticed, otherwise. Don't do yourself down.'

Daniel smiled at her, kind of her to say so, and to be honest, she had a point. Sue smiled back, but held her smile longer than the exchange demanded.

'What?' Daniel asked.

'It's just that I've not seen you so alive since you were a DI; it's nice to see you so engaged.'

Daniel smiled back again, and said, 'Thanks, it's like a drug, I guess. Even being involved vicariously, as I was as a DI, it still gave a high. I suppose this transition into retirement is a bit like a detox; coming off the buzz so to speak.'

'Does that mean having slipped off the wagon you'll go back to being mega grumpy as opposed to just being a pain?'

They both burst out laughing, and Daniel guessed she had a further point, even in jest. But then he thought about the poor sod in the van, and hoped the man was OK. The thought brought him out of his self-indulgence and he felt a tad guilty. He hoped Wellard wasn't in too much peril - though it hadn't looked good from where he and Jill had been standing.

The sound of the doorbell broke his thoughts. Sue said she'd get it, she was nearer. Daniel took an easy chair in the rear living room of their house. They had two living rooms, one for Sue and all the soaps, and one for Daniel and all the car shows. He'd just sat down and picked up the TV remote when he heard multiple footsteps in the hall, followed by Sue appearing in the doorway.

'Someone to see you, Daniel,' she said and stepped aside to reveal Detective Superintendent Peter Bartholomew, head of serious crime. He had always got on with Peter professionally but had never warmed to him as a person. He was too full of himself, though it probably went with the rank. Someone had once said that to be a superintendent you had to be able to walk around with an imaginary ten-gallon hat on.

'I believe you've been busy, Daniel, can't leave it, eh? Once a cop and all that?' Bartholomew said.

Daniel grinned at the banter and waved towards a seat. Sue offered him a brew, but he declined as he wasn't staying long. Sue nodded and left them to it. 'Just in the right place at the right, time, Peter. But to be honest, you'd be better speaking to Jill, she saw more.'

'I will later, I just wanted to have a quick chat with you wearing your old intel head, and wondered if you had a view of what had happened? And I know I'm asking for nothing more than supposition.'

THE CABAL

Before Daniel answered him directly, he asked him for a quick update on Bartholomew's team's investigation; it might help put some context on the day's events.

After Bartholomew had finished, Daniel said, 'Bail, how did he manage that?'

'After the last collapsed trial, the odds were in his favour. Plus, he drew the same judge at the bail app.'

'How did that happen?'

'Your guess is as good as mine. But I've got a little surprise planned to wipe the smile from Johnny Piper's face, but I can't go into that.'

'I understand,' Daniel said, and he did. He was no longer in the circle of 'need to know.' He sighed inwardly; he did miss it sometimes. Then he gave Bartholomew's question some further consideration. From what he remembered of the intelligence package, or indeed from what was not in it - the sensitive stuff - he couldn't think of anything that helped. He guessed it was Daniel's previous access to the sensitive stuff, such as informants' reports etc. which was the real reason for the visit. Even at his rank and position, Bartholomew would be barred access to such information in-force.

'I probably should say, I couldn't possibly comment on my knowledge of the sensitive material one way or the other,' Daniel said.

'Which is what I thought, you'd say.'

'But to be honest, I can't actually think of anything which could help you, and that's the truth,' Daniel did say. And it was.

'OK, fair enough, worth a try,' Bartholomew said as he stood to leave. He looked in a hurry.

'But for what it's worth, I'd guess that it is some low-level dispute, one of their own who has been a bit naughty and might be in for a slap or two. Hopefully no worse. But I appreciate that you must assume the worst until you know otherwise.'

'I actually do know but can't go into it,' Bartholomew said.

'Oh OK. Good luck with your spoiler for Piper, I hope it works.'

'That's one thing you can be sure of. I'm looking forward to it,' Bartholomew said without elaborating, and hurried out the room to see himself out.

Daniel sat for a while chewing over the conversation and trying to fill in the blanks which of course he failed to do, so he reached for the TV remote.

THE CABAL

Chapter Nine

Bartholomew jumped behind the wheel of his BMW and turned to face Don Merson in the passenger seat. 'You should have come in and said hello, after all, he was one of your DIs.'

'We didn't part on the best of terms, as you know, so bad idea.'

'Well, you shouldn't have shafted him, then.'

'We all have to make difficult decisions; again, as you know.'

'Nothing to do with your affair with his replacement, then?'

'All rumour and supposition.'

Both men laughed together. 'Aye, course it is. And now he has got what he wanted; you are stymied should you ever want to move him,' Bartholomew added.

'Come on, just drive.'

Bartholomew grinned as he drove away from Daniel Wright's home and headed for Piper's. According to the observation post, which was in the back of a mocked-up SKY van, Piper arrived home about thirty minutes ago. Then two other blokes arrived carrying crates of beer and bottles of wine, he was clearly not planning to leave home anytime soon.

A twenty-five-minute drive later, Bartholomew pulled up on a car park behind Fulwood Fire and Rescue station, in the north end of Preston. They were using it as a forward RV. He left Merson in his motor and had a quick word with the officers amassed there. There was a full uniform search team headed up by a sergeant, and four DC's and one DS from his dept. The plan was to do a rapid entry, which the search warrant allowed for as they were looking for drugs. The DS who had obtained the warrant an hour earlier, said the magistrate had at first been reluctant, given the circumstances, and said she would take a very dim view if the information proved to be false and no drugs were found. The DS had assured her that the intelligence was A.1. - know to be true from a trusted source. This is where Detective Superintendent Don Merson had come in, and he'd done a good job. The report was a wonderful work of fiction, and Bartholomew had jibed that he should take up creative writing as a career when he left the police.

But it had done the trick. The DS applying for the warrant had believed it totally, which had made him an excellent witness in front of the magistrate. Bartholomew knew that they would not find any drugs, but that they would find the money. And courtesy of Carol Winstanley, it now had heroin particles all over it. The lab would quickly identify it as from the same batch of drugs already recovered and in the evidence chain.

Bartholomew sent the troops on their way and told the DS, a detective called Ron, to ring him as soon as the premises and its occupants were secure. Then he would join them. He climbed back into his car and waited. Piper lived in a plush detached house about a five-minute drive away on a tree-lined avenue called Cromwell Road. Most of the houses there were worth a substantial amount. 'You coming in with me?' Bartholomew asked Merson.

'As head of the department that gathers the intelligence, it's a big no, no to actually be seen at the business end, as you know,' he replied.

'I know that; firewalls and all that. But you didn't personally gather any of the intelligence, as you actually made it all up—'

'Yes alright, not out loud,' Merson interrupted.

'So, no problems then, and they won't know who you are, especially dressed like the oldest teenager in town,' Bartholomew added. He had never understood why Merson dressed down the way he did. He always thought that a quality suit helped carry the gravitas of the rank of detective super. 'And you'll miss the fun bit,' he added.

'OK, but let's not hang about.'

'Suits, me, quick in and out and then leave my staff to sort it,' Bartholomew said. Then he got the call from Ron. The house and its five occupants were all secure, but two had to be decked and cuffed as they had kicked off. They were not happy bunnies.

'Where is Piper?' Bartholomew asked.

'Sat at his desk in a study, with one of my DC's standing over him. The search team have just started in the other rooms, but we'd better find something, boss, he's threatening blue murder, and has already rung his brief to turn him out.'

'Be there in five; but keep the search team out of the study until I've spoken to him.'

THE CABAL

'Will do, boss.'

Bartholomew started his car engine and set off at pace. He was soon outside the des res and bounded upstairs to the first-floor study followed by Merson. They entered the office to find a red-faced Piper at his desk. He was on his phone. The DC stood over him shrugged an apology to Bartholomew, who nodded back. He knew they couldn't stop him doing anything normal during the search until he was under arrest, and that depended on what was found. Bartholomew quickly ascertained that when the DC had rushed into the room Piper had been stood behind his desk. The room itself had a lock on it, and Piper confirmed that only he had a key.

'Why's that,' Bartholomew asked, 'got something in here you don't want anyone to see?'

Piper ignored him.

Turning to the DC, Bartholomew asked, 'Have you searched, Piper?'

'No sir, the DS said to just guard him until you arrived.'

'Good man, but can you take him into his bedroom to afford him some privacy and then search him. We'll guard in here until the search team arrive.' The DC nodded and led Piper away. As he opened the office door, Bartholomew could hear shouts of 'clear' repeatedly from downstairs. He'd better move quickly. He checked the drawers in the desk and opened the only unlocked one and took the bundle of money from his inside pocket and was about to put it in the drawer when Merson, interrupted him.

'A desk drawer, twice? Might raise an eyebrow.'

Bartholomew nodded; he was right. Then something else caught his eye in the open drawer, but before he could look further, he heard footsteps on the stairs and knew time was short. Behind the desk was a floor to ceiling bookcase stuffed with books and ornaments, he quickly pulled three paperbacks out and stuffed the drug money into the space before replacing the books. The novels now stood proud, so he pulled the rest in that segment of shelf forward too, so as not to look obvious.

Voices on the corridor told him that the search team had gone to Piper's bedroom first, and were being told by the DC, to give them a minute. Bartholomew returned to the open drawer and to the shiny object which had caught his eye. It was a one-kilogram gold bar. The office electric light had reflected off it and initially grabbed his attention. He quickly picked it up and held it up to show Merson. It was surprisingly heavy for a relatively small item.

'What the hell are you doing?' Merson asked.

'Where are you taking Piper?' A voice from the landing said.

'We've done in here, now, we are going back to his office,' the DC replied.

Bartholomew and Merson looked at each other in a moment's stationary pause.

'Your prints will be all over that now,' Merson said.

'We'd better keep it then,' Bartholomew replied and swiftly put the bar in his inside coat pocket. The weight of it immediately pulled his jacket out of shape. He put his hand in his outer pocket to use the crook of his arm to support the bar in his sagging jacket. Make it look less noticeable.

'Peter, for God's sake, put it back,' Merson said, as the office door started to open.

Bartholomew quickly pushed the desk drawer shut using his knee just before the DC walked Piper back into the room.

'What are you doing behind my desk?' Piper asked.

'Just admiring your bookshelf,' Bartholomew replied as he made way for Piper to retake his seat. He then turned to face the DC, and said, 'Sounds like the search team will be in here in a minute, so we'll leave and give you some space.'

'Yes, sir,' the DC replied.

'Come on, Don,' Bartholomew said to Merson, but without looking at him. He rapidly left the room and took the stairs two at a time and was relieved to hear that Merson was following him. He was even more relieved to get out of the house and feel the cool refreshing easterly breeze on his face as he strode towards his BMW. A silent Merson closely followed him.

They both jumped in the car and Bartholomew sped off down Cromwell Road in the direction of Fulwood Barracks, the headquarters of the army in the Northwest of England. Neither man spoke for minutes which felt like an eternity to Bartholomew.

Then Merson did; 'I can't believe what I've just seen.'

'Spur of the moment decision.'

THE CABAL

'It's one thing fitting up Piper, who is public enemy number one, and deserves to be sorted, but this? Just theft, pure and simple.'

'Is it so different?'

'Of course, it is.'

'So why didn't you stop me?'

Merson didn't reply. Bartholomew knew he'd made a good point. Not that he would have expected Merson to intervene; one, he didn't have the guts, and two, he was already in it up to the guts he didn't have.

'I was just stunned,' Merson did eventually say.

'Look, Don, you say it's different, and perhaps it is on a higher moral ground. But you and I both know that the money used to buy this gold was dirty money.'

'Which the courts would have confiscated on conviction. A conviction that the drug money would guarantee.'

Bartholomew didn't answer.

'And remember we got in this to end Piper and his gang's reign, not to become bent, thieving crooks.'

'So, you won't want half of it, then?'

'I'll not blow you out, because as you are abundantly aware, I can't. But I want no part of it. It's all yours.'

'You sure? Must be worth between forty and fifty grand.' Bartholomew turned to look at Merson for the first time since he'd picked up the bar. He could see genuine surprise on his face. He didn't answer, so Bartholomew added, 'Last chance; fifty - fifty, and we keep shtum to the others.' He glanced at the road ahead, and then turned back to face Merson who nodded reluctantly. 'Yeah?' Bartholomew asked. He wanted to hear Merson agree out loud.

'OK, yeah, but this is a one off, no matter what else we may come across.'

'Deal,' Bartholomew said, and sighed with relief as a huge euphoria washed over him.

Chapter Ten

Since he'd taken his brother's call, Johnson had been pacing around the warehouse aimlessly; he punched Billy each time he passed him. How dare the filth hit Piper again, and as soon as he'd got bail, too. They couldn't even wait until the following day or so. It was a total piss take and the lead filth was making this all very personal as far as Johnson could see. It was the only explanation. And what the hell did they expect to find? Johnson knew that Piper's gaff was sweet; that was the whole point of having him as the figurehead running the legit haulage company. There was much more behind this; that, he was sure of. He paced over towards Billy and took out his flick knife and extended the blade. He held it close to Billy's face and told Goon One to hold his head still.

'No for God's sake, no,' Billy screamed.

Johnson pointed the knife towards Billy's left eye and said, 'If this is also your doing, I will torture you until you beg to be killed.'

'Please, Tommy, I've no idea what you are talking about.'

Johnson retracted the blade into its sheaf and nodded at the goon to let go of Billy's head. He needed to be patient. The first call from Piper was to alert him of the raid and that there was nothing to find, though they'd thought that last time. The warrant said drugs, and they both knew there were no drugs. And the scum who had planted drugs before was here hanging on a rope. After Piper had been nicked at the haulage office, Johnson had done a thorough search of Piper's gaff, just to be safe. There was nothing incriminating there, as it should be.

As soon as he'd spoken to Piper, who couldn't say too much as the filth was looking over his shoulder, Johnson rang their brief, a senior partner at Wales Solicitors. He told Johnson to sit tight until he rang back. He was on his way to the house to represent Piper during the search, which he immediately said was an abuse of process and that there would be hell to pay. The brief had no idea how true his last comment would be. Then Johnson's phone rang. He looked at the screen; it was the brief, again. He quickly accepted the call.

'It's Gerald Wales here, Mr. Johnson.'

'Is it over?'

'For now, but we will not let this matter rest.'

'Which outfit, was it?'

'The same as last time; Lancashire Serious and Organised Crime Dept.'

'Impure weasels.'

'Quite; and their commanding officer himself, no less, was there, I apparently missed him by minutes, which is a shame.'

'Is that usual?'

'Very unusual in my experience.'

'What's his name?'

'Detective Superintendent Peter Bartholomew.'

A name to remember, Johnson thought, and then asked, 'Is Johnny alright?'

'Well, there's the thing; they have arrested him. I'm about to head to the police station to continue his representation.'

'THEY'VE DONE WHAT?'

'I'm afraid so, Mr. Johnson.'

'On what grounds, the house was totally clean?'

'They found a large amount of cash hidden on the bookshelf in his office, and one officer made a comment that it was covered in a brown powdery substance.'

This time Johnson didn't shout, he did the opposite and fell silent as he rocked from the shock. He glanced at the hanging man as he computed what this all meant. Then asked, 'Are you sure they *found* it?' accentuating the word *found*.

'I was there when they unearthed it. And the look of utter shock on Johnny's face struck me as a hundred percent genuine.'

'Of course it would be genuine; this stinks. The dirty skunks.'

'Quite,' Wales said again before making his excuses and rushing off the phone to head to the police station.

Johnson leaned back until his neck cracked and then straightened up, aware that both his goons were watching him intently. Billy couldn't have planted the money, which means he didn't plant the drugs. But it was now obvious to Johnson who had. 'Cut him down,' he yelled at his goons, and as they did, he walked to the front of a bewildered Billy. 'You have my sincere apologies, Billy, I know now that it wasn't you, but you can surely see how it looked?'

Billy didn't answer, just nodded; he looked too thrilled to be free to risk saying the wrong thing now. 'But you can rest assured those responsible will pay an extra price for your inconvenience. There will be a couple of grand extra in your wages next month by way of compensation.'

Again, Billy just nodded. Johnson turned to the lead goon, 'Get him cleaned up, give him anything he wants to make him comfortable tonight, look after him.'

The lead goon nodded, and Johnson headed to the warehouse exit. If those filthy cops wanted a war, they could have one.

***

Piper was stood in a queue at the Preston Central Police Station custody suite waiting to be booked in by the arresting officer, DS something or other. He felt some relief at having his solicitor Gerald Wales with him from the off. But he was very afraid. He'd absolutely no idea where that money had come from, just as he'd had no idea where the heroin had come from the other day. But two finds, twice with him present, and in his private areas was bad, really bad. He didn't need seven years at law school to know that he was proper stuffed. But what he didn't know was who was responsible, and why? He never hurt anyone. All he did was run the haulage business. He knew that Johnson dealt with the loads, well the dodgy ones, like the drug runs or the gun shipments - but that didn't involve Piper upsetting anyone. If any other outfit had a beef with their gang, then surely it would be Johnson they'd come for. And why set them up in this way? There were rules of engagement, criminal ethics to be observed. If someone was gunning for them, then they would use guns, or other forms of violence and intimidation, not plant evidence on them. That was below the bar. As bad, if not worse than grassing.

THE CABAL

Chapter Eleven

Two days later Daniel was enjoying his mid-morning coffee in the rear lounge at home. He used to drink buckets of the stuff, but since retiring Sue managed his intake. So, his mid-morning brew was a treat to savour; then his mobile rang interrupting events. He was going to leave it until he saw who was calling, it was Jill James. He hadn't spoken to her since the incident with the red van, he'd better take the call. He put his cup of freshly ground Kenya coffee down, looking longingly at it as he picked up his phone from the chair arm. 'How's it going?' he started with.

'Just had an update from one of my old team.'

'Go on.'

'Apparently, Bartholomew's mob hit Piper as soon as he arrived home from the bail hearing.'

'That'll will have gone down well.'

'And they have re-arrested and charged him.'

'What with?'

'They found a wedge of money - so money laundering, as he can't or won't account for it. And the lab has said it has traces of heroin on the notes, and get this, they have matched the traces to the kilo seized on his first arrest.'

Wow, Bartholomew hadn't been kidding when he said he was on his way to spoil Piper's welcome home party. 'Well, any chance of bail now is gone; even in front of Judge Carmichael. All good stuff, let's hope they don't stop at Piper.'

'What do you mean?'

'The entire organised crime group need dismantling, if they stop at Piper, a new Piper will soon emerge. They need to take down everyone involved in The North End Crew.'

Jill agreed and said that Bartholomew must know this.

'What about the bloke we saw snatched?'

'Found safe and sound but refuses to make a complaint or say what happened, other than it was a misunderstanding.'

'Do the police believe him?'

'No, as his nose was upside down, but they can do little without his complaint or other evidence.'

With one eye on his cooling coffee, Daniel thanked Jill for the update and said he'd keep in touch. She took the hint and sent her love to Sue before ending the call.

Daniel mused over what Jill had told him as he finished his coffee, and then recalled his conversations with Bartholomew. He had seemed animated and greatly confident the other day when he said that he had a surprise for Piper: they must have a good source into his firm.

Then Sue joined him, must be lunchtime.

'Who was that?'

'Just Jill with an update,' he replied and then filled her in.

***

George Dawson was pleased that Johnny Piper was back in custody, and as this was his last day, it meant he could retire with some good news. He had avoided Peter Bartholomew as it would mean congratulating him; churlish and petty, he knew, but he couldn't stand the man. And as it was his last day as chief constable, then he would allow himself one act of unprofessionalism. He'd told his staff officer, Shirley Lancaster that he would be leaving at 12 noon and was disappointed that she was not there to see him off. It was 12.30 p.m. already, and he wasn't inclined to wait further. He had of course said goodbye to her earlier, when the senior command team had met him for a breakfast meeting. They had given him a lovely handmade crystal trophy with a touching inscription thereon. He had then officially handed over command to his deputy, whom he hoped would get his job. He'd given him his support the previous day when he'd had a farewell lunch with the Mayor.

He'd cleared his desk and handed in his warrant card and appointments to Shirley earlier, so planned to just leave without any further fanfare. He felt emotional as a compendium of competing feelings raced through him. End of an era and the beginning of another, he thought. And as for Lancashire Police, he was satisfied he was leaving it in good shape. At the last

THE CABAL

Home Office inspection, the force had been rated as outstanding; nice to go out on a high - and not a low - as many of his peers had suffered.

He was just about to close his email down for the last time, when he noticed one marked 'Urgent.' It was also marked 'Private and Confidential.' It was addressed to Detective Superintendent Carol Winstanley - head of anti-corruption at Professional Standards. He'd been cc-ed into it. It had been sent an hour earlier. He speed-read it before deleting it and then picked up his desk phone. The missive had been short and was from the senior scientist at the forensic lab. He had concerns about an exhibit in the R v Piper case. An amount of recovered cash had tested positive for heroin, and that heroin had matched a previous exhibit of seized drugs from the same defendant. No problem with that. But it was the amount of the traces on the money which concerned the senior scientist.

He was about to ring the scientist, a man called Jordan Cummings, but as the email was an hour old, he reckoned Carol had probably already done that, so he rang her instead.

Pleasantries, and all the best for the future platitudes over, he explained the reason for his call.

'You should be at home now cracking open the champagne, boss, not worrying about work stuff,' Carol said.

'Trust me, I will be shortly; do I need to ring the lab?'

'No, no, I've already done that,' Carol said, hurriedly.

'If you are busy, I'll call back if you want?'

'No, no problem,' she said, slower, 'I've already spoken to Cummings, it is nothing to worry about, it was just that the notes were quite heavily covered in the heroin powder. More so than they would have expected to find unless the cash had been accidentally dropped into a bag of the stuff. Probably a mistake by Piper or one of his gang.'

'I see.'

'But the subtext in the email is obvious.'

'Granted, which is why I promised Professor Cummings that I would take a personal look at it in order to rule out his concerns.'

'Well, glad to see that you are all over it and I appreciate you dealing with it yourself, just to show transparency.'

'Of course, no problem.'

'And do keep the dep updated, won't you?'

'Goes without saying.'

Dawson said his goodbyes and Winstanley again wished him all the best in his retirement. He put down the phone and turned off his computer. That was it; his last act as chief constable. Time to go home.

THE CABAL

Chapter Twelve

George Dawson hadn't wanted a big do when he retired from the police, and since that letter had landed the other day, he was more determined to keep it low key. He'd always thought that big lavish leaving dos were a thing of the past. And in any event, it was something that the junior ranks did. He wasn't being elitist in his thinking, but he did consider that there was a lot of vanity involved. He'd known many senior officers who'd put on big dos for only a handful of peers to turn up. How embarrassing must that be? He'd had lunch with the Mayor and the breakfast meeting with his senior officers - several of whom weren't present, he'd noticed - which only reinforced his view about leaving dos. And with all that done, all he wanted to do was spend a pleasant evening with Joan, his wife of thirty-two years, and his two grown up sons and their partners.

And a great evening he'd had too. It was the following day in the conservatory at home, he was enjoying the sunshine on his face through the open doors. He listened to the sound of birdsong from the garden. The number of times he'd sat in this very chair mulling over a stressful situation which needed an immediate response. And every time he'd done that, he'd never heard the birdsong. He reflected on things and being the man he was, he focused on his regrets rather than his many achievements.

Joan walked in and joined him. Also in her mid-fifties, she was as attractive as she'd always been, and could no doubt still fit into her wedding dress, if she were ever minded to try. He looked at her as she sat in the chair opposite. 'Sorry,' he said.

'For what?'

'For all the times I wasn't here over the years. For all the times you had to struggle with two kids on your own. For all the times we've had to cancel a holiday because work got in the way.'

'You don't have to apologise; I knew what I was taking on when I married you. And anyway, we are still relatively young, we have our health. It's our time now. We can do what we want, go where we want, whenever we want.'

Dawson smiled at his wife with all the warmth he could muster.

'So, stop this self-indulgent maudlin, and cheer up,' she said, grinning.

'You always did straighten me out.'

'So why the long face?'

'I was just contemplating my regrets.'

'Regrets?'

'Well, more about what I hadn't managed to finish.'

Joan, looked nonplussed, and rightly, so. Whilst chief he'd always been discrete at home, no pillow talk. But he was no longer chief and it felt liberating that he could confide more with Joan. So, he did. He told her of his dislike of Bartholomew, of how he suspected him of running a corrupt agenda, of which he could never prove. Of how the arrogant man had invited him 'to join *them*' proving that he had others working with him. When Dawson had finished, Joan sat back in her chair and he guessed she was putting her magistrate's head on. She was chair of Leyland Magistrates' Court, though she was planning to join Dawson in retirement very soon. Then she replied, 'What makes you suspect that whatever it is that Bartholomew is up to, is illegal?'

It was a good question. He knew what Bartholomew had said about the 'join us' remark relating to a coalition of public servants working together, but he explained to Joan about the many things that hadn't quite seemed right over the past few months.

'Who did the enquiry into him?'

'Carol Winstanley, head of Anti-Corruption at Professional Standards.'

'And you trust her?'

'Never had any grounds, not to.'

'That's not what I asked.'

Typical Joan, direct and to the point, maybe he should have discussed things with her long ago. One trouble with being chief constable was that rarely did anyone really challenge you. People told you what they thought you wanted to hear. Even when you gave them free reign not to. The only person he had to report to was the Mayor in his role as Police and Crime Commissioner, and then that was never on operational matters. Here at home, there was no rank structure. He pondered Joan's last question, and said, 'I trusted her, but didn't believe she was as capable as I would have liked.'

'You were the chief; you should have moved her.'

Dawson really wished he'd sought, Joan's counsel more often, but then realised in the same instant why he never had. Operational security aside, she was giving him a hard time. 'Believe me, even at my level, it's not easy to move a detective superintendent without a solid, evidence-based cause. Impressions and gut-feelings can easily be misconstrued as being personal, or worse, bullying or misogyny.'

It was now Joan's turn to consider before replying, but she eventually, said, 'We, as a society, have got ourselves in a bit of pickle. Scared to act out of good sense in case we are accused of doing so inappropriately; I get your difficulty.'

'As I said, I have no proof, though our last phone conversation jarred with me.'

'What was that?'

Dawson told her about the email from the lab and his subsequent phone call, and then added, 'She seemed in a hurry to appease me, even though she'd yet to look at the issue properly.'

'Maybe she was just busy?'

'Could have been.'

'Look, you trust your dep implicitly, I know that.'

Dawson did.

'And you told her to liaise with him.'

He had.

'So, leave it to him. You're now retired George, and it's time you took me out to lunch as you promised last night.'

'I was dead drunk last night.'

'You'll be dead now if you don't.'

They both laughed and the mood lifted. It had been good to chat it through with Joan, and her direct responses had helped clear his misgivings. And she was right; it was the dep's problem now. She stood up and Dawson followed her out the room.

They were soon at their favourite lunchtime pub-cum-restaurant in the village of Longton, situated about five miles south-west of Preston. As soon as one left the city you were in the sticks, which was why the village was so popular. The pub was reasonably busy, about half-full and they both treated themselves to fillet steaks. They cooked them perfectly here. Dawson liked his steaks rare, which elsewhere often meant medium-rare as far as Dawson was concerned. When he asked for rare, he wanted rare. 'Cut the horns off and wipe it's backside' was a joke he'd often used when ordering in the vain hope they would take notice. Here they did just that. When his steak arrived, he turned to Joan and had started to say another of his stock refrains: 'A well-trained vet could have this back on its feet in five minutes.' He got as far as 'vet' before Joan had silenced him. Fair enough, he needed some new one-liners.

'I bet you were never like this when you were chief.'

'Never,' he'd replied, 'I save the real me for you.'

'God help me,' she'd said and they'd both laughed.

He looked at Joan's steak which was well-done, as always. It was the one way of cooking a steak that everywhere seemed to do consistently. Well, in the UK that was. They'd once been on a weekend break to Paris where the chef had refused to cook her steak well-done. When Joan had insisted, he reluctantly agreed, but what came out of the kitchen was medium at best.

As Dawson considered these daft thoughts, he realised that he had started to relax; filling his head full of trivia. It made a nice change from more demanding issues. He was waiting for Joan to finish, but enjoying not feeling under any sort of time pressure. He glanced around and noticed Professor Jordan Cummings sat a table with three others. He'd no idea that the man lived local. Cummings saw him looking and nodded. Dawson pondered if Cummings thought him rude for not responding to his email yesterday. And as he thought this, he noticed Cummings get up and head to the gents. Dawson needed to go before they left so he followed him. He would explain whilst Joan finished her meal. He could see that she was nearly ready to go.

At the next urinal and pleasantries done, Dawson quickly thanked the professor for his email and explained that he'd spoken to Carol Winstanley. He repeated what she had told him. That she and the dep would look at his concerns as a matter of urgency. He also explained that yesterday had been his last day in office.

Cummings turned to face Dawson; his face full of concern. 'That's odd.'

'What is?'

'Carol Winstanley told me that there was no need to worry, no need for further investigation into my concerns.'

'Why would she say that?'

'Because she said that the money had been found in Piper's office as per the lab submission form, but found in a container which had clearly been used to contain drugs. That was her explanation for the over-contamination of the banknotes. And when I asked about the container, she said the cop searching had not recovered it at the time. And when sent back to get it, it had already been moved and probably destroyed. And as regrettable as this was, it didn't affect the primary evidence. We had the money with drugs on it, and the rest of the drugs from the earlier seizure.'

Dawson couldn't believe what he was hearing. Winstanley had lied. Fact, not superstition. 'That's not true.'

'How'd you mean?' Cummings asked as he made his way to the wash basins.

'Well, for a start, the money was found on its own on a bookshelf behind some paperbacks.'

'Now I am worried.'

Dawson joined him at the wash basins. 'It stinks, doesn't it? Look, I'll speak to the dep who is now acting chief and forward your concerns, he'll no doubt want to speak to you.'

'Thank you, George, I'd appreciate that. And sorry for bothering you on the first day of your retirement.'

'Not at all, it was me who interrupted you.'

'I'll try and keep an open mind until it's resolved.'

Dawson nodded and both men made their way back into the restaurant. Joan was waiting for Dawson at the exit, and just before Cummings headed back to his table, Dawson touched his arm to pause him. 'Just to put context on it, have you ever seen drug money with that much contamination before?'

'Had it been in a container full of drugs as Superintendent Winstanley stated, then it would explain it. But once removed, the excess powder would easily fall off leaving a fine particle layer almost invisible to the eye. But detectable to the touch.'

'I see.'

Then Cummings added, 'We often get money to examine which has been in the same environment as the drugs, on the same table as the commodity when it is weighed and bagged, or cut with additives, that kind of thing.'

'How much more was there on our exhibit compared to that?'

'Educated guess - which is provable by way of comparison from previous seizures and resultant analyses - I'd say many hundreds of times more.'

THE CABAL

Chapter Thirteen

Daniel had spent an hour in his greenhouse, and as relaxing as it had been thinning out his bedding plants and vegetable seedlings, he knew that sooner or later he would have to occupy his time with something far more constructive. Just not as demanding as he had been used to. There had to be a happy medium. He knew some officers who retired from the police in their fifties and were content to fill their time doing nothing, or playing golf, or whatever. But that would drive Daniel insane. Plus, as good as his DI's pension was, it was still a massive drop in income which he needed to supplement at some stage. Especially if Sue chose to work reduced hours so they could spend some quality time together. That would be a novelty. In fact, he was slightly trepidatious about it. Sounded daft, but over the many years they had been married, the amount of time spent together had been whatever it had been. Not much. Now, that would be multiplied many times. He just hoped they didn't end up bugging each other.

As if on cue, he glanced towards the back of the house and could see Sue waving from the kitchen window. He checked his watch, nearly time for lunch. But lunch today would be different. They were going out to dine as it was Ruby Tuesday. Daniel had lost both of his parents years ago and they still crossed his mind often. And when they did, he felt that tinge of sadness which always came in the bittersweet moment of recall. His father had been the last to go, and although they used to have heated political debates - which at the time used to wind him up - he would give anything to have a further one with him now. With or without a row attached.

Sue, on the other hand, had only lost her surviving parent, her mother, Ruby, three years ago, and it was still raw for her sometimes. Grief is a multi-faceted thing. As time goes by, one thinks one has moved on from a loss, and then out of nowhere you can get blindsided by the simplest of things. In Sue's case it was often shoes; every time she bought a new pair of shoes it brought back memories of her mother who had owned more than Imelda Marcos.

After the funeral Daniel had welcomed Sue to 'The Club.' And when she'd asked what he meant, he'd replied, 'The Old Farts' Orphan Club;' as they were now both parentless. He'd hoped the quip might make her smile, but it had the reverse effect. This made him feel guilty; obviously too soon for a gag. Not the first occasion he'd got his comic timing wrong.

Anyway, to repair the damage, he'd suggested that once a year they had a celebratory meal to commemorate all four of their parents. And to hold it on the first Tuesday after the anniversary of Ruby's passing as she was the last to go. Hence, Ruby Tuesday. Plus, they were both big fans of The Stones' early stuff, and all the 70s and 80s music.

Daniel made his way back into the house and ten minutes later was ready to join Sue. As neither of them had to rush back to work, they could both have a drink. She'd taken the afternoon off, which she usually did on Ruby Tuesday. And Daniel - who usually drove as he always had to be somewhere afterwards - was looking forward to having a proper drink too. Consequently, they decided to walk into Longton. Plus, it was a beautiful spring day. They hadn't booked a table, but didn't expect a problem on a weekday lunchtime. There were several pubs to choose from if the first one was busy.

A short walk later and they arrived at the first hostelry, the Golden Dragon, which had been taken over a couple of years ago and now concentrated on its food customers more than its ale-only drinkers.

'This one do?' Daniel asked. 'Doesn't look too busy through the window.'

'Sure, the reputation has really gone up since it changed hands,' Sue answered.

Daniel knew neither of them had been in since the change, and hoped they would now have the chance to get out more. 'Happy days, then,' he replied and started to head towards the door, closely followed by Sue.

THE CABAL

Daniel then came to an abrupt halt as he'd started to open the swing door to the pub. He let go of the handle and the door closed.

'What's up?' Sue asked.

Daniel turned around to face her, 'Let's try the White Ram instead?'

'Why, what have you seen?' Sue asked and then quickly added, 'It's not someone you've arrested, is it?'

Daniel noticed the look of worry across her face. 'Nothing like that, so don't panic.'

'Well, what then?'

'George Dawson, the chief constable is in there with who I presume is his wife.'

'So?'

'He's the man who ended my career, as you well know.'

'No, he's not, he was just the figurehead; it was your super Don Merson who ended your career.'

Daniel didn't reply, he knew she was technically correct, and he also knew he was being churlish.

'For God's sake, Daniel, let it go. Just ignore that he's there.'

'I know you're right, but I'd hate it if he came over all pally and chatty, not sure what I'd say, especially with a pint in me. Plus, I don't want to spoil our lunch, its Ruby's, and the others' Tuesday after all.'

'OK, you big baby, the White Ram it is. But if the food is crap, you're cooking tonight.'

'Deal,' Daniel said, and set off again before anyone noticed them.

Chapter Fourteen

'Don't keep telling me to calm down, I'm not paying you to tell me to calm down,' Johnson spat into his phone.

'Look, I understand your disquiet—' Gerald Wales, started to say.

'Disquiet, disquiet, who says disquiet? Drop your lawyer speak and talk proper.'

'We need to look at things through calmer eyes, is all I'm trying to say.'

'And another thing, why can't you get Johnny out like last time?'

'Believe me, I'm trying my best, but it's just got a lot harder, even if we were to gain an audience before Judge Carmichael again.'

'Audience, audience; there you go again. We're not going to the theatre,' Johnson said in frustration, as he paced up and down in front of Piper's desk.

'That's not exactly true, in court it is very much about performance sometimes rather than substance.'

'Yes, yes, whatever.'

'Where are you now?'

'I'm in Johnny's office.'

'At the haulage firm?'

'No, at his house. I'm looking at the bookshelf; there is no way even Johnny is daft enough to keep money there.'

'Quite.'

'And in any event, it's not illegal to have cash around the place, and what's it got to do with the drugs they claim they found at the haulage yard?'

'Normally, I would agree, but that's why I'm ringing you.'

Johnson plonked himself down in Piper's chair; he knew the imminent news would not be of the good variety. 'Go on,' he said wearily.

'We've just had some additional advance disclose served on us by the CPS,' Wales started.

THE CABAL

Johnson had to grit his teeth, why couldn't this man ever speak normally.

As if sensing his frustration, Wales quickly added, 'Additional evidence that the prosecution intend to use.'

'What additional evidence?'

'They have found particles of heroin on the seized money.'

'This just gets worse.'

'And worse still, I'm afraid.'

Johnson said nothing.

'They have linked the particles of heroin on the cash to the kilo they seized from Johnny's desk drawer at the yard.'

Johnson was stunned. This was turning into the mother and father of all set ups. The bent filth had really gone to town. For once he took Gerald's advice, and instead of exploding he calmed himself. This was serious and he needed a cooler head to think it all through.

After a long pause, the solicitor asked if he was still on the line. He said he was thinking. Wales said that as a matter of course they would seek their own examination of the drugs and money, and if the CPS refused, they'd get a judge to order it. But he expected the result to be the same.

'What else can we do in the short term?' Johnson asked.

'I'll be looking into the legal opportunities later and let you know of any options I can come up with. But it might help if you make a formal complaint.'

Johnson nearly laughed at the suggestion; coppers investigating coppers was never going to end well for them, and said so. Then Wales went to great length to explain how the new-ish Independent Office for Police Conduct worked, and even if they just supervised a complaint run by the police's professional standards department, they were, as the name says, independent.

'Depending on the severity, they can use their own investigators in isolation from the police,' Wales added.

'That's all well and good, but firstly, we have no evidence to back up our claims, and secondly, how do we know which cop is the bent one?'

Wales explained that the IOPC would be duty bound to revisit all the gathered evidence to look for anomalies. It would put pressure on the police knowing that they were being scrutinised. It would stop them coming up with any more surprises. Johnson shuddered at the thought of anything else; surely the bent swines had already done enough. But he could see the validity of Wales's point in making the complaint, and asked how best to do it.

'Either I can do it as Johnny's solicitor, or you could do it in person on his behalf. It needs to be done to a uniform inspector not involved in the case.'

'Won't they just tell me to sod off?'

'The uniform inspector won't, or else they'd be the one in trouble. So, to cover his or her back, they would fill in a special form outlining your complaint and send it to their professional standards. We can of course complain direct to the IOPC who will in first instance send the complaint to the force involved. This would normally be my suggested option, but in this case, I think it would serve our purpose to complain direct. Put them on notice quicker. But I would add that we tell them that a copy of our complaint has also been sent to the IOPC; just to make sure nothing goes missing.'

'Sounds like a plan,' Johnson said, as he started to feel better. The sheer fact that they were doing something gave him a boost. And it allayed his guilt a little. The whole point of using his half-brother Johnny was to have a clean skin as the North End Haulage Company's head. Allowing him to stay under the radar and run all the criminal side of the business. But when they had set it all up, they couldn't have envisaged the police would fit Piper up. Or try to take the whole crew down, if indeed, that was their intention. 'OK,' Johnson said, 'I'll do the complaint at Preston Central nick, if you do the IOPC thing. But it would be better if we had a name to accuse?'

'We do; Detective Superintendent Peter Bartholomew.'

'Of course. That's the pig who came to Johnny's house when they hit it.'

'And he was apparently at the yard when the drugs were found, too. I think it's highly unusual that a man of his rank turns out to attend search warrants being executed - twice.'

'Dead right, I've never known that, or heard of it before.'

THE CABAL

'Nor me, usually they're run by a sergeant or in exceptional circumstances, an inspector. They are specially trained to search and are usually in uniform and not involved in the actual investigation, well not one on this level.'

'And as he was in here with Johnny, just before the search filth found the dosh. It's got to be him who planted the stuff, it must be.'

'Whether it is, or not, will remain to be seen, but we should mention all this in our complaint. And in any event, he's the SIO of the investigation and the head of the unit doing it.'

Johnson thanked Wales, who said he would text him the bullet points to mention as a reference guide. He didn't need it, but it wouldn't hurt. He grabbed his coat and headed out to the red van he was using.

A short drive later, Johnson was sat in the enquiry area at the front desk at Preston's central nick. There were several people ahead of him in the queue, all sat in a row on metal chairs which were bolted to the floor. Taking up everybody's time was a fat woman at the enquiry desk moaning about this and bloody that. Johnson couldn't make out what her problem was; he just wished she'd hurry up. The police civilian counter clerk looked fed up. He almost felt sorry for her. Next in line was a guy with a cracking black eye. Johnson would have been proud to have been the inflictor. After him was a boy-girl, or it could have been a girl-boy. Johnson couldn't work out which way around they were. Not sure what their problem was, but they didn't look happy.

***

Peter Bartholomew had called into Preston nick to speak to the CPS just to make sure they were happy with everything in Johnny Piper's case. And they were. They were gearing up for his solicitor to try a further bail application, but he would need a change of circumstances to do so. They would scrutinise and challenge heavily should one happen. He then popped into the canteen for a coffee and saw Don Merson sat on his own. He nearly didn't recognise him as he was wearing a suit instead of his usual casualwear. He plonked himself down next to him. 'Who got you ready?'

'Ha, ha,' Merson replied.

'Not got a promotion board, have you? Can't have you making chief super before me.'

'Just been to Preston Crown to deliver a brown envelope to a sentencing judge. I'm just waiting for a lift back to headquarters.'

'Anyone I know being sentenced?'

'You know I can't tell you that.'

'Promise I won't tell.'

'All I can tell you is that he is a burglar called Billy.'

'Billy the burglar - yeah right.'

'He actually is called Billy.'

Bartholomew laughed and then asked, 'Do these brown envelopes actually work that well?'

'All depends on what's in them; as in how much help the individual has been to the police. In this case we have Billy who is up for burglary, but he solved an armed robbery, so he'll get a hefty reduction in sentence.'

'Is that why you are wearing a suit, so no other criminal would recognise you sneaking into the Judge's chamber?'

'You can try, but your wit will never match mine.'

Bartholomew shrugged and then said, 'I popped in for a brew, but can sack it and give you a lift to HQ if you want?'

'That's good. Could do with calling home on the way and get out of this suit, if that's OK? I'll make you a brew at ours, I've just got a new coffee machine, be better than the sludge they serve here.'

Bartholomew nodded and both men made their way down the stairs towards the front office. He was leading with Merson following closely behind. They exited through the police-only door into the front foyer. Bartholomew glanced at the members of the public sat waiting. One had a corker of a shiner. He was just standing up as a large woman stormed out looking less than thrilled.

The enquiry assistant was on her desk phone, and he heard her say, 'He's here now,' and she slammed the phone down whilst looking their way. 'Sir, sir, Mr. Bartholomew,' she shouted.

THE CABAL

Both Bartholomew and Merson looked at her and came to a halt.

'That was CPS, you left your briefcase in their office,' the enquiry assistant added.

Bartholomew was about to answer her when his mobile rang. He took it out of his pocket and looked at the screen, and then turned to face Merson. 'I'd better take this.'

Merson said, 'You take it, and I'll nip back and get your case if you like?'

'Cheers, Don,' Bartholomew said, and turned and put the phone to his ear as he strode out of the police station's front door.

***

Johnson was already studying the two suited men as they emerged through the 'Police-Only' door into the enquiry area. Obviously, detectives, not CPS, there was a difference. They just looked different; their body language was different. These were detectives, and looking by the superior quality of their suits, senior ones at that. He couldn't believe his luck when he then heard the enquiry clerk shout out the name Bartholomew. He watched intently as the two men spoke to each other, though he couldn't hear what they were saying. They separated and one strode out with his mobile ringing and the other went back inside. The latter must be Bartholomew. His interest was now firmly on the 'Police-Only' door, and five minutes later it opened again and the same detective came back through. But this time he was carrying the errant briefcase. And just in case he was in any doubt, Johnson noticed P and B in gold lettering on one corner of the reddish-brown leather case.

He took the man in as he walked right in front on him with the case; stocky, in his forties or fifties with wild bushy black hair and a prison shade of pallor. And even though he was wearing an expensive looking suit, he somehow looked scruffy in it. Johnson couldn't believe it; the formal complaint would have to wait. He was now in reconnaissance mode as he quickly gave up his seat to the next in the queue and shuffled out the police station following the man with the case.

Chapter Fifteen

'Yes, yes, I'm aware, thanks for the call though; my colleague has nipped back to your office for it, thanks,' Bartholomew said as he finished his call. His BMW was in a small car park near the front entrance to the nick. A short time later, Merson appeared with his case. He jumped into the front passenger seat and threw the case into the back. 'Thanks for that,' Bartholomew said as he started to reverse out of the parking space. He edged out slowly as his view was restricted; some idiot had parked their red Transit van behind, blocking his view. 'Bleeding van drivers,' he muttered.

'What about them?' Merson asked.

'All ignorant. They park where the hell they like, have no consideration for other road users, and they all think they are driving sports cars and not diesel vans.'

'Strong views.'

Bartholomew had to do a five-point turn to get his car facing the right way, and then drove out of the little car park and headed to the main compound gates. He checked his mirror instinctively before turning left onto Lancaster Road North, and could now see that the red van was manoeuvring on the car park. 'He's bloody moving now.'

'What?'

'The red van.'

'Probably watched you struggle before approaching his motor, just for fun,' Merson said, grinning.

'Wouldn't surprise me. Anyway, where do you live?' he asked Merson, who told him. It was off the main road in Penwortham, a suburb south of the city and on their route to HQ. It wouldn't be a huge detour. Once they were on the main drag through the city centre Bartholomew commented at how the last two days or so couldn't have gone much better. They at last had Johnny Piper by the jangly bits, and their annoying chief constable was no more.

'What about the other thing?' Merson asked.

THE CABAL

Bartholomew glanced at Merson to assess what he was talking about. 'If you mean *that?* Then I have already made a couple of calls and it's going to be worth at least forty; that's twenty each.' He noted that Merson looked uncomfortable, and added, 'Too late to change your mind now.'

'I know, I know.'

'And remember, not a word to the other two.'

'I know that, too. Anyway, when are we going to meet with Carol and Shirley?'

'We'll have to ring them and arrange a proper debrief somewhere, and soon.'

'That country pub again would be good.'

Bartholomew smiled and nodded as his mobile rang via the car's Bluetooth. It was his office chasing him; he should have been in a meeting ten minutes ago. Damn, he'd forgotten all about it. He told his secretary that he'd be ten minutes, so to break out the coffee and biscuits, and as he was chairing the meeting they'd have to wait. When he ended the call, he turned to Merson, 'Do you mind if we go straight back?'

'I need to get out of these clothes; this shirt collar is rubbing my neck.'

Should wear it more often, then, Bartholomew didn't say.

'If you can just drop me, I can get picked up from home.'

'OK, fair enough.'

***

Johnson realised that a big red van was not the most discrete vehicle to use to follow the BMW, but if they stayed on the main road, it wasn't too bad. He kept his distance as much as he could, but wasn't sure what would happen if they turned into a side road. He was expecting them to drive to the police HQ on the southern outskirts of Preston, where he would just have to sit and wait for the end of the day. Then his phone display lit up, 'Gerald Wales Calling', he took the call.

'Have you made your formal complaint yet?' Wales asked, with a discernible haste in his voice.

'Had to delay it, something else has cropped up, but I'll do it later or tomorrow, why?'

'Because you're going to need to add to it.'

'Christ, what else has happened?'

'When I spoke to you before, I was at the Prison waiting to see Johnny on a legal visit, just to check on him and see if there was anything he might be able to think of to help us get a bail app.'

'And now you've seen him.'

'Yep.'

'How's he bearing up?'

'Actually, a little better than last time.'

'That's good. What about the bail app?'

'I'm going to try, but don't hold your breath.'

'OK.'

'But that's not why I'm calling. This is the first time I've been able to talk to Johnny properly without someone lingering on the other side of a door, like at the police station.'

Just then a car in the next lane piped its horn and the driver gestured at Johnson about his use of his phone whilst driving. The guy got some swift gestures back and a tirade of abuse.

'Do you want me to call back?' Wales asked.

'No, no it's OK, but make it quick; I'm drawing attention to myself.'

'Johnny's girlfriend managed to get a quick visit with him while he was still at the police station. He asked her to check something, and he rang her just before my visit.'

Johnson didn't like the sound of this and told Wales to get to the point.

'Apparently, he had a gold bar in his desk drawer at home before the police raid, and now it's disappeared.'

Johnson nearly rear-ended the car in front as traffic came to halt at traffic lights. 'The dirty, thieving, bent swines. This is un-be-live-able.'

'Because interest rates are so bad, Johnny keeps buying gold bars as an investment. His broker had only just dropped it off minutes before the police arrived. He hadn't had chance to put it away in his safe.'

'It the safe, OK?'

THE CABAL

'Apparently so. It's hidden in the floor; the police don't know about it.'

'Neither did I; but thank God for small mercies.'

'Quite.'

'How much is the nicked bar worth?'

'Forty-five grand.'

'Those pigs will pay for this, ten times over.'

Then Wales launched into his 'don't do anything rash' warning speech, and Johnson had to dig deep to control what he said. It was easy to forget sometimes that he was talking to a brief and not one of his men. 'No, of course not, I'm not daft; it just makes me so angry.'

'I'll text you the broker's details so you can include them in your complaint, as will I. It'll be harder to ignore when we have a reputable witness like that.'

'Sure, got to go, just doing some business, I'll speak to you tomorrow,' Johnson said and then ended the call. He could now let his anger and other emotions come to the surface. He was white hot with temper. He couldn't remember a time when he'd been angrier. He accelerated and pulled in one car down from the BMW, there was no way he could afford to lose sight of it now.

Chapter Sixteen

George Dawson had spent the 24 hours since bumping into Jordan Cummings mulling over what he'd been told. He was considering what he should do. Carol Winstanley had lied to him about the drugs being found in a drug-drenched container, and not on a bookshelf. If she was in cahoots with Bartholomew, then no wonder her proactive investigations into him had come to nothing. The sheer thought that she could be part of the Cabal had shaken him to the core. He'd totally trusted her. Was his judgement that poor? Maybe he should have left years ago.

Joan wandered into the conservatory where Dawson was pretending to read the paper, and said, 'You look a treat; anyone would think your retirement had been cancelled.'

Dawson smiled at her, and for the second time in 24 hours - and thirty years - he confided in her and told her what Professor Cummings had said.

'Now, you do have a fact to base your suspicions on,' she said.

'What should I do about it?'

'It's not actually your problem anymore.'

'But I wouldn't be able to relax without dealing with it. It would haunt me.'

Joan didn't answer at first, she nodded with a knowing look on her face; she knew Dawson inside out. He waited, then she said, 'Ring the dep, it's his call now, and then tell Cummings that you have, and leave them to sort it out.'

'That's pretty much what I told Cummings that I'd do.'

'Well then, get to it, then perhaps you can shift that look from your face and we can go for a stroll in the sunshine,' she said, before turning and leaving the room.

As soon as he was alone, Dawson picked up his mobile. The dep - Bernard Darlington - was another who Dawson trusted; he just hoped he'd got that right. He had always found him supportive when he was the chief, not in an obsequious way, but an honest one. If he disagreed, he always did so constructively and with alternative suggestions - one of the few who did. And

THE CABAL

was always polite, Dawson really hoped he got the top job. Darlington picked up straight away, and pleasantries over, Dawson got down to business. After he had finished, there was a long pause before Darlington spoke; 'No offence, George, but I've heard all this before, I get it that you don't like Bartholomew, but it's time to move on.'

Dawson was shaken by Darlington's reply and the coldness in his tone which accompanied his words. 'But that aside, what is irrefutable is that Winstanley lied to me, and that Professor Cummings is genuinely concerned. I bumped into him yesterday and told him I'd ask you to liaise with him.'

'George, you are not the Chief Constable anymore. I am not your deputy, in fact, I'm Acting Chief as you know, so it's not for you to make arrangements on my behalf.'

'So, you are not going to oversee this?' Dawson asked, struggling to keep his tone mellow.

'Of course I will. But unlike you, I will not jump to conclusions, I'll let Carol Winstanley investigate it and await her report. Then I'll speak to Professor Cummings and take any appropriate action.'

'Look, I'm not trying to step on your toes, Bernard, but what Carol said just—'

'I've got to go George; I've got a police force to run, just leave things with me. And no need to call again, bye.'

Dawson was left staring at his disconnected phone; his uneasiness was deeper than ever.

He wandered into the kitchen and told Joan what had been said.

'Hasn't taken him long to get his feet firmly under your old desk,' she said.

'Is that all you think it is?'

'I'm sure of it, a bit rude, but yes. Reverse the roles, how would have felt with your old boss ringing to check on you after just one day?'

'But I wasn't criticising him, just wanted to make him aware.'

'Well, he probably took it that way, and in any event, you've made him aware, so let him do his job. Come on, grab your coat, there's a slight easterly breeze.'

'Do you think I should ring the Mayor?'

'For God's sake, George, you'll really upset him then. Do you want to ensure that he does nothing? Because that'll probably do it. Plus, the Mayor isn't involved in operational matters, as you have often recited.'

'OK, you're right, I guess,' Dawson said as he reached for his light windcheater. But he knew it would take more than Joan's wise words to appease him.

***

Johnson was forced to take over the running of the haulage firm in Johnny's absence and was sat at his desk. It was 24 hours after he'd first followed the BMW, and he was still just as angry about the gold bar. Even madder if that was possible. The BMW had turned into a residential housing estate in Penwortham, which was halfway between police HQ and Preston. Not what he'd anticipated. He'd thought they would head straight to the top cop shop. It had taken more self-control than Johnson knew he had, not to follow the car from the main road. But he knew his big red van would have stuck out more than a gold bar in a bent copper's back pocket. So, he'd let it run and parked up on the main road outside a Subway food outlet. Only a minute or so later, the BM had reappeared on the main drag and turned in the direction of the head pig farm. But as it waited at the junction, Johnson could see that the car was now minus its passenger, so he took his chance.

He darted down the road it had come out from but could see no sign of the briefcase carrying scumbag, who he now knew must be Bartholomew. It was a longish street with a side road fifty metres up on the left. Given the time the BM had been gone, the man must have gone into one of the houses soon after being dropped off, or had made it to the side road. Johnson knew he couldn't hang about so turned down the side road and trusted to fortune. He reckoned one drive through was OK and shouldn't draw any attention.

He was in luck, as soon as he turned into the side street, he saw the briefcase-carrying thief on his left walking down the driveway of a house. But curiously, now without his briefcase.

THE CABAL

But it was him. As Johnson passed, the man opened the front door and stepped inside; he noted the house number was forty-three. He drove on with a smile on his face.

Back in Johnny's office, he was grinning again as the office door opened and in walked Goon One and Goon Two. They were like Tweedle Dee and Tweedle Dumb. Both heavy set six footers with shaven heads and no necks. Bookends, or opposing walls of the same brick-built outhouse. They were both called Gary, just to further complicate things, which is why Johnson thought of them as Goon One and Goon Two. But that said, Goon One had a distinctive z-shaped scar on his right cheek which set him apart from Goon Two. It was an old injury caused by a nutter with a retractable bladed knife. It caused a lot of banter between them. Goon Two always teased his mate as being the ugly one, whereas Goon One said it made him look tougher. As far as Johnson was concerned, they were both ugly and as hard as each other. But he also knew that they were totally loyal, and not put on this planet to pass any exams. They had other skills. Goon One was the tallest of the pair but not by much. Johnson called him G to his face, to differentiate from Gary the slightly smaller of the two.

'G, you take the blue Vauxhall, and Gary, you take the silver Mondeo,' Johnson said.

Both Goons nodded.

'Don't take chances, stay out of sight, and move as soon as you feel you are drawing attention,' Johnson added.

Two more nods.

'You can keep going back and forth, if need be, just don't hang around too long at a time. The road's a sleepy one and not that long.'

'What then, boss?' G asked.

'I want to know all the comings and goings, if he lives alone, that sort of stuff. We need to send a message, and it needs to be done right, so no cockups.'

More nods.

'Once we know more, then we'll move it up to the next stage; which will be message-time,' Johnson said as he threw two sets of car keys across the desk. Each goon picked a set up, and then turned to leave in unison.

'Just one last thing, Johnson said, and both men turned back. 'Have we done the last of that dodgy batch?' Johnson knew that the last heroin they had banged out had had mixed reviews. It had been bashed up with the wrong bulking agents. They wouldn't be using that supplier again. Perversely, the stuff the cops planted had been top stuff. According to Wales, the police reckoned it was high quality and twice as strong as the norm. It almost surprised him that Bartholomew hadn't kept that to have dealt on his behalf, and just used poor stuff to fit Johnny up with. He wished he knew where it had originally come from; he could do business with them.

G with the scar, answered, 'Two ended up in hospital, and one didn't even get that far. So, I binned what was left.'

'Good, I'll let you boys get to it, now, cheers.'

Both Garys nodded and left.

THE CABAL

Chapter Seventeen

Dawson knew that he was about to break every police code imaginable. But he felt he had no option. He'd turned it over in his head a thousand times and felt the straitjacket of his retirement adding to his frustrations. He couldn't deal with the situation his chat with Professor Cummings had left him in. He couldn't direct others to do his bidding anymore, either. And he knew he would never get any peace by standing by and allowing an innocent man to go to prison. Even one as unsavoury as Johnny Piper. Whether thereafter, anything could ever be proved against Bartholomew and Winstanley, he'd no idea. He knew that was firmly out of his hands now, and in those of Bernard Darlington. He only hoped for Darlington's sake that he made the right call, or else his heady honeymoon period in the top chair would end before he knew it. Only to be replaced by the heavy monolith of responsibility that came with having nowhere else to go; it's where the buck truly stopped.

He could do little to influence that side of things, made only too plain by Darlington's attitude when he'd called him. But he could do something about the horrendous miscarriage of justice he feared was about to unravel. He just had to break ever copper's code to do so.

With a heavy heart he took up position in his favourite chair in the conservatory, the French doors were already open; he heard no birdsong as he picked up his phone and dialled.

After he outlined, albeit briefly, the reason for his call, the shocked recipient agreed to meet him straight away. He'd also agreed to meet on neutral ground at a coffee shop in Longton in forty-five minutes. He was clearly dropping everything, which Dawson thought was a good start. He decided to walk to the rendezvous; it would take about thirty minutes and give him chance to consider what he would say. He didn't tell Joan about his call, or his arranged meeting, he didn't want scrutinising until he'd done it. He just said he was meeting and old colleague for coffee and picked a name at random.

As Dawson approached the café frontage, he could see Gerald Wales already sat by the window table with a yellow pad already open next to a coffee pot. He joined him and ordered a flat white and got the preliminaries out of the way.

Straight to business, Wales said, 'I have to say I would have bet your pension against receiving such a call from you.'

'It's not one made easily, and if you double-cross me in blind pursuit of your client's nefarious needs, I'll spend my pension on discrediting you as much as I'm able.'

Ice shattered.

'I give you my word that whatever we say to each other here, stays here, and that whatever we jointly agree I can take forward, is all that I will act on.'

'Are you recording our conversation?'

'I am not,' Wales said and removed his smart phone from his pocket and turned it off with great theatrics before placing it on the table.

Dawson did the same, but without the fanfare. He knew that Wales could easily have a Dictaphone in his jacket, but could do no more than follow his own instincts. He'd feel his way in, a bit at a time, mentally redacting what he was to say. 'I suspect that one of the exhibits in the Piper case has been tampered with.'

Wales's didn't seem shocked, Dawson noted, and then he asked which one.

'I suspect that the recovered cash has had some of the drugs from the recovered kilo added to it. The custard may have been overegged to use a worn-out metaphor,' Dawson said and then sat back as his flat white arrived. He took a sip as Wales's appeared to be considering his own words with care.

'So, do you suspect my client is still guilty, notwithstanding that the evidence has been tampered with in order to ensure his finding of guilt, or do you suspect that he may actually be innocent?' Wales eventually asked.

'I'm not sure to be honest; but as he has been public enemy number one for a long time it could be either. But it's a slippery slope that needs flattening.'

THE CABAL

'Do you know who may have tampered with the money exhibit?'

Dawson obviously did, but without proof he was not prepared to say, so just shook his head.

'I see. Can I first thank you for your honesty, a rare commodity sometimes.'

Dawson didn't know if Wales was having a dig at the police in general or not, but decided to let it ride and just said, 'I don't need your thanks, just your honesty in dealing with it.' He hadn't meant to add the last part of the sentence, but it slipped out.

'OK, here goes; but you won't like what I am to say.'

Dawson just nodded for Wales to continue, but could not have expected what he was about to hear. It left him reeling. According to Wales, he believed that the tampered money had been planted, and that the kilo in Piper's office from which the inordinate amount of drug particles had come from, had also been planted.

'Have you any evidence of this?' Dawson asked, having got over the initial surprise.

'No, but Superintendent Bartholomew was present at both finds. I find it highly unusual for a man of his rank to have been present at both searches and at both finds, don't you?'

Dawson did, but didn't say so. He could almost believe it of him. And if he'd roped Winstanley into his little conspiracy of corruption, then no wonder her investigations into Bartholomew had always drawn a blank. It all made perfect sense.

Then Wales hit him with his trump card, and told him about a missing kilo gold bar.

'Are you absolutely sure of this, I mean, this adds a new depth to it all.'

Wales said that he was, that the dealer was a reputable witness who will say that he gave Piper the gold bar not thirty minutes prior to the raid, and watched him put it in the drawer from which it went missing.

'Granted, but that doesn't mean it was stolen by the police.'

'Just to be sure, I met the witness at the house; he had a full itinerary of all the gold that Piper had bought. It was all accounted for. And as no one left the house, or had access to Piper's office, there is no other explanation.'

'Hang on. What other gold, I'm not aware of any being found during the house search?'

Wales didn't answer straight away; Dawson could tell that it was his turn to wrestle with what to say next.

'OK; my turn to be honest; but in absolute confidence.'

'As we agreed, everything said stays here, unless we both agree it can leave,' Dawson said.

'OK, Piper keeps his gold in a hidden safe within the property. All his gold investments are in there, and all are accounted for. Had the police raided thirty minutes later, that missing gold bar would have been in the safe. Piper just didn't get chance to do it. And this information stays firmly in this café; I don't want any secondary searches at my client's home.'

'You have my word.'

'And guess who was in Johnny Piper's office leading up to the search of it?'

'I'm guessing Bartholomew?'

'You'd be guessing right.'

Dawson sat back to compute it all, it was worse than he'd imagined.

They ordered more coffee and talked asides for a minute, let the pressure ease. Then Dawson asked, 'I fully accept that Piper is probably innocent on this occasion, and I know we need to discuss what to do next. But it is ironic that he may be not guilty here, but has no doubt been guilty of many a crime for which he has always got away scot-free.'

'So, it doesn't matter what you catch him for, is that what you are saying?' Wales said, stiffening in his chair as he spoke.

'No of course, *I'm* not saying that, though others no doubt may do. I wouldn't be here if I subscribed to that way of thinking. I'm just pointing out the irony of the situation.'

'I'll let you into a secret; just to allay such thoughts,' Wales said, but was halted as the waiter brought their refills. Then he continued, 'Johnny Piper is not who you think he is.' He sat back to sip his hot coffee.

THE CABAL

'Well, as a defence lawyer, you would say that.'

'And I'm not what you think.'

Dawson wasn't sure what the latter meant, but asked Wales to clarify his former comment, first. Wales elaborated that Piper just ran the haulage business, that he was a 'clean skin' - to quote from the real strength behind the throne. Any criminal activities which the company is involved in will be at the behest of that strength from behind the chair. Which is why he passionately believes his client is innocent.

The shocks just kept coming. 'So, Johnny is just a front?'

'I believe so.'

'So, who is the real villain in charge?'

'That, you know I can't tell you. The fact that I have told you that there is someone operating under the radar, someone whom you are unaware of, is probably much further than I should have gone. I just wanted to convince you of Piper's innocence and the level to which he has been falsely accused.'

Dawson gave Wales a resigned nod.

'If you were to ever pass on even the hint that there is a secret number two who is really in charge, you must never say it came from me,' Wales said, and Dawson noted real concern in his voice.

He gave Wales his word again, but then pushed further. 'A lot of defence lawyers hide behind their profession's raison d'être to excuse what they do. Irrespective of what they are told by their clients, or what they believe of their clients' guilt. Many see it as their duty to help the guilty avoid justice.' Dawson fell short of asking the obvious question.

Wales pondered for a moment before he answered it anyway, 'I know the police tend to group us as all the same, but we are not. I am first and foremost an officer of the court, and my priority is seeking justice. Our codes tell us that we should not represent in court someone whom we believe to be guilty. I always remind my clients of this.'

'Before they tell you something you don't want to hear?'

Wales smiled and said, 'None of us like moral dilemmas.'

Wales then explained that he often had to befriend his clients' and their families in a way which went far beyond what he was ever comfortable with. How they started to treat him as their friend, when he often despised them as human beings. He just believed that all deserved representation and a fair trial of ones' peers under the law.

Dawson had never thought about it from this way around. 'When my detectives see your colleagues' cosying up to society's dregs, well, it looks bad.'

'I know, I get that, but it's just business. The most senior partners at the practice demand we do it,' Wales said, and then added, how he had been invited to birthday parties, christenings and get out of jail dos; all hideous. How one client wanted him to be a godparent to his kid, and how his own father, the lead partner, had tried to persuade him to do it until he threatened to quit. His father had only just backed down. It was fascinating for Dawson to see things through Wales's eyes, and it felt as if once he'd started, he couldn't stop. Dawson kept a dignified silence and resisted the opportunities to throw in negative quips. He did feel sorry for the man.

When he had finished, Dawson offered him his hand, and Wales took it. A bond of trust had been built.

'OK, what do we do about it?' Wales asked.

'Well, I came here today to warn you of a great injustice awaiting, but to be honest, you know far more than I, and I'm the one who has had his mind opened further. What I had intended to suggest was that you set your enquiry agents on the case. I was just aiming to point you in the right direction, but you are already there.'

'To be honest, my enquiry agents are little more than process servers. We need ex-detectives to work for us, but as you can imagine, getting an ex-cop to cross the divide would be like getting a Preston North End fan to name his child after a Blackburn Rovers player. Plus, I'm no real judge of detectives. I wouldn't know a good one from a bad one until it was too late.'

THE CABAL

Dawson thought for a moment, and then said, 'There is one retired detective I can think of: honest, decent, effective and I believe currently not doing much.'

'Would you approach him or her on my behalf, I'd pay them a generous wage.'

'Therein lies an issue. I had to fire the bullet retiring him four months ago on behalf of his super, so I am probably not the top of his Christmas card list. How to get him on board, I'm afraid, is down to you.'

'OK, who is he?'

'Ex-Detective Inspector Daniel Wright, I'll just dig his phone number out for you.'

Chapter Eighteen

Johnny Piper couldn't believe his bad luck. He couldn't believe that he was back in Preston prison so quickly, and according to what Wales had told him, with little chance of getting bail this time. He lay on his bunk contemplating the fast-moving events of the last few days. First, the drugs, then the money, and then the theft of his gold bar. He always knew that being the figure head of North End Haulage came with risks. And that he turned a blind eye to what really went on, and for that much he was morally guilty. But it afforded him a wealthy lifestyle in a nice house in a posh district of Preston. He'd been a greedy fool. He knew that Tommy - he refused to call him by the stupid name of Toe Jo - was as unpredictable as a Pitbull terrier, but with all the aggression. But they were blood after all; well, half-blood at least.

It was plain that with everything Tommy got involved in, the police must think it was all down to him; either directly or indirectly. But Wales reckoned that the detectives didn't know about Tommy, well, not as head of the North End Crew. Wales had said that they probably just thought of him as a local nutter. But Johnny knew he was far more astute than his rugged persona suggested. He was totally in his hands now. The last conversation he had had with him - via the wing phone – he had told Johnny just to keep his head down, wear his fake title, and leave the rest to Tommy. He'd been dying to ask him what exactly he planned to do, but knew that the screws could be listening in, so had kept it vague. He thought about asking Wales, but knew that as loyal as he was to the family as their retained brief, he was still a lawyer and according to Tommy, not to be trusted with anything dodgy. The man was unfortunately honest, which is what made him such a good advocate in front of the local judges.

There was nothing Johnny could do, so it was pointless to keep going over it; he was just tormenting himself. He lay back on his bunk and tried to relax. His pad mate was playing pool and had left the cell door open. All the clatter and noise flooded in;

THE CABAL

Johnny was about to heave himself off his bed to close the door when it suddenly went dark. A huge man, who he didn't know was stood in the doorway facing in. Johnny could see that he had a couple of men stood on his shoulders.

'Don't believe we've been introduced,' Johnny said as he realised who he was addressing. It was a vast lump of muscle named Big Simmo. He'd been shipped in from Stangeways jail in Manchester the previous day. A local nutter who was no doubt pleased to be back in Preston.

'We're about to be,' Big Simmo said.

Johnny sat up straight; he didn't like the tone in Big Simmo's voice.

'This is what your mongrel of a half-brother did to me before I got sentenced,' Big Simmo said as he pointed to his face.

It was only then that Johnny realised that the man was blind in one eye. His left eyelid was stitched shut. 'Look mate, any beef you have with Tommy, is between you and him.'

'True.'

'So, if you don't mind, let's have a bit of respect,' Johnny said with all the gusto he could marshal. His insides were turning, but he knew he had to 'wear his fake title' as Tommy had told him.

'I don't respect pussies.'

'You obviously know who I am, so you know I'm no pussy. So back off with the insults,' Tommy said as he slid off his bunk and stood up. Big Simmo had walked into the cell a foot or two, uninvited: which was an intrusion. An insult, a lack of reverence. He noticed that the two grunts behind Big Simmo had stayed in the doorway, they didn't look as sure of themselves. 'Take your issue up with Tommy, not me. I'll be sure and tell him that you feel wronged by him. But until you both meet again; I suggest that we show each other some respect.'

'I know it's all bull, all front; Tommy's the top dog in your outfit. I mean, look at you?'

'Last chance; you're pushing it.'

'Not so bold without an army around you.'

Johnny looked over Big Simmo's shoulder and cocked his head as he did so.

Big Simmo took the hint and told his two underlings to scram. They both looked mightily relieved to be stood down and turned to leave. Big Simmo added, 'Just keep nicks and keep the landing clear. Shout "turd" if any screws come near.' They both nodded and shot off out of view.

Johnny was relieved to reduce the odds to one-to-one; but knew he was still hopelessly outgunned. He considered dropping the act and offering the man money; he knew it would shatter his façade and make him liable to all sorts of attacks. And he would no doubt become Big Simmo's bitch, too. But humiliation might be better than a kicking.

'It's just you and me now, and I need to send your half-brother a message; a hint at what will be waiting for him when I eventually get out of here.'

Johnny was about to launch his plan B when Big Simmo's next words froze him to the spot.

'An eye for an eye,' he said, just before he launched himself at Johnny.

THE CABAL

Chapter Nineteen

Daniel Wright was sat in 'his' sitting room enjoying an old episode of Top Gear when his mobile rang. He looked at the screen but didn't recognise the number calling, other than it was a Preston dialling code. The days of having to slavishly answer his phone were over. Generally, now if he didn't know who was calling, he'd leave it. If it was important, they'd leave a message. Just one of the freedoms most people took for granted, of which he'd been enjoying immensely since he'd left the force. He turned his attention back to the telly when his phone tinged to announce that a voicemail had been left. He groaned as he realised he'd better listen to it, so did. But the message was unusual to say the least. It was from a solicitor called Gerald Wales who worked for a firm in town which usually represented all the dregs. This one said he needed to talk to Daniel about his client - Johnny Piper. Now his interest was piqued. As he was considering whether to call Wales back, his phone rang again, same number. He answered it.

Daniel was stunned to silence at what Wales had to say and allege, and if that wasn't enough, he then tried to offer him money to help prove his wild conspiracy theories. When he'd eventually finished, Daniel asked where he had got his private mobile number.

'Your ex-chief, George Dawson gave it me, he couldn't recommend you enough,' Wales said.

Initially, Daniel thought he had heard wrong, but as the words took root, he felt utterly flabbergasted. Why would Dawson recommend Daniel to try and get the likes of Johnny Piper off. Especially as it had been Daniel's old unit that put Piper up to be looked at in the first place. It didn't make sense. And why had Dawson had gone over to the dark side suddenly, that made even less sense. And why did Dawson recommend Daniel. The man had ended his career. 'If I didn't know better, I'd guess that this is some sort of major league piss-take.'

'I can ensure you that it is not, and all is not what you think it is. If you would just meet me for coffee and give me ten minutes to explain further, I'm sure it would then all make sense. If you then decided to walk away, fine, I'd respect your decision.'

'"Respect my decision," that's bleeding good of you.'

'There's a nice coffee shop in Longton, I could meet you there tomorrow? Any time to suit you?'

'Actually, I'm OK for coffee, and tomorrow I will be mainly washing my hair. The answer's no, Mr Wales. And please don't call this number again,' he said and ended the call. 'Sue,' he shouted, 'you won't believe what's just happened.'

***

As usual, Bartholomew arrived at The Higher Lock pub first. If he didn't know better, he'd believe that the others hid until he'd landed and got the drinks in. This time he only bought half pints of Naughty Witch and a single G&T but a full pint of lager for himself; they'd get the message. Once they were all there and settled, they all quickly went through where they were up to. Then Shirley Lancaster surprised Bartholomew with what she said next.

'If we have finally nailed Piper, then should we carry on taking risks? Do we need to?'

'It's not over until he is convicted,' Bartholomew said, noting silence from the other two.

'But there is clearly no way out it for him now. Plus, I'm a little superfluous to the group now that Dawson has gone,' she replied.

'Granted, but we don't know who the new chief will be yet, or what his or her policies will be. If the new chief is another risk averse tosser who is happy to let the likes of Piper run riot, we may need to do it all again,' Bartholomew said.

Shirley didn't respond to what he had just said, but she looked far from convinced.

Then Carol Winstanley waded in, 'I must admit I nearly had a heart attack sorting out the money exhibit, especially when I had to appease the lead scientist.'

THE CABAL

'How are we with that?' Bartholomew asked.

'I'm happy it's all sorted now, but it gave me heartburn I can tell you. And to add to what Shirley has just said, my original responsibility here was to watch your back, Peter, which, as you know, I have done explicitly. Now Dawson has gone, no one is asking for you to be investigated, so I'm becoming redundant to the cause, too.'

Bartholomew sat back in his chair; it was obvious to him that the two women had had a conversation. 'Look, I know we all came together for a common purpose; the removal of Johnny Piper and the destruction of the North End Crew, but there is more to do,' he said.

'How do you mean?' Merson chipped in.

'OK, he was the top man, but the rest of his gang need toppling; the whole organised crime group need destroying.'

'But you always said if we removed Piper, the rest of the gang would implode?' Winstanley said.

She was the same rank as Bartholomew, but she was in professional standards for a reason as far as he was concerned, and that was because she was a rubbish detective. He breathed in and gave himself a moment, but before he could answer her, Shirley turned to face Merson and spoke.

'Do we have any actionable intelligence suggesting other gang members are active, or taking control, or able to take over in Piper's absence?'

Merson shook his head, and said, 'To be honest, since DI Daniel Wright left, we have had little about anything, not least about the North End Crew. I reckon they will all scatter, not that we know much about who Piper has grafting for him.'

'Christ, not you, too,' Bartholomew said.

'Look, Peter, we all came together born out of much frustration in our inability to pin anything on Johnny Piper; that was our objective,' Merson started.

'Main objective,' Bartholomew spat.

'Only objective,' Winstanley added.

'And we have achieved that, not least by all your efforts, but also with the superb support from Shirley and Carol. So why push our luck when the job is done?' Merson asked.

Bartholomew didn't answer straight away; he took a moment to gather his thoughts. These three were ganging up on him. It was a bleeding conspiracy against him. But he knew now was not the time to lose his rag. 'OK, OK, when the job *is* done, then I might agree with you, but it is far from done. You all think it is, but it isn't.'

All three looked nonplussed. Bartholomew added, 'OK, look, I have it on good authority that Piper is not actually the head of the criminal organisation. He runs the haulage company, and no doubt knows a lot of what goes on, but he is not in charge as he purports to be. This is why we have always failed to find enough evidence against him. There is someone else behind Piper who is really running things and until we flush him or her out, and remove them, our core objective is not complete.'

The other three all sat back in silence, all looked stunned. Merson spoke first.

'I've never heard of or seen any intelligence which has even hinted at someone else being in charge.'

'That's because you run a shoddy department, gathering poor info about car thieves and the like when you should be focused on serious crime. The only decent manager you had was Daniel Wright, but you binned him off so you could shoehorn your boyfriend into his place,' Bartholomew said, immediately regretting his defensive outburst; especially the last bit. Merson looked wide-eyed and shell shocked. Bartholomew quickly jumped in to try and repair the damage. 'Sorry, mate, I shouldn't have said all that, lost my rag, I didn't mean it.'

Merson didn't reply; he just glared at Bartholomew, who noticed the two girls exchanging a look.

Winstanley spoke next, 'Putting your nasty little outburst to one side for a second,' she started, and then raised her hand with a smile towards Merson who looked like he had recovered his voice, or was about to. 'What you are now saying is that Piper is not the man in charge?'

THE CABAL

'Exactly,' Bartholomew said.

'And his removal was only ever intended to flush out some mysterious crime lord that no one has hitherto heard of?'

'Yes, so you can see why we can't give up now?' Bartholomew said.

'Even Don Merson's department with all its resources in terms of undercover operatives and informants - shoddy or otherwise - have never heard of this elusive crime lord.'

'Well, I guess not, but that's not really a reflection on—'

Merson interrupted, his voice a seething whisper, 'Where have *you* come by this information?'

'Well, I can't er say, er, you know how it is?'

'A good point, Don, but what I'm leading up to is the realisation that we have just put an innocent man in jail,' Winstanley added.

'Well, he's hardly an innocent, is he, he's—' was as far as Bartholomew got. Merson reached over and poured his half pint of ale over Bartholomew's head as he stood up. 'You're on your own now you arrogant maniac. I'm out of it. And if you try and threaten me with you-know-what, I'll take you down with me. Never contact me again regarding any of this.' He then apologised to Carol and Shirley.

Bartholomew used his hanky to mop his face and head. He was glad he'd only bought halves. Merson then marched out of the pub drawing a few glances from other punters as he did.

'You asked for that,' Winstanley said.

'I know I did; he'll be OK when he's calmed down, I'll apologise properly when he has.'

'Christ, we've put a completely innocent man in jail,' Shirley said, as if the reality had only just struck her. God, Bartholomew wished he'd worded it differently. 'Look ladies, Piper may not be strictly guilty of anything, as such, but he must know what's going on, he must know who is really running the show.'

'That's if this mysterious crime overlord exists. God, I hope he doesn't, I hope Piper is really the boss, and what we have done to him is justified,' Winstanley said.

'And if he does exist, as he thinks he does,' Shirley said as she pointed at Bartholomew, before continuing, 'then I'm not sure how we can ever rest at night herein after.'

Winstanley turned to face Shirley, 'Let's hope this dickhead has got it wrong.'

Shirley nodded at her, before turning her scowl back towards Bartholomew. 'Either way, I'm also done.'

'Me too,' Winstanley said, and both women stood to leave. 'You're on your own now, Peter,' Winstanley added.

All Bartholomew could do was watch both clip clop out the pub. Damn his temper, and his bloody mouth. But he'd give them a couple of days, too, and then sweet talk them round. It would be OK. The job was still only half done.

THE CABAL

Chapter Twenty

Johnson was about to pack up and head home as he closed the laptop on Johnny's desk at the haulage yard. Then he received a phone call from some screw at the prison, Johnny's personal officer - whatever that entailed. But his reluctance to engage the caller soon evaporated as he listened in silence. He could barely take on board what he was being told, and screamed at the caller who simply ended the call. He slammed his phone down on the desk and cracked its screen in the process. On seeing this he sideswiped the laptop onto the floor and rushed around the desk to stamp on it.

G - Goon One - rushed in, 'Boss, what's up?'

Johnson came to a stop and looked at G, momentarily at a loss at what to say. Then as he calmed a little, his speech returned. 'They've put Johnny in the hospital wing.'

'Christ, boss, is he OK?'

'No G, he's not. They've blinded him in one eye.'

'Wow, that's serious. Who would do that?'

'Directly, some nutter with a grievance against me.'

'But why attack, Johnny?'

'Easy target, G, but the arse wipe will pay a heavy price.'

'Anything me and Gary can do?'

'There is.'

'Name it, want me to burn his house down, do his bitch, or whatever, just say the word.'

'All in good time, yes, but first I want you to do something else. I want the scum who is indirectly responsible, and I want him now.'

'Sure thing.'

'Go and grab Gary, it'll take two of you.'

***

Bartholomew wasn't sure whether to leave Merson overnight to calm down, but he was panicking that the whole team was breaking up. So, he decided to go straight to his house and wing it. Plus, he had a present for him. Thirty minutes after leaving The Higher Lock he pulled up outside Merson's house in Penwortham. At first Merson refused to answer the door, but Bartholomew knew how to get anyone to answer their door, always had. Just keep knocking as loud as you can until the occupant can't stand it any longer. They may come to the door in a less than friendly mood, but come to the door they would.

He employed the same tactics here, and eventually Merson succumbed. 'What do you want now?' he'd started with.

'Just five minutes to apologise, honestly Don I'm so sorry for what I said.'

'Just proves what you really think of me, though. You're a user, you always have been and I'm not interested in anything you have to say,' Merson said, and then started to close the door.

Bartholomew stuck his foot in the door jam.

'Now just a minute,' Merson started to say.

Bartholomew put a hand into his jacket inside pocket, and held it there. 'I didn't get chance to give you this earlier. So let me in unless you want me to give it to you here in full view of your neighbours?'

Merson opened the door and Bartholomew stepped into the hallway, but Merson blocked his path from entering the front room. Bartholomew pulled the inch thick wedge of crisp fifty-pound notes from his inside pocket and offered it to Merson, who just stared at it. 'Twenty grand there, as we agreed; fifty-fifty.'

After a minute's stand-off Merson scooped the money from Bartholomew's hand. He had him back under control.

'This changes nothing, I'm still done.'

'We still have a job to finish, and then we can both rest.'

'But what about Piper? The man's innocent!' Merson said.

'Look, I can understand the other two going all Judge Rinder about it, but not you. You're a seasoned pro like me, and we both know that Piper is up to his neck in it. Plus, he's no doubt been paid very well by whoever is behind him. Just to play the role, so he knows the risks in doing so. He's fair game.'

'I'm not sure.'

'Sleep on it, Don, and we'll chat tomorrow. If I'm wrong, then what we have done is a hundred percent proper, and if I'm right but you are still unhappy, then walk away and I'll not trouble you anymore. But please stay on-board until you know for sure. Does that sound like a fair deal?'

Merson didn't answer right away, and Bartholomew knew he'd won him back.

'OK, I'll sleep on it, but if I do carry on, it'll only be to prove you wrong and ease my own mind about Piper's guilt.'

'That's all I can ask.'

Merson nodded and Bartholomew returned the gesture before leaving him in peace. He waited until he was driving away before he allowed himself to smile. Even if the other two had bottled it, it didn't really matter that much, he didn't need them now. It would be much easier with just Merson and him.

Bartholomew reached the junction with the main road and contemplated going for a beer, but that would mean turning right against the traffic, and there was a blue Vauxhall and a silver Mondeo waiting to turn into the road he was on, and they were obstructing his view. He took the easy option and turned left and headed for home.

Chapter Twenty-one

Daniel Wright woke the next day still seething from the phone call he'd received from the solicitor Gerald Wales. Not so much about Wales, he was just trying his luck, he realised that. But the fact that George Dawson of all people had not only recommended him - when only a few short months ago he'd been surplus to requirements - but that he'd given out his personal number. Sue walked back into the bedroom with a mug of tea for Daniel. 'And another thing, you'd have thought that Dawson would have had the common decency to speak to me in first instance; before he handed my number out,' he said.

'Make the shower cold when you get up, it might calm you down,' Sue said with a smile on her face before she turned and left.

He knew she was right, and he had to stop badgering her, too. He picked up the remote and turned on the morning TV, just because he'd never had the time to watch it until recently. Two minutes later he turned the TV off; he'd not been missing much all these years so headed to the en suite. By the time he was dressed he'd decided to drop the Wales thing, though he may ring Jill later to tell her, but he'd leave Sue in peace. He was just readying himself to leave the bedroom when he heard Sue's voice shout from downstairs.

'Daniel, you have a visitor.'

'Coming,' he replied. He wasn't expecting anyone and hadn't heard the door go; perhaps it was Jill popping by. He quickly came downstairs and took his dirty mug into the kitchen. Sue was sat at the dining table with her works laptop open and headphones on. He put the mug in the sink and asked her who had called. She was just about to answer when her machine pinged and she put her hand up. He realised a work call was coming in so left it.

Daniel popped his head around his lounge door but the room was empty. She must have shown the visitor into the front lounge, which he thought odd. Until he opened the door and saw

THE CABAL

a sheepish looking George Dawson sat uncomfortably on the edge of the sofa, opposite an armchair. The rear lounge just had a settee in it at the moment, until the new armchairs arrived.

'Christ, you've got a cheek,' Daniel said as he closed the room door behind him and headed for the recliner.

With both hands raised in submission, Dawson said, 'I know I should have rung you first, but—'

'But you knew what I would have said,' Daniel said, interrupting him.

'True. But if I could just have five minutes of your time to wrap some context around it; which is what I should have tried to do, firstly.'

Daniel was intrigued to know what had driven an ex chief constable of all people, to get on the same merry-go-round as a solicitor defending the likes of Johnny Piper. He'd give him his five minutes.

Ten minutes passed and Dawson stopped to draw breath, and it was only then that Daniel noticed no complimentary cup of tea in front of Dawson. Nice one Sue, he thought. He then sat back and considered all that Dawson had told him. How he was convinced that Piper had been set up, and how Dawson had long suspected a corrupt senior officer was involved. And how he had coerced others into his illicit 'Cabal' as he termed it. Initially, Daniel became defensive; after all, Dawson was calling into question the validity of the target intelligence package which his old unit had produced. This had justified the investigations in the first place.

Dawson threw his hands up again, and said, 'This is in no way a reflection of you, or your unit's work.'

'But it has to be.'

'Not if you've been played. Not if we've all been played.'

Daniel had no idea what the man meant, and said so. The reply surprised him. According to Wales, the police were always led to believe that Piper was in charge of the North End Crew in order to protect the person who was really giving the orders. All sounded a bit convenient to Daniel. 'So, who is in charge?' he asked.

'Wales hasn't disclosed that yet. He said to even admit to me that there was someone else driving things was a huge risk on his part.'

'Sounds, like you are being royally played to me. Sounds like the opening statement of a defence case at trial. And you are being prepped to be the defence's star witness.'

Dawson didn't answer; he sat back again and looked as if he was taking on board what Daniel had suggested.

'I have to admit that that's a possibility I'd not considered,' Dawson eventually did say.

'You were the policy maker, I was the detective,' Daniel said, assuming the conversation was coming to an end.

'But for one fact, probably the only fact I have to give you.'

Daniel asked what that was, and Dawson told him about his lunchtime chance meeting with Professor Jordan Cummings and his disquiet about the drug drenched money exhibit. And how that proved to Dawson that Carol Winstanley had lied to him.

'Maybe Carol was just guessing in order to appease you on your last day?' Daniel said.

'That's what my wife, Joan, reckoned.'

'Pardon?'

'Nothing, sorry, And there's something else.'

Daniel just nodded for Dawson to continue; he may as well hear it all.

'Wales reckons the police involved stole a gold bar worth forty-five grand from Piper's house.'

Now this was really taking things to a new level of fiction as far as Daniel was concerned. It was plain to him that for all Dawson's acumen as a chief constable, he was almost gullible at a more operational level. This was clearly a clever manipulation by a sharp shark of a defence solicitor. Throw enough mud at a jury and some always stuck, and a defence brief only ever needed to seed the tinniest doubt and the case would be unproved. A conviction had to be beyond all reasonable doubt. It only took the slightest chink in a prosecution case to ensure its failure. Wales would know that as well as anyone. Dawson, for all his good intentions had been played. No doubt about that! And he told him

THE CABAL

so as he stood to signify that the five minutes promised were long over.

'Please think it through, and if you change your mind, call me,' Dawson said, leaving a calling card on the sofa as he stood.

'It would take a lot for me to "cross the aisle"; and to do so to work for Piper's lawyer would be like surfing a tsunami. Sorry, no deal.'

Then Dawson smiled weakly but coughed harshly. Daniel was about to offer him a glass of water when it stopped. 'You OK?' he asked.

'Thank you, it's just a tickle I sometime get when I talk too much, my throat gets dry.'

Daniel felt a hint of guilt in not offering the man a brew. And seeing him in that moment's discomfort made him appear more human. Vulnerable, even, he was no longer looking at a chief constable, but just someone else, an equal, who rightly, or misguidedly, was on a mission of honourable intent.

'You know it was never personal,' Dawson said.

'What wasn't?'

'Your removal from your unit. Just business; and it was Merson, your detective super's decision.'

Daniel almost felt sorry for the man; he had only ever been the firer of the gun. He had worked that out at the time.

'And for what it's worth,' Dawson continued, 'I'm sorry, and regardless of your decision here today, I realise it was wrong back then. I should have been stronger and overruled Merson. If it's any consolation, the wonder kid that took over from you turned out to be far from what Merson had claimed. I'd been played then that's for sure.'

Daniel appreciated what Dawson had just said and told him so. It had a very cathartic effect on him. Perhaps he could now let it all go, put the torment in the ground and out of his mind for good. If nothing else, the chat with Dawson had done Daniel an immense favour.

'Before you go, just one question?' he asked Dawson as he ushered him towards the front door.

'What?' Dawson said as he reached the door and turned to face Daniel.

'Who is this leader of this corrupt Cabal?'

'I could only share that if you were on board.'

Daniel realised that Dawson was right about that. He told him that if he genuinely believed that this Cabal existed, he should tell professional standards and leave them to investigate it.

Dawson smiled and said, 'And therein lies another problem.'

Daniel didn't know what he meant, but as Dawson walked through his front doorway, he gently placed his hand on Dawson's arm, pausing him, 'George, I really think you are being used and played by Wales. Just be careful,' Daniel said with genuine affection.

'I will, and thanks for your time.'

Daniel smiled and watched Dawson as he walked towards his car.

THE CABAL

Chapter Twenty-two

Johnson had to go for a walk around the haulage yard's curtilage, and then the perimeter around the block when that wasn't enough: in order to calm down. He would need to direct his anger, shortly. Well, for starters. But it wasn't easy as he thought of Johnny lying in a prison hospital bed permanently blinded in one eye. Simpson, when his turn came, would suffer long for this, and Johnson would need his self-control to ensure that he achieved this in a systematic and elongated way. To maximise the torment, both physically and mentally, and not to jump in with all his blind fury as he was used to doing - as he had often done when younger. But that was for the near future, he had a far more pressing issue to enact against, and to ensure he enjoyed it fully he needed a cooler head.

He checked his watch and realised that they would probably be back soon, but allowed himself a further few minutes as he wandered from the rear of their premises into a small area of greenery. Hardly big enough to call it an urban park space, but a small relief in among all the industrial units and terraced streets in this part of the city. He sat on an old bench at one side, where he and Johnny had often sat as kids. The area was lacking love, full of dog turds and syringes. When this was all over, he'd pay for it to be straightened out. And it was time the area had a new bench; the wooden slats were nearly rotten through. But for its concrete legs some scumbag would have nicked it years ago. He stood up after a few minutes and put the thoughts out of his head; he had to get back on task, get his mind set back where it needed to be. As he walked swiftly back to the yard, he thought again of Johnny lying in the prison hospital wing, and his seething anger came flooding back.

He entered the main hall of the enclosed yard and saw G and Gary stood in the middle, where Billy the driver had recently been. There would be an extra slap or two on his behalf for their new guest. Like Billy had been, the new occupant was also strung up by his arms with his toes just touching the floor. Unlike

Billy, the man had a black bag over his head, and Johnson could see the material around the mouth area going in and out at a rapid pace. The man was wearing casual clothes rather than the sharp suit he'd had on the last time Johnson had seen him. He must have heard Johnson's approaching footsteps as the bagged head turned towards him. He noted that his goons had done things properly, the bag was gathered in around the neck to keep it on, and contain any claret that got spilt.

'Any dramas, lads?' he asked his goons.

'None, boss, all sweet as…' G replied.

'Then let us begin,' Johnson said as he backhanded the hooded man, hard. He yelped in pain.

'That is just for starters. How bad things get is entirely up to you.'

'Look, I've no idea what this is all about, but you are making a big mistake.'

'Am I?' Johnson replied, followed by a backhander from the opposite direction. The man let out another yelp. 'Anything on him?' Johnson asked G.

'Nothing boss, but we did find this on a table in his lounge,' G said, and took out a roll of fifty-pound notes.

'How much?'

'Twenty large.'

Johnson told G to stick it in the office. He knew straight away where the money had come from. 'Looks like you've been ripped off,' he said to the hooded man.

'I don't know what you mean?'

I mean, that bar was worth twice that, Johnson didn't say but did punch the man's midriff. He bent as double as his restraints would allow and coughed into his hood. But didn't reply, which told Johnson all he needed to know. Bartholomew had nicked it, not that he had been in any doubt.

'Do you know who I am?' the hooded man eventually said.

Typical cop arrogance, Johnson thought. 'Of course, I know. I saw you only yesterday, but you didn't see me.'

The hooded man turned his head towards Johnson, 'What, where?' he said, suddenly sounding even more nervous.

THE CABAL

'Let's just say near one of your places of work.'

'Then you'll know I'm a detective superintendent?'

'Yes, I'm aware of your rank and status. That's why you are here.'

The man didn't answer.

'And I saw what you were carrying.'

The hooded man's head shot up, and said, 'What, the brown envelope?'

Johnson had no idea what Bartholomew had been carrying in his poncy monogrammed case, nor was he interested, but this envelope seemed to matter to him.

'It's not what you think; it was just a report for the judge.'

'And what do I think?'

'Some snout's up at court to be sentenced and you think the envelope was his get-out-of-jail card.'

Johnson wasn't interested in some secret report about some grassing Judas, or any other envelopes in Bartholomew's briefcase. It was time to come to the point. 'Look, this is just a friendly warning, just a chat, and it can all be resolved quite simply.'

'Anything, look, I'll not come after you or anything if you stop this now. We can call it quits.'

'Quits, quits, you arrogant toad,' Johnson said as he felt his temper start to rise. He turned around until he saw what he was after and picked it up. He then turned back to face Bartholomew and said, 'I hope you like cricket.' He then started to swing the bat at the man's torso and struck him several times, before stopping to catch his breath. The man screamed out in pain as the bat struck home on every strike. Once Johnson's breathing had calmed, he spoke, 'I hadn't meant it to go this far, but you are winding me up. If you want this to end, it's simple, lose the bent exhibits and all associated paperwork so Johnny Piper can be released. You agree to do that, and this ends now. As regards the other 20K you owe, and compo for the eye, we'll have to come to an arrangement. Maybe you can pay off the debt with future help; whenever and whatever we ask of you.'

The hooded man didn't answer right away, he just shook his head. And then he said, 'You are obviously an interested party in the Piper case.'

'You could say that.'

'But you have to understand, that that has got nothing to do with me.'

Rage briefly took over Johnson once more, and five minutes afterwards he again paused for breath, almost oblivious to the screams which echoed around the warehouse.

'I'm not the SIO… I can't access the stuff…honest,' the hooded man said in between gasps.

'Yes, you can, or do you want some more persuasion?'

'Oh my God, you think I'm Peter Bartholomew?'

'Don't think; know. So don't insult my intelligence.'

'My name is Don Merson, you have to believe me.'

'I don't have to believe anything coming out of your lying mouth.'

'But it's true.'

'That's why you carry a briefcase with the letters P.B. on it?'

There was a pause as the man in the hood dropped his head.

'Well, do we have an agreement?'

'You really have got the wrong man, but I know why, and it's an easy mistake to make.'

'So, you didn't plant drugs in Johnny's desk?'

'No.'

Johnson hit the man's right thigh with the bat. 'Or plant the money on his bookshelf?'

'No.'

Johnson hit the left thigh. 'Or steal his bar of gold?'

The man didn't answer. Then did.

'OK, I didn't take the bar, but I didn't stop it. Keep the cash, it was my half.'

'Oh, I intend to. Who has got the other half?'

'Bartholomew.'

'Do you enjoy pain?'

'Of course not, look I've just admitted about the money, so I couldn't do anything about today now, even if I wanted to. So please just let me go and I'll see what I can do about the exhibits.'

'What does that mean, exactly?'

'Keep one eye on things, so to speak, until I get chance to do something.'

'What? You are taking the piss?' Johnson said, as he felt his temper rising up once more.

'No of course not. I'm good at the sneaky stuff. Good at keeping an eye out on things. They used to call me cyclops when I was a younger detective.'

Johnson couldn't believe what he had just heard, nor could he staunch the eruption of white-hot wrath which engulfed him seconds later.

Chapter Twenty-three

Bartholomew was glad he'd not gone for a nightcap as he knew he needed a clear head the following morning. He was in his office before eight and straight on the phone to Carol Winstanley. As limited as her help was, and notwithstanding that the tosser of a chief, Dawson, had gone, he still wanted to persuade her back on board. For moral support if nothing else. He smiled at the thought, it should be *immoral* support. But then snapped out of it. For once he knew he had to be less arrogant and more contrite - or appear so an any rate. If he could get Winstanley back, then he was confident that Shirley Lancaster would follow. He'd already bought Merson's acquiescence, and he was desperate to achieve his ultimate goal, his only true goal. Piper was only ever a means to an end.

'Morning Carol, look, before you say anything, just let me apologise for my behaviour last night. And for not being totally upfront with you from the start. Can we put this behind us?' Bartholomew opened with when his call was answered.

'Apology accepted; life's too short. And we will have to work together in the future no doubt many times, so bad blood would be no good for anyone,' Winstanley said.

'Brilliant, that's very gracious of you, can I buy you lunch and we can discuss the way forward?'

'I don't need you to buy me lunch, and there is no way forward.'

'But I thought you said—'

Winstanley cut across him, 'There you go again with your arrogant assumptions; there is no way I want any part in anything else. I've accepted your apology; end of. We've achieved what we set out to, and I just hope and pray, for the good of my conscience, that we *have* put Lancashire's number one criminal behind bars thereby disproving your wild conspiracy theories. I will not be part of a further witch hunt on God knows who you conceitedly decide should be next.'

'But, but—'

THE CABAL

Interrupting again, Winstanley continued, 'No buts. And I must go; the chief's office is trying to get through.'

Bartholomew was left looking at his phone after the line went dead. He must be losing his touch. Then a text message came through: it read, 'Pls attend A/CC Darlington's office, ASAP. S.O.'

There must be a job on he thought, noting the message had come from Shirley Lancaster who had signed off S.O. - Staff Officer - not the usual, 'Shirl'; a bit abrupt. She was obviously not on speaking terms with Bartholomew either.

Ten minutes later, a very curt Shirley Lancaster showed Bartholomew into the acting chief's office. There was a hum of quiet chatter from within, and once inside, he could see that all eight of Lancashire's detective supers who could SIO a job was present. There were only two exceptions, as always. Firstly, the counter terrorism super who was only available to SIO terrorist related jobs. This always wound Bartholomew up; how many terror jobs did he have to SIO in a year? Not that many. And secondly, the other exception was covert policing, which Bartholomew did understand. There had to be a firewall between the gatherers of intelligence and the operational detectives who acted on it.

The head of CID, Detective Chief Superintendent John Jones, an insipid skinny sycophant in his late forties - who Bartholomew usually avoided whenever possible - was stood next to the acting chief, Bernard Darlington. They looked comical next to each other as Darlington was the total opposite to Jones; a six-foot four-inch ex-guardsman in his fifties who could grace any Rugby scrum. Also stood at the front was ACC Marty Mathews, a fast-tracked graduate entry in his mid-thirties, who probably had started shaving, but only just. Bartholomew thought that a full moustache and beard were probably still beyond him.

Darlington called the meeting to order, and the hum died down as the eight supers turned to face the front.

'Thank you all for dropping everything and coming here at short notice; I wanted to catch you all before you disappeared on your normal duties. Consequently, I haven't all the details I would wish yet, but we have a grave situation in front of us. Chief Super Jones will give what specifics he can in a mo, and then I'll address you all as to why I'm sending this out-of-force.'

Bartholomew's first thought was that this must be an extremely sensitive job, such as a high-level corruption enquiry requiring an independent lead investigator. He immediately panicked with his own guilty knowledge, and tried to catch Winstanley's eye, but she steadfastly ignored him from all of ten feet away. He turned to look at Shirley Lancaster at the rear of the room, and she too looked away. He was starting to worry now.

John Jones thanked the chief and then cleared his throat before he spoke, 'Just over three hours ago as the sun was coming up, a dog walker saw a body in the River Ribble. Near to its estuary with the Irish Sea at Lytham St. Anne's. A search was instigated and the RNIB lifeboat from Lytham recovered a human body of a male in his late forties.'

John Jones paused and took a deep breath, here comes the sensitive bit, Bartholomew reckoned. But before he could continue, someone behind Bartholomew, asked, 'Any clue as to cause of death?'

'Obviously the post mortem has not been carried out yet, but the man had injuries which appeared pre-mortem and are not consistent with the circumstances,' Jones replied.

'So, he'd been beaten prior to death, but that may not have been the actual cause of his death?' the groveler from behind said, stating the bleeding obvious. Bartholomew now realised that the recently over-promoted tosspot was showboating for his own vanity.

'It's classed as suspicious until the pathologist has completed the PM, which will be later this morning,' Jones said.

Bartholomew was impressed that they had managed to get a Home Office Pathologist in so quickly. Then he found out why as Jones took a further deep breath.

'Unfortunately, I have the sad task of informing you that the deceased was one of our own. He is Detective Superintendent Don Merson, whom you all know well.'

THE CABAL

The words hit Bartholomew hard. Stunned, he questioned what he had heard, but knew that there was no mistake. He'd only seen him twelve hours ago when he'd left him settling in for the night. How had he ended up in the river miles away.

Jones let a couple of moments pass to allow the shock to kick in and for the resultant mutterings to subside before he continued. 'His partner, DI Jack Reynolds is now on companionate leave and I have taken the pre-emptive step of allocating a family liaison officer straight away. He has said that he would appreciate any contact, however well intentioned, to go through thc FLO.'

'Could still be a tragic accident?' The tosspot behind said.

Bartholomew would punch him in the face if he didn't shut up. He was barely keeping it together as it was, without added irritation from him.

'Again, pre-emptive of any SIO command, we actioned immediate house-to-house enquiries and have a witness who saw him leaving home around nine last night with two men, whom she described as 'bouncer types.' They escorted him to a car and sped off. She said it caught her attention - not least because the two men looked 'rough' - but also that they were extremely close to either side of him.'

'Like he was being frog-marched?' Mr. Pot asked.

Jones nodded and Bartholomew turned to face his irritant and said, 'Yeah, I think we all got that. You should consider becoming a detective.' Then the second shockwave hit Bartholomew. He must have only just left Merson's gaff before his burly visitors arrived.

'So, you will understand that due to the sensitives, and the fact that you all knew Don, you are all far from impartial. This is why I have asked for an SIO from a neighbouring force to come in,' the acting chief added.

'Who is it?' someone asked.

'Detective Superintendent Joanne Hargreaves from Greater Manchester. Now, if you'll all excuse me, she is due here any minute,' the acting chief finished with.

As everyone started to leave, Bartholomew pushed his way to the front and addressed Jones and the acting chief, 'Gents, I think I may have been the last person to see him alive.'

'You'd better stay then.' Jones said.

Bartholomew turned around half expecting to see Carol Winstanley and Shirley Lancaster heading to join him, but both had already gone. He was mightily relieved. The meeting at The Higher Lock was irrelevant; the chief didn't need to know that bit. And after all, it was Bartholomew who would have been the last to see him from their group.

THE CABAL

Chapter Twenty-four

George Dawson was watching the evening news and was shocked to see the headlines in the local bulletin. He called Joan through from the kitchen as he took in the scant details that were being made public.

'What is it? I'm trying to…' she started to say as she entered the room, before looking at the TV and then glancing at George. 'That's not the Don Merson who used to work for you, is it?'

'I'm afraid so. Detective super in charge of the force's Covert Policing Department found dead in the water by a dog walker at first light.'

'What a dreadful accident,' Joan said.

'It's no accident.'

'Have they said so?'

'Just said it was being treated as "unexplained".'

'Well, there you go, then.'

Dawson didn't reply; he couldn't be bothered in debating it with his magistrate of a wife, who always kept an open mind. And as admirable as that was, Dawson knew she considered it sport to disagree with him whenever it suited her. As soon as she left the room, he muted the TV and picked up his mobile. No point ringing Darlington, he'd try the ACC in charge of crime, a graduate entry called Marty who was destined for extremely high places. A young man for his senior rank, but what he lacked in time-served experience he made up for with natural acumen. Dawson had tasked him many times with complex issues and had never had to explain anything twice. The man was academically sharp and could look through heavy narrative and see outcomes as if they were jumping out with his name on them. Tactically was where he lacked depth, and he would be the first to admit it.

Marty answered on the third ring and pleasantries over, Dawson conveyed his shock and concern over Merson, and then said, 'I hope it was an accident, but suspect not. Not that it matters to poor old Don Merson, I guess.'

'The results of the PM have just come back, and it's definitely murder; all things considered George, but you didn't hear that from me.'

'That's just awful. Who's SIO-ing it, not Peter Bartholomew I hope?'

'God, you really don't like him, do you?'

'Sorry, force of habit,' Dawson said, knowing he had to hide his feelings before he blew the phone call.

'I've had to bring an out-of-force SIO in, not least because of the sensitivities of what he did for a living, there could be hundreds of MO suspects. And in any event, Bartholomew couldn't run it due to a conflict of interest.'

'Dare tell, Marty?' Dawson asked, knowing that he was pushing it.

'No biggie, really, but he'd been for a pint with Merson shortly before he was, er, I mean, that he was the last person to see him alive. Look, I've got to go; we have a briefing in five.'

'Sure, sorry to bother you. I was only ringing to say if I could offer any help with my established contacts at the College of Policing or the lab, just give me a shout. I realise that you have not been in post too long,' Dawson partly lied.

'Sure will, and thanks for that,' Marty said before ending the call.

Marty was holding something back, and understandably so, but it suggested a premeditated event. And not a random spontaneous act by someone near the estuary. He may not be a seasoned detective like Daniel Wright, but even Dawson could read the subtext. He was sure this was nothing to do with someone Merson may have pissed off as head of Covert Policing. His role was not public knowledge, and as departmental head he never got involved in the operational end. Merson didn't work undercover, or handle informants, or follow criminals around. And as for being social chums with Peter Bartholomew, that was news. The more he thought about it the more he suspected that Don Merson was also in Bartholomew's Cabal. It made perfect sense to have the head of covert policing on board. That way, Merson could skew any intelligence that went to the intelligence

THE CABAL

unit. Bartholomew could orchestrate - through Merson - any rationale he wanted to justify any action he wanted to take; against any one he chose to target.

Dawson slammed his hand down on his sofa arm knocking a cup and saucer onto the floor. Merson was Cabal, had to be. And his death was surely linked with it in some way, which probably meant Piper. Perhaps Merson was going to blow Bartholomew out. My God, has he gone that far down the slurry pit of corruption, so that he'd even kill one of his own to protect himself. Dawson would be shocked if that were true, but not surprised.

The more he turned it all over in his mind, the more he came up with unanswered questions. But he was sure of the following: Merson's death was nothing to do with his position on the force, it had to be the Cabal, and Piper's case's footprints were all over it. And he also now knew who three members of the Cabal were: Peter Bartholomew, Carol Winstanley and Don Merson.

He picked his phone up and searched for Bernard Darlington's number, he knew this next call was not going to be easy, but he had to try. He took a deep breath and pushed the call button.

Two minutes later Dawson was left staring at his phone after the call had been brought to an abrupt end by Darlington. 'The absolute cad. And to think I recommended him to the Mayor.' Then his mind was distracted by the ticker tape running across the bottom of the TV screen: *"Prisoner blinded in attack at HMP Preston is named as Johnny Piper, who is currently on remand awaiting trial."* Dawson unmuted the TV as it cut to a shot of a reporter stood outside the prison main gates. *'The man who attacked Piper, who has been described as a local businessman, has been named locally as Simpson, a convicted criminal with a violent past. He has been placed in solitary confinement whilst police probe the incident. Back to you in the studio.'*

Dawson muted the TV once more. Another coincidence? No way.

***

Johnson was in Johnny's office at the haulage plant watching the regional TV news with G and Gary. When the news cut to the weather, he turned it off and turned to face two stunned looking faces. 'Who the hell was that?'

'It said Detective Superintendent Don Merson,' G said.

'I know what it said; and it wasn't Bartholomew.'

'The report showed his warrant card photo, which was definitely the same guy,' G said.

'We lifted the bloke you showed us, boss,' Gary joined in with.

Johnson didn't answer, he knew it wasn't their fault. He just couldn't understand how he had got it so wrong. 'Must have been the other pig,' he said. 'That Merson must have gone for his briefcase for him.' He looked at both goons and could tell that they had no idea what he was saying, but it didn't matter. What did matter was that they have stiffed the wrong cop. Not that they had intended to stiff him at all. It was all just supposed to be a 'friendly' warning. In fact, as soon as he had coughed up to the money being from the gold bar, Johnson knew he had him in his pocket. He would have been an especially useful asset going forward. That was until he decided to die. Johnson had been taking a leak when it had occurred; he turned to G and said, 'Tell me again what happened?'

'It's like I said, boss, neither of us was hitting him, he just started panting and shouting about a pain in his chest.'

'That's true, boss,' Gary said. 'We just thought he'd cracked a couple of ribs from the slapping. Always hurts like hell to breathe with cracked ribs, especially when your hands are tied up above your head.'

'Must have had a dodgy heart or something. But it lands us in a whole world of trouble. They'll throw everything at catching us.'

'But they don't know we took him, boss,' Gary added.

'And it better stay that way. So, you two keep shtum; got it, it stays in here. No pillow talk, nothing.'

Both Garys nodded furiously.

'But that still leaves us with the problem of the real Peter Bartholomew.'

'Do you want us to lift him?' G asked.

'Yeah, that would be a really wise move now we've offed one of their own. No, of course I don't, you idiot. We'll just have to find another way to get Johnny out and free. If we need to sort out Bartholomew later on, then that's a different thing.'

More nods.

'But for now, you two do one and burn your clothes and the motor you used, but do the car well away from here so it doesn't get linked.'

Further nods from both Garys who then left. Johnson needed to give this whole crock of crap some serious thought.

Chapter Twenty-five

Daniel Wright turned the TV off, and sat back in his chair looking into the rear garden through the patio doors. Stunned. He hadn't liked Don Merson, especially at the end of his own career, but he would never have wished him harm. The news report had been understandably brief, but had mentioned where the body had been found. Daniel couldn't even speculate as to what he was doing at the Ribble estuary at daft-o'clock in the morning. It all sounded very suspicious. He resisted the temptation to ring any one of his friends who were still serving; he knew they would be up to their necks in it. The first day of any murder investigation was always manic as the infrastructure was set up and the urgent lines of enquiry were actioned. The news report had said the police were treating the death as 'unexplained', but he knew that they would run it as if it was murder, until they knew that it was not. If that indeed ever happened. The first forty-eight hours of any murder enquiry were crucial for obtaining what had often been termed as 'The Golden Hour' of evidence. Not least at the crime scene, or the postmortem examination which were always done by a Home Office warranted pathologist. They carried out far deeper PMs than the local pathologist would do in non-suspicious deaths.

Then his phone rang, it was George Dawson who immediately linked the death to the Cabal and threw in the attack on Piper for good measure. The latter Daniel didn't know about. 'Steady on, George,' he started, feeling slightly odd at calling him by his first name. The sheer thought of such a slight when he'd been Daniel's chief constable would have been unthinkable. But he was just Joe Blogs now, just like Daniel. 'You're not seriously suggesting that Merson's death is linked to Bartholomew in some way, are you?'

Dawson filled him in on Bartholomew being the last person to see Merson alive, which proved absolutely nothing. He then went on about Piper's attack, and the timing of it. This could have been done by any nutter inside who fancied a crack at Piper the

Mr. Big. It often happened, and he said as much. Eventually, he had heard enough, and he told Dawson so. 'There is no way I could live with myself if I worked as an enquiry agent for the defence trying to get Piper off charges - which have culminated from investigations led by an intelligence case put together by my old unit. If Bartholomew has somehow, unethically assisted things, as you suspect, then let professional standards do their thing.'

'How about this for a compromise: instead of working for Wales and his defence team, we do our own independent enquiry. After all, we are free citizens now, not badged and shackled.'

'To what aim; we are polar opposites?'

'Exactly, we could provide a check and balance to each other. I may be trying to prove that Piper is innocent, to prove the existence of this corrupt Cabal run by Bartholomew. And you may be trying to prove his guilt, to try and justify his charges, and therefore the justification to investigate him in the first place. We will both be after the truth. It's just that we both believe that truth to be different.'

Daniel was unconvinced how this could ever work, even if he were interested, which he was not. It would prove adversarial with no arbiter. It would be akin to a crown prosecutor and a defence solicitor joining sides, but with no judge. 'Never work, George, we'd end up rolling around on the floor trying to knock lumps out of each other.'

'But, but—'

'No buts, George; let justice take its course against Piper. Let the SIO from Manchester investigate the death of Merson, and let the rubber heel squad look at Bartholomew and Winstanley. You and I are retired; go for a walk, put your feet up, but don't call me again,' Daniel said and ended the call before Dawson could draw breath.

But before he could chew over the details of the phone call, his wife Sue walked into the rear lounge. She was pulling her phone away from her ear, and looked ashen. Her eyes were staring into space and she seemed to focus on Daniel belatedly, unaware of his presence. Then she was. But before he could speak, she burst into an avalanche of tears. Deep wracking sobs from her very core. Daniel couldn't imagine what was wrong, but could see it was bad. He sprang to his feet and put his arms around her as the tears continued to teem down her face. She held onto him and buried her face into his shoulder, muffling her anguish.

A minute passed, at least, before her heart-breaking howling subsided into a cough. She raised her head and answered Daniel's unasked question.

'It's Sally, my niece. She's dead.'

Daniel sat Sue down and let her recover from her shock some more before he gently probed her for the details. He had dreaded that this day would come, but knew it probably would if things ever went backwards.

'Eighteen, Daniel, she was only Eighteen.'

'I know love, I know,' he answered before asking her for more. He knew that Sally had had her problems, but all the indications from Sue's sister, Melanie, were that she was turning a corner. She'd been an addict for over two years, and at the worst of it, Daniel had sat down with her, and shown her some brutal photographs of addicts who had taken things too far. The shock had seemed to reach her as she promised her mother that she would accept help. Daniel knew that the first stage of any addict's journey of recovery was an honest recognition by themselves that they needed help. And that they wanted help, and were not simply saying what loved ones wanted them to say.

He also knew how convincing addicts could be, especially heroin abusers, driven by the uncontrollable need to satisfy the wickedly painful cravings. But even he had believed her. He'd arranged for her be appraised for a fast-tracked treatment programme which she passed with honours. No nepotistic queue jumping, she was adjudged like all others. But they took her on because of her youthful age and their assessment that she wanted to, and could succeed. That had all started three months ago, and she had been receiving a reducing amount of Methadone - the heroin substitute - for some time. But something had obviously gone very wrong. She had also been prescribed with Naltrexone,

THE CABAL

the drug which blocks receptors in the brain disallowing the euphoria, and helping to block, or reduce, the withdrawal led desire for heroin. And as far as he and Sue were aware, she was making progress, slow, but heading in the right direction.

When Sue had calmed further, she turned to face Daniel, 'Melanie is in bits, as you can imagine.' He could only imagine, and made worse by the lack of any spousal support. Her husband had left her years ago, and although he was fully supportive of Sally: he was not so of Melanie. This was always in the back of Daniel's mind when he had tried to help. 'You know, I really thought we'd turned a corner with, Sally,' he said.

'We all did, even her mum.'

'Now, I feel like we were just kidding ourselves, I feel like I've failed her.'

'It's often the way with addicts and addiction, you know that more than most,' Sue said.

'I know but I feel that I, of all of us, should have realised, and if I had, maybe I could have done something else,' Daniel said.

'None of us knew she was back using. Melanie is of the opinion she had only just relapsed, so no good will come from beating yourself up,' Sue said. 'And in any event, it wasn't her relapse that killed her.'

Daniel turned fully to face Sue, surprised. 'How do you mean?'

'Apparently, she was found in a known drug users' squat, and still had the syringe she'd used next to her.'

Daniel's surprise grew; he knew that Sally had smoked the heroin whilst she had been using, but she had never ever injected it. He had spent ages with her when she'd been at her lowest explaining the dangers of injecting. She had thought injecting just gave you a quicker fix - which was true. But he had gone to great effort to explain that if she were smoking it, the ingestion process was measured and gradual in a way she could control. So, if she were ever given a bad batch with toxic adulterants, or just a batch way stronger than she was used to, she would realise as she smoked it that something was amiss. She could stop immediately. But once a syringe plunger is depressed, then that's it; it's done. All gone, and there is nothing you can do about it.

This was all very troubling to Daniel, how Sally could have gone from rehab, to relapse, to injecting for the first time, so quickly.

'Melanie has asked me to ask you for a favour,' Sue said.

'Anything.'

'She said that the officer who is investigating the death had an air of "open and shut case" about his demeanour when he broke the news to her. She felt unconvinced he would chase the scumbag who had dealt to her. And when she told him Sally never injected, ever, even at her lowest point, he had looked at her with scepticism.

'She knows you have retired, but wondered if you could try and find out exactly what the police are doing?'

'Consider it done.'

THE CABAL

Chapter Twenty-six

Daniel spent the rest of the day on and off the phone. He eventually spoke to the reporting officer dealing with Sally's death, and soon started to fear that Melanie's assumptions were correct. This cop had already moved on, as far as he was concerned this was just another non-suspicious drug overdose. Though, to be fair to him, he had requested samples from the PM to go for toxicology, just in case there was a bad batch of gear out there, from a public health warning perspective. But it wouldn't be fast-tracked without any intelligence suggesting anything out of the norm. Daniel understood that. In fact, the body was to be released back to the family later today so that they could start to make funeral arrangements. The officer asked if he would pass that on to Melanie. Lazy cretin. Daniel refused, said it should come from him.

Daniel was more interested in who supplied the gear and why Sally had chosen to inject it. It soon became apparent that the cop wasn't chasing an investigation into the dealer, and with nothing to suggest foul play, the CID or Drug Squad wouldn't be getting involved. Daniel shook his head and had to dig deep to keep his emotions out of his tone, just in case he needed to speak to the officer again. But the one highlight he managed to ascertain was the details of the drug squat where Sally was found. It was a local doss hole in the Ribbleton area of Preston, east of the city centre. He thanked the officer for his time, ended the call and grabbed his car keys.

It was late afternoon by the time Daniel parked his car around the corner from the address. It was situated at the end of a cul-de-sac off Ribbleton Lane - which is a busy thoroughfare that runs east out of the city. Not the best of areas, but busy, so he hoped his new Jag would survive the visit. It was a retirement gift to himself. Sue usually ran the family car and Daniel had a runabout when he'd been in the police. He wished he still had it. As soon as he started to walk away from his car, he saw a couple of youths with their hoods up eyeing it.

'Nice wheels, man,' the taller of the two said as he walked past.

Daniel was about to go back and move the car, but he'd no doubt face the same dilemma anywhere around here. So, he chose a different approach. He turned and addressed the two of them, whom he now realised were even younger than Sally. Products of their environment, he felt sorry for them, not that they would appreciate such sympathy. 'I'll be ten minutes, max; there's a tenner here if you stay and watch the motor, and another tenner, if you're still here when I get back,' he said.

The two youths looked at each other and grinned, and then the taller one spoke, 'Make it fifteen both ends and you have a deal.'

Daniel knew better than to negotiate but also knew that communication skills were everything. When in the police it was always important to speak to people on their personal level, but to guard against appearing patronizing. If you connect, they'd think 'he's OK.' So, he chose his words with care. 'Christ lads, this ain't Wheeler Dealers, and that ain't some modern classic, but they are the only wheels I've got, just got them, in fact. You should see the sack of crap I used to drive.'

Both hoodies half smiled, and the taller said, 'If you have to wait to get to your age to get decent wheels, you're doing the wrong graft.'

'Now I find out.' Both smiled again. 'Look, ten each way, and an extra ten for each further ten minutes if I'm late?'

'Fifteen for every extra ten minutes, and you've got a deal,' taller hoodie said.

'Sorted, then,' Daniel said, and handed over the first tenner and agreed the time. There was a clock on the wall opposite above a pawn broker's shop, so that took any debate out of it.

A minute afterwards, Daniel was at the address and could see that the front door was just pulled to, on account that it was only hanging on its top hinge. As soon as he pushed it open a stench hit him. It was the smell of ground-in dirt and bacteria. Daniel had always noted that the stench from a dirty home was the same fetid smell as the stink from a dead body. Both contained rotting organic matter.

THE CABAL

He entered gingerly, there were no carpets or undelay, just a few scattered newspapers on the floor. The walls were covered with graffiti on the bare plaster where wallpaper had once hung. It was hard to imagine that this had once been someone's family home. The front room of the end terraced property was empty, which was a shame. Daniel really didn't fancy having to do a return trip. The staircase was missing, so upstairs was out of bounds. He wandered into the kitchen/diner at the rear and saw a man in his thirties sat on the floor among newspaper, dog muck and discarded needles. He glanced up lazily at Daniel with little concern on his gaunt face. His pupils were like saucers; he had recently shot up. Daniel said hello as friendly as he could and told the bloke his name and asked him what his was?

'Names don't matter, Danny boy, and if you're after a working boy, I ain't it. But for a tenner I'll tell you where to go.'

Christ, were they all free marketers around here. And then he shuddered at what the man was suggesting. 'No way, that's not my thing either, just after knowing summat,' Daniel said, trying not to over-accent the word 'summat'.

'You are not the filth, are you?' the man asked with a touch of concern now on his otherwise placid expression.

Daniel told him about Sally.

'Ah, I'm really sorry about that, she was a cool kid, shouldn't have happened.'

'How'd mean?'

'She cranked up for the first time, shouldn't have done her gear like that.'

'Were you here?' Daniel asked, surprised to learn that the man must have been.

'Yeah, I'm sorry. I was in the other room with another user when she came in. The Man was here and giving her it large about cranking it.'

Daniel guessed The Man was the dealer, and it sounded as if it was him who was pushing Sally to inject the heroin rather than smoke it. He could feel his blood start to boil, but had to keep it under wraps, for now. 'Why would The Man, give a toss how she did her gear?' he asked.

The man tapped the side of his nose and said, 'They get you cranking the stuff, and your bads go through the roof. More bads, and you need more gear.' He tapped the side of his nose again, 'Just business to those monsters. It's why I only smoke it,' he said, before tapping his nose once more.

The heartless scum must have realised how naïve and vulnerable she was, but hadn't cared a jot. It was all about business. He shook his head.

'She wanted to social her stuff with me and the other bloke, but he shouted her off in here to do it. Bad form to crank up in front of others.'

It was at this point that Daniel wondered if this addict was sat where Sally had been. He felt tears pricking his eyes, he shook head again; he had to stay focused. 'Who was The Man?'

The addict hesitated, and then said, 'He's a bad man, but I can't afford to cut him out.'

'There are other dealers, and as you have already said he was a bad dealer, a "monster". I'll make it worth your while.'

'How much?'

'Something worth more than money.'

Then he sat up straight against the wall, 'You've got gear? You carrying?'

Daniel didn't answer him straight away, he left the man to believe what he wanted for a moment, and then said, 'Do it for Sally, you're a smart guy, but Sally was not much more than a kid, and there will be other young people overdosing because of that dealer.'

The addict nodded, and said, 'OK. For Sal, a nice girl. I don't know the man's name, but he's a big mother, everyone is scared to death of him.'

'What does he look like?'

'Like a say, a big mother; white bloke with a z-shaped scar on his cheek, that's all I got.'

Daniel thanked the addict and then pulled his wallet out and saw his eyes widen more if that was possible. But he didn't take money out, he couldn't in all conscience feed this man's habit. He pulled a calling card out instead and handed it to him.

THE CABAL

'What's this? I thought you had some gear?'

'The details of the head of the local Drug Treatment Team, they'll assess you fairly and might take you on, help get you clean.' Daniel would put a call in to them later as a courtesy, but he didn't tell the addict this, it would only raise more questions. The addict took the card and looked at it.

'It's worth far more than gear or money if it helps you get clean,' Daniel said, as turned to leave.

The addict was still staring at it, and then he looked up and said, 'OK, cheers, I might give it a go,' and then he put the card in his jeans pocket.

Daniel could only hope that he would. 'Just say Daniel gave you the card,' he said, and quickly left before the man could respond.

He rushed back to his car and was relieved to see both hoodies still sat on a low wall next to the Jag. They both pushed themselves off the wall as he approached. 'I know, I know,' he said as he glanced at the wall clock opposite. Five minutes late. He quickly took twenty-five pounds out and handed it to the tall hoodie, and then said, 'Another twenty if you can tell me where a big white dealer with a z-shaped scar on his face can be found. And before you ask, I'm not filth. It's just business, need a chat. That's all. No beef.'

Both youths looked at each other, and the smaller one nodded, then the taller one said, 'You talking about Capone?'

Daniel grinned, 'I guess.'

'He's a bad man, pissed off loads of folk around here. You need to watch yourself doing trade with him.'

'Appreciate the warning. Another twenty sound OK?'

'Thirty,' the smaller youth said, speaking for the first time.

Daniel knew now was not the time to barter and quickly handed the thirty over.

'Name's Gary and he works for the North End Crew,' the taller one said, before they both turned and headed away.

Piper's mob, that swine's lot. Daniel was incandescent now. He'd make sure that Piper, and particularly this z-faced Gary, paid for their crimes.

Chapter Twenty-seven

George Dawson was sat listening to the birdsong at home, it was a mild day and he had the patio doors open. His phone rang; it was the solicitor, Gerald Wales.

'I'm really quite concerned, now,' he started with.

'So, you've heard the news, then?'

'It was on the local teatime broadcast, didn't say a lot though.'

'And your concerns are?'

'Maybe I'm putting two and two to get five, but Piper has been attacked, and then this.'

'Merson wasn't directly involved in the case against your client,' Dawson said, playing reverse thinking.

'I know, but if he was, or thought to be…' Wales said, leaving his sentence unfinished.

'Do you believe your client and his associates are capable of murder?'

'Before today, I'd have said no. But I've just come off the phone to, erm, the person running their business in Piper's absence and asked him if he was involved.'

'I'm guessing he said no.'

'He did, as you might expect, but the way he answered has left me very uncomfortable.'

'How do you mean?'

'Very, very aggressive, an overreaction. It was almost as if he exploded before reigning himself back in trying not to show a disproportionate reply.'

'You could expect him to be upset at the suggestion?'

'I know, but it didn't feel right.'

'So where does this leave you?'

'First and foremost, I'm an officer of the court, and I represent Piper, not this other man. I'll do my job and then that's it. I'll cut the lot of them adrift, and if my firm don't like it, I'll quit. Soon get a job elsewhere.'

Dawson was surprised, Wales was clearly rattled.

'I could really do with your mate to act as my enquiry agent.'

'Sorry, Gerald, I tried, it's never going to happen.'

'A shame.'

'Look, I'll strike you a deal.'

'What is it?'

'If you come across anything that further adds to your disquiet, you can tell me in confidence and I'll make sure it gets to the right ear, leaving you out of it.'

'Are you allowed to do that?'

'You're forgetting that I'm no longer in the job, and as a private citizen I'm a free agent.'

'Well, that gives me some solace. Had Mr. Merson a family?'

'He was single, but had a boyfriend who is in bits as you might imagine.'

'The poor man. Do we know how he died?'

'Suspected heart attack, but he had a lot of fresh injuries from a very recent beating which probably brought it on, but you didn't hear that from me.'

'Fair enough.'

Dawson knew he was taking a risk at passing this info on to Wales, but it was a calculated one. The details would no doubt be released to the press by tomorrow at the latest, when the force would announce it is treating the incident as murder. But having appeared to be giving Wales something, and taking him further into his trust, it cleared the way for his next question. 'In a spirit of détente, perhaps you could help me out, now?'

'What is it?'

'The new figurehead of the North End Crew, or North End Haulage Company, if you prefer. The person who has taken over from Piper.'

'What of him?'

Dawson now knew it was a man and not Piper's wife as he had suspected. 'I just want his name, that's all.'

There was a long pause on the other end of the line, which Dawson took to be a good thing. Then Wales spoke.

'He's a thug who has been operating behind the scenes all along. He'll have form, which is why I am still firmly of the opinion that Piper has been set up, because your lot knew nothing of him. Well, in relation to running the North End empire, that is.'

This was indeed news to Dawson, and he was sure that it would be news to Bartholomew, too. Not that he ever intended to share it with him, he'd probably only try to fit him up as well. 'I appreciate your honesty, Gerald.'

'I'm out on a limb here, and I'm trusting you massively.'

'You have my word.'

'Fair enough.'

'Just need his name now, Gerald?'

'Shouldn't your old mob be able to find that out, now they know that they are looking for someone else, and that he has form?'

'That may be true if I were to tell them, but I'm not. I simply don't trust them; or know who not to trust. And I know that's a dreadful thing to say, but until I can be sure of the integrity of whom I would seek to pass that on to, I'll keep it to myself.'

'In that case, his name is Tommy Johnson, he goes by the ridiculous nickname of Toe Jo, and he's Piper's half-brother,' Wales said and then ended the call.

THE CABAL

Chapter Twenty-eight

Daniel walked into the café and sat down in the window seat where a freshly prepared flat white coffee was waiting for him next to his host. He nodded a greeting and took his seat and a sip of the brew, also nodding his thanks for the beverage.

His host, George Dawson, replied, 'I have to say, Daniel, yours was the second of two phone calls I would have least expected to receive over the last twenty-four hours.'

'A day ago, it wouldn't have happened. And still might meaning nothing. I just want to hear more of what you had in mind.'

It was Dawson's turn to nod as Daniel added, 'Tell me about your first unexpected call.'

Dawson explained to Daniel generally what Wales had said to him.

'It's good he's reaching out to you, seeing the light, even about the scum he represents, but I will never, ever do work for him to help him represent Piper,' Daniel said, before stopping himself from going into a rage-filled rant. He caught his breath and took a further sip of his brew. The truth be known, his emotions had been all over the place since learning of Sally's death, massively compounded by what he had learnt at the drug squat.

'Don't panic, Wales is under no illusion about you helping him. I iterated that on your behalf.'

'Good,' Daniel said, feeling a little calmer.

'But before you come on to what has brought you here today, of which I am intrigued to say the least, have you ever heard of a thug named, Tommy Johnson?'

Daniel rocked back in his chair as he thought, the name was familiar. Then it hit him.

'Nickname is a ridiculous Toe Jo, to his friends,' Dawson added.

Daniel never understood why some criminals insisted on giving themselves stupid nick names in a vain attempt to add gravitas to their reputations. 'Or Toe Jam to his enemies,' Daniel said.

'Yeah, he's a low life thug with delusions of his own criminal importance, allegedly a minion in the North End Crew.'

'Would it surprise you to hear that he is now running things since Piper was locked up?'

'It would amaze me.'

'Or shock you further, to hear that he has always been running things?'

Daniel was astonished by this but immediately disregarded it. He had read the intelligence case which had justified and initiated Bartholomew's investigation into Piper. There had been little information about the specifics of the rest of the gang, and no mention at all of Toe Jam. He told Dawson this.

'I'll come to the intelligence part in a bit. But according to Wales, Johnson is running things now for sure, whether you believe he always was or not.'

'Two questions then,' Daniel said, 'why is Wales telling you all this, and why would Piper let an idiot like Johnson sit in his chair?' he said before finishing his coffee. He loved flat whites but being essentially a double shot, they were always served in a small cup. He caught the waiter's eye and used two fingers in the Churchillian way to order more brews.

'Firstly, he says that his client is Piper and not Johnson, whom he clearly doesn't like and is even afraid of. When the case is over, he wants away from them,' Dawson started with.

'Interesting,' Daniel said.

'And secondly, because Johnson is actually Piper's half-brother.'

This really was news to Daniel, 'Brothers conceived under different covers?' he said.

'You could put it that way. And if it is true that Johnson has always been running things, it then adds weight to my worry that Piper is an innocent man. Whether Bartholomew ever knew, or later found out, I've no idea, but if he did, it didn't stop him.'

'What about the intelligence case pointing everything at Piper?' Daniel said, still feeling defensive towards his old unit.

'Two possibilities occur to me; the latter one I hope is not so.'

'Go on,' Daniel said.

THE CABAL

'Maybe the gathered intelligence was skewed. If Piper gave the appearance of being the head of the gang, then any sources reporting the facts would be doing so honestly, but mistakenly.'

Daniel mused on this for a moment. It could be possible, he knew. But as with all intelligence, corroboration was always sought and usually obtained, certainly in part, if not in full. 'And the second scenario? The one you wish not to be true?'

'That the intelligence in main or significant parts is false. All made up to justify a proactive investigation by Bartholomew.'

That was a huge leap as far as Daniel was concerned, and would take some doing. He was beginning to wonder if Dawson's hatred of Bartholomew was clouding his thinking. 'Just a minute George, that would be nigh on impossible to pull off.'

'Normally, I would have agreed with you.'

'Apart from anything else, all submissions to the intel unit have to be signed off by the departmental head.'

'Who is?'

'The detective superintendent in command of The Covert Policing Department.'

'Who is?

'Don Merson,' Daniel said, immediately realising where this was going.

'Who was murdered yesterday. Not common knowledge yet, but he'd had a severe beating which brought on a heart attack. Apparently, he had something wrong with his ticker that no one knew about.'

'I haven't seen that on the news.'

'You won't have yet, Marty Mathews - ACC Crime told me.'

Daniel was not convinced Merson's death could have had anything to do with Piper or Toe Jam. He was still to be convinced that a violent half-wit like Johnson could have been secretly running the North End Crew all this time without it leaking out. 'Well George, there is a lot of conjecture in all this, and if my narrative is correct, then Piper and his henchmen are guilty as hell, and I want nothing more than to prove it. And I'm particularly interested in his henchmen.'

The brews arrived, which was probably good timing as it created a pause. He had grown to like George the more he saw of him without his chief constable façade. The last thing he wanted to do was engage him in a heated debate of 'Oh yes they did,' and 'Oh no they didn't'. And when Dawson spoke next, Daniel was relieved that he wasn't bouncing back into defence of his theories, but instead, said, 'What about Piper's henchmen?'

Daniel took a long slug of coffee and a deep breath and then told Dawson all that had happened in the last 24 hours. When he finished, Dawson couldn't have looked more shaken and offered heartfelt condolences.

'Are you going to pass on what you've learnt to the officer dealing?' Dawson asked.

'Not yet, he's a waste of time. I'm not convinced he'd do anything with it, or if he did, that he wouldn't muck it up.'

'So, what are you planning to do with it?'

'Corroborate and add to it. If I can prove what this z-faced monster did, and therefore further implicate the North End Crew, then I will. I'll only pass it to the police once it's at a stage where even a quarter-wit couldn't cock it up.'

'I see, and I totally understand, but what of me did you wish to hear more of?'

'When you last pitched to me to work for Wales, you said you had a theory of how we could both work, albeit from differing agendas.'

'I did, but the events of the last 24 hours put us even further apart.'

Daniel thought about this, and it was true. Maybe he didn't need the help of Dawson after all, he was the detective. But if Dawson went off on his own agenda it could prove catastrophic should they'd end up in a blue-on-blue situation. He was driven to try though, with or without Dawson, but was still a little unsure as to George's true motivation, so asked him to elaborate.

'Some may think that I have an unreasonable distrust of Bartholomew, and they might be right. But it is my one remaining regret that I didn't nail the bent swine when I was still chief constable. This is now magnified by the death of Don

THE CABAL

Merson, whether connected or not, and if I'm right, an innocent man has lost the sight in one eye and is about to lose his long-term liberty and good standing.'

'If this bugs you so much, why didn't you stay on as chief until you had achieved your aims? Why go now?' Daniel asked. Dawson didn't answer right away, and seemed to be troubled by the question, or by what his response should be.

Then he said, 'I thought I could trust Carol Winstanley to honestly investigate Bartholomew. By the time I realised that she had lied about the drug money exhibit, and that she was probably therefore part of Bartholomew's Cabal, it was too late. I'd already gone.'

Daniel knew this was true, but couldn't help feeling that Dawson was holding back on something. He shrugged it off for the moment. 'OK, how do you see this working?'

'We are both seeking truthful answers, whatever they may be. You want justice for your niece, and I'm happy to help all I can with that. If what we find justifies new charges against Piper or whoever, then that is right and proper. If, however, we also discover that Piper is innocent of the current charges he faces, then we deal with it, but not as Wales's agents, but as private citizens.'

'Whatever we find in relation to your agenda, we discuss together and agree what to do?' Daniel asked, then added, 'Not working for Wales would give us the freedom to do that. We would not be duty bound to pass it on to him.'

Dawson considered the caveat which Daniel had laid down and started to nod. 'Agreed. Because if we found incriminating evidence and gave it to Wales, he is under no obligation to share it with the prosecution, which when it's the other way around they are obliged to do.'

'We decide together, if it supports the defence then we let the CPS have it first, knowing that they will pass it on if appropriate. And if it supports the prosecution then they'll use it as they see fit,' Daniel added.

'Again, agreed, but in principle only; each on its own merits to be jointly agreed.'

Daniel nodded, and then added, 'But what if we find evidence of the Cabal?'

'Again, we jointly decide who has the safest pair of hands to receive it. I still have a close relationship with the Mayor, so that is one option. Marty Mathews ACC Crime is another.'

Daniel could now see where being an ex-chief constable brought skills to the party which he could never access. This could work. His last question was what if they uncovered evidence in relation to Merson's murder? Dawson reminded him that the SIO was an out-of-force Manchester officer, so impartial, and Marty Mathews could be the conduit for any approach.

They shook hands, and as unlikely bedfellows as they were, Daniel looked forward to having someone else to bounce off. It also felt good to be doing something for Sally; he just regretted that he couldn't have done more for her whilst she had still been alive.

THE CABAL

Chapter Twenty-nine

After Daniel had told Sue all that had been agreed between him and Dawson, they both wandered from the kitchen into the rear lounge. The patio doors were ajar and the waning sun was throwing shadows across the rear lawn into the sitting room. The thought of just curling up on the sofa to an old episode of Top Gear, seemed a long way off. He would never be able to relax until he had found justice for Sally, Melanie, and Sue.

'I want you to be careful, and promise me that you will not take any silly risks, you're not a detective now,' Sue said.

'I know, but it feels so liberating without all the rules and authorities needed to even take a dump.'

'I'm being serious, Daniel. As much as Melanie and I appreciate what you are doing, I don't want you doing anything stupid.'

'I know, but I'm a big boy.'

'Promise me.'

'I promise I'm not stupid.'

Sue sighed in obvious exasperation, but dropped it as she moved on and asked, 'Looks like you've formed an unusual alliance?'

'I know, I wasn't sure at first, but it's clear that he has ins at a different level to me, which can only help.'

'How do you mean?'

'Well, he's already rung to say that he's spoken to the ACC Crime to keep him warm and found out that the last person to see Merson alive was Bartholomew. They had apparently been for a drink, but the SIO is concentrating on a witness who may have seen Merson being 'escorted' from his home.'

'I'm guessing the former is not relevant,' Sue said.

'I would have agreed with you, to a point; a fuller timeline of the hours leading up to a murder often contain golden nuggets. But I also find it strange as they were not social buddies, so what were they talking about over a drink, and in the middle of nowhere, too?'

'I guess you're going to find out.'

'It's somewhere to start.'

'How will that help Sally's cause?'

'Probably won't as it's on Dawson's agenda, not mine, but it'll keep him sweet.'

'Where are you going to start on our agenda?'

'Probably some low key obs on the haulage yard to see who comes and goes and take it from there.'

'Well, be careful.'

'Honestly, I will.'

'Why don't you ask Jill to help?'

'It's an idea, but I'll wait until I need a third pair of hands.'

'I still can't believe you and Dawson; talk about the odd couple,' Sue said and started laughing. It was good to hear her laugh, and lowered the overarching tension a little. Daniel threw a cushion at her, and then felt immediately guilty at the moment of levity. He saw Sue's face drop, too. 'It's OK to smile, you know,' he said. 'Breaks the tension.'

'I guess,' she answered as Daniel stood up and grabbed his car keys from the coffee table.

'Just promise me—' Sue started to say.

'I know, I'll play it safe,' Daniel interrupted with.

'We've done that bit. Just promise me that you will catch that horrible, horrible man, who has shattered my sister's world,' she said as tears filled her eyes.

Daniel gave her a long hug and told her to keep strong. The tears stemmed and she said that she would. He walked down the hall more determined than ever.

Twenty minutes later, he'd collected Dawson who almost looked excited. Daniel guessed it had been many, many years since he'd done anything remotely operational. He'd had to explain why he needed him. That two people walking into a pub were less noticeable than one. Daniel had chosen the covert approach for now, just to weigh the place up. If he felt that they would have to ask questions, then they'd need a cover story, so he warned Dawson about this. It took a further twenty minutes until they neared the pub, it was truly in the middle of nowhere on the outer edges of Ormskirk, a West Lancashire market town. A strange place to come to for a casual meet. 'And you're sure the SIO hasn't actioned a visit to this place?' he asked. The last thing they wanted was to be clocked by the murder investigation team. That would take some explaining.

'According to Marty, they have started the investigation after Bartholomew left Merson at his home. They see this drink thing as a non-relevant event, for now anyway.'

'And Marty Mathews isn't suspicious of your questions?'

'No. I'm being careful; he just thinks I'm being nosy. Plus, he wants to keep me sweet because if the deputy gets my old job, he wants to apply for the dep's job and I said I'd help him prepare.'

Dawson was really proving his worth. It was Daniel's turn to deliver to their partnership, so he gave Dawson a few brief instructions as they pulled onto the car park of The Higher Lock pub.

The place was quiet with only a handful of punters in, who all looked like local farm workers. They were clearly the teatime trade. The clientele would no doubt change later. But from an outsider's point of view, it was more the location to bring someone you were having an illicit affair with; or for a clandestine meeting. Not a quick pint after work. Especially, when work was a thirty-minute drive away.

The hardwood flooring announced their arrival and they drew a couple of momentary glances as they made their way to the bar. Daniel ordered a shandy, and Dawson went for a craft ale called Naughty Witch. They settled on their barstools and took in the environment. A TV hung from the far end of the bar and was muted. A news channel was on and a picture of Don Merson flashed across the screen. Daniel saw that the barman was watching it intently. Great timing, so Daniel jumped at the chance to capitalise on it. 'Bloody strange job that,' he said in a raised voice aimed at the back of the barman's head. The news item shifted to something else and Daniel repeated his remark, even louder as the bar man turned back around to face them.

'Sorry, it sure is. Used to come in here with his mates now and again, didn't know he was a copper though, and a senior one at that.'

'You get much passing trade in here?' Daniel asked.

'Bit out the way really, usually just locals.'

'It's a lovely spot, must admit me and my partner were just having a drive in the country when we spotted your place, thought we'd have a shifty,' Daniel said, risking a quick glance at Dawson's startled face.

'You're always welcome to come back.'

'Sadly, that guy won't be back,' Daniel said and nodded to the TV.

'Not sure he would be anyway.'

'How do you mean?'

'Last time he was in, he was with his mate, and the usual two women,' the barman started.

Two women? Daniel thought.

'But they must have had a fall out.'

'That so?'

'Reckon. That dead cop poured his ale over his skinny mate's head, and stormed out, closely followed by the ladies, then the skinny bloke left.'

Skinny bloke; Bartholomew, Daniel thought.

'What was it about?'

'No idea, the skinny man apologised as I went over with a mop, said it was his brother and it was something and nothing.'

'When was that?' Daniel asked, wondering whether he was pushing his luck beyond a normal bar chat.

'Reckon it was the night before they found him in the River Ribble.'

'You told the police about it?'

'I was going to, but that skinny bloke came back yesterday. He said he too was a cop, so not to worry about the previous evening. It was not related.'

THE CABAL

Daniel and Dawson shared a further look, and then Daniel, said, 'Oh that's OK then, I guess.'

'Yeah, he showed me his badge and everything. You just never know who you've got in your pub.'

Daniel emptied his glass, and saw Dawson take the hint and do the same. 'Well, I hope his brother catches the maniac who did it,' Daniel said, as he stood to leave.

The barman picked up their empty glasses, and said, 'Yeah, me an' all. Hope you two call again when you're not just passing.'

'We'll be sure and do that,' Daniel said as his parting remark.

As soon as they were back in the car, Daniel said, 'Now wasn't that worth a visit?'

'Bartholomew's taking a chance; what if the real police do follow up on that place?' Dawson said.

'He's obviously panicked and tried to close it down.'

'Still a risk.'

'He'll have an answer ready no doubt, but he is probably confident they aren't going there.'

'But why lie?'

'Yeah, the "brother" thing,' Daniel said.

'Probably trying too hard to reassure the barman, to stop him calling it in.'

'Which means he's hiding something,' Daniel added.

'Certainly, looks that way. Told you he's bent.'

And for the first time, Daniel was beginning to wonder if Dawson wasn't right.

'Anyway, what's all this partner malarkey?' Dawson asked, with half a grin.

'Basics,' Daniel replied, also grinning, 'couples look less suspicious.'

Chapter Thirty

Bartholomew had just about got over the shock from the day before, but as far as he was concerned, nothing had changed. Piper was out of the way and the real force behind the North End Crew would now have to rise and put its neck in open view. Bartholomew wouldn't stop until he'd beheaded the Crew. Then his job would be done, and everything else would fall into place. The one thing he did miss with Merson gone, was the ready access to all things intelligence. But they'd never been able to identify Piper's lieutenants previously, so he could manage without Merson now. The thing he really missed was the twenty grand he'd given Merson to keep him sweet only hours before his death. If only he'd known. And having heard no mention of it being found at Merson's house, he could only surmise that whoever took Merson had also taken the cash. Probably for the best, as his fingerprints would have been on some of the notes.

He spent the day after the briefing in the chief's office, nosing around and trying to find out what was happening with the murder investigation, but he hadn't got far. The ACC Boy Wonder knew nothing, and as the SIO was from Manchester, he couldn't really approach her. He didn't know her, but had heard of her, another ruthless bitch destined for the top by all accounts. But he still had Carol Winstanley keeping an ear on the professional standards side of things and Shirley Lancaster with the acting chief's ear; or so he hoped. Neither were currently returning his calls.

He'd just finished a strategic tasking meeting where the only outcome was the bleeding obvious, iterated by those intent on crawling up the head of CID's arse. And as far as Bartholomew was concerned, none were more sycophantic than John Jones himself. The deputy chief was acting chief and wanted the top job, and the Boy Wonder wanted his job. John Jones, who Bartholomew used to think was OK, had suddenly gone uber corporate as he no doubt wanted to become ACC - Crime. All only concerned with self-advancement rather than doing the job they were actually paid to do. Bartholomew believed he was one of only a few senior officers doing the job of taking on criminals like the North End Crew - whilst others hid away and concentrated on promotion.

He left the meeting room and headed to the canteen. After filling his tray and paying for it, he looked for an empty table where he could eat in peace without having to make polite conversation with some crawler with an agenda. That was until he saw Winstanley and Lancaster alone at the rear of the hall. He quickly joined them and saw their faces drop as he placed his tray down on the table. 'Hello, ladies, piece of luck running into you two, especially as neither of you appear to be speaking to me.'

'We both told you the other night, the night poor Don lost his life that we are done. Piper is on remand and that's that,' Winstanley said.

'But as I said, the job's only part done.'

'It's done as far as we both are concerned,' Lancaster added.

'How are you getting on with the acting chief?' he asked Lancaster.

'Fine and he is by far the front runner to get the job. And he's totally different to how George Dawson was, so I'd be careful what you say around him if I were you,' Lancaster replied.

'I'm fifteen years older and one rank higher than you Shirley, so don't treat me like a numpty.'

'You're also an arrogant son of a bitch, which can cloud your judgement,' she replied with.

Bartholomew knew he had to reign himself in otherwise he'd lose his audience before he'd started. He threw his hands up to gesture peace. 'The last thing I want is to fall out with you two. We've all had a shock after poor Don's death. Nerves are bound to be raw,' he said as conciliatorily as he was able, which he knew could come out as patronising.

'Look, Peter, we don't want to fall out either, it would serve none of our purposes, but you have to respect our decision,' Winstanley said.

'Fair enough, but I'd just hoped that as our little team had worked so well, we could always do it again, on an ad hoc basis. Obviously, just when another untouchable, like Piper, popped up.'

'Well, I always thought this was a one off to remove Lancashire's worst criminal,' Winstanley said.

'It was, it was, but I just thought that as it had worked so well, it would be a shame not to do it again.'

'Be a bit hard now Don's gone,' Lancaster said. 'He controlled the intelligence side of things.'

As far as Bartholomew was concerned, this was the first sign that Lancaster might be swayed.

'True, Shirley, but possible. And only to be done if we all agree, like before.'

Winstanley then looked at Lancaster and said, 'Surely, you're not thinking of doing this all over again?'

Lancaster replied to her, 'I wasn't, but you have to admit we did achieve that which every lawful investigation failed to.'

'Failed, perhaps, as we now suspect, because Piper may have been an innocent puppet,' Winstanley said.

'Tell you what ladies, let's find out. Let's park any decisions about the future until we finish the job at hand. Deal with Piper's number two, and leave the North End Crew dismantled, then reassess. All decisions joint with no more gung-ho from me. What do you reckon?' he said and sat back to take a mouthful of his cold lasagne, as both women whispered to each other. He could only pick up the odd word with all the background chatter around, but ignored them and gave them some peace as he wolfed his food down while it still had some heat in it. As he wiped his mouth, both women turned to face him and leaned in.

'OK, but only to clarify exactly what the hell we have done, and if it turns out that Piper is totally innocent, then we find a way to put this right,' Winstanley said.

'Of course, scouts honour,' Bartholomew lied.

'And if we get past this, then we will consider doing it again against a suitable target, but we must all concur,' Lancaster added.

THE CABAL

'Also agreed,' Bartholomew further lied, as he pondered the sudden turnaround. He'd worked out Winstanley's angle; fearful that they'd fitted up Piper, an innocent man - which Bartholomew knew he was. Didn't matter. It was just important to get these two back on side. But he couldn't see Lancaster's angle, so asked, 'Why the change of heart, Shirley?'

Lancaster flushed, if only for a second before she answered, 'Well, the acting chief, who will no doubt become the new chief, wants me to lead a strategy to reduce serious crime. I can say I've linked in with you without him knowing how we intend to achieve it, so long as we get results. That's all that matters to him. I can soon make something up to fit afterwards.'

Bartholomew could see how they could swing that, but was still at a loss as to why the acting chief would want his staff officer to take the lead on such an initiative, so asked, 'OK, but why you?'

The flush came back for a further millisecond as she answered, 'He says that if I can achieve this, then he'll support me for the next round of promotion boards to superintendent.'

Now he got it. Another self-serving career hungry parasite. But at least he had control of them both again. Things were looking up.

Chapter Thirty-one

Johnson was sat at Piper's desk in the office at the haulage yard, in the Deepdale area of Preston. Business was carrying on as normal, with the HGVs continuing their legal and illegal runs to the continent. The whole administration of which was a nightmare post Brexit. But fortunately, Piper had put all the necessary systems in place to facilitate things. The checklist he had written was straightforward but a pain in the arse. He was more accustomed to the other side of the business. Both Garys were with him, and G had produced a half decent idea. After they wrongly fingered the driver Billy, why not promote him to office manager while Piper was away. It would make up for his wronged treatment, and as a driver himself he would understand all the customs' rubbish. 'You must have eaten clever pills for breakfast, G, that's a top idea.'

Goon Two - Gary - laughed, and G threatened to put an x on his face to match his own z-shaped scar.

Johnson joined in the banter, 'Good idea, then I can call you x and z. But what happened to y?'

'Thicko can't count,' Gary said.

'Letters isn't counting; double-thicko,' G replied.

'OK, you don't know your alphabet then,' Gary added.

'OK ladies let's get back to business. What's the street update?' Johnson asked.

Gary answered first, 'The last consignment of handguns has all been shifted, three sold to that firm in East Lancs, three to the firm in Cheetham Hill in Manchester, and two to that mob in Toxteth.'

'How'd it go with the Tockie crew, we've not worked with them before?' Johnson asked.

'Scousers are Scousers, boss, so long as you don't rip them, and make them think they are getting a solid deal - which they are - and have a bit of craic with them; all sweet.'

'Good. Are we sure there is no beef between them and the Cheetham Hill mob? Wouldn't want to get caught up between a

THE CABAL

Scouse versus Manc thing?'

'No, I checked; they're good with the Mancs; it's a Birkenhead firm they are at handbags with.'

'Good man,' Johnson said, and then turned to face G, 'How's the gear runs doing?'

'All of the last batch of heroin and crack have gone out; I've taken a backwards step and brought a lad in to coordinate the street level dealing.'

'Problem?'

'No, all sweet, he only knows that he's working for me. He thinks I am top of the North End Crew,' G said.

'Delusions of grandeur for one so illiterate,' Gary threw in.

Ignoring Gary, Johnson pressed, 'I mean, is there a problem with you? You know I like you to be hands on, stops anyone taking the piss.'

'Only temporary, just operational security after that daft bitch went over. Thought I'd keep a low profile until it died down; just in case the cops started sniffing around it.'

Johnson nodded; it made good sense. For all their lack of academic wisdom, both Gary's made up ten times over in street smarts, plus he knew he could trust them totally. 'OK, no probs, if the kid does good then keep him on, but micromanage him.'

'Will do, boss,' G replied.

'And talking about cops, we still have a problem to solve. We still need to stop this Bartholomew and get Johnny out of the nick.'

'What about the scum what done, Johnny?' Gary asked.

'All in good time, boys, but trust me, you'll have your fun and Johnny will have his revenge, but it'll have to wait a short while.'

'What do you want us to do first?' G asked.

'We need Johnny sorted first, and I've got an idea how to do it. But first, let's get hold of Billy the driver then I can give it my full attention.'

'I'll go get him,' Gary said.

***

Daniel picked Dawson up, but not because he really needed him. In fact, it would look less obvious alone, he'd just seemed keen to come along. Daniel only planned to keep watch for a couple of hours, just to get a feel for the normal comings and goings, and would not stay long enough to draw attention. Each observation job was different, each with its own limitations based on the environment. North End Haulage Company was situated in the Deepdale part of Preston, and as its name suggested, that was in the north end of the city. In fact, Preston North End Football Club was within sight of the premises. The company included an open, but covered yard, occupying a whole block of what was once a mill, stuck in the middle of a bunch of terraced streets.

Daniel had picked a spot roughly one hundred metres back from the main vehicle entrance and exit to the covered yard, which in turn was next to the frontage and main doors to the premises. After thirty or forty minutes, Dawson's excitement at doing something operational was starting to wane; he'd lost that cheesy glow from his expression.

'How long do we stay here?' Dawson asked.

'As long as we feel comfortable.'

'When will you know when it's been too long?'

It was a good question, which Daniel answered as best as he could. It all came down to a sixth sense honed from years of doing observation jobs as a DC and a DS. You just knew when you started to feel uncomfortable, often for no singularly obvious reason. A case of going before you get clocked, going just before you would have been noticed. Spooky, really. If you wait until you have been seen - even if unnoticed - it was too late. Dawson nodded after Daniel's explanation, but didn't look as though he fully understood. Daniel didn't really; he just knew that when that itch to move came, only a fool ignored it. Then Dawson started coughing, and even though they were in an enclosed vehicle, noise, any noise could travel and draw attention.

'Dry throat,' he managed to say between splutters, as Daniel reached for a flask on the back seat and poured Dawson half a cup of coffee. Dawson took it and two or three gulps later his coughing stopped, much to the relief of Daniel who was scanning via all the car's mirrors to see if anyone was looking at them.

THE CABAL

Fortunately, it was a quiet side street and Daniel couldn't see anyone as he took the empty cup back from Dawson.

'I never thought to bring a flask,' Dawson said. 'I'll know next time.'

'Serves two purposes, though it's a long time since I've actually done any obs work.'

'What's the second purpose?'

'Once the coffee's gone - depending on how long the job is - it serves as a mobile toilet, too,' Daniel said, and enjoyed the look of horror on Dawson's face.

'I hope that's a new flask?' he said.

It wasn't, but Daniel spared him by saying that it was. Then his eyes were drawn to his driver's side door mirror as a motor approached. It had only been the second car that had passed them since they'd arrived, which made it a noteworthy event. Daniel slunk down in his seat and saw that Dawson immediately followed his lead as the BMW saloon passed them. It was travelling slowly as if it was looking for somewhere to park. It pulled up in front of them fifty meters further down the road, just short of the company's main doors. Opposite the company was a row of bordered up houses, so this looked promising.

And then it became even better, or worse, depending on your point of view. The driver's door opened and Peter Bartholomew alighted and stretched his back as he stood up straight. Fortunately, he didn't look back towards Daniel and Dawson, for which Daniel was extremely grateful. It would take some explaining as to what he and Dawson were up to. Bartholomew was too preoccupied looking towards the front of the haulage company.

'I knew it, I knew that swine was bent,' Dawson said.

Daniel didn't answer, as he wasn't too sure why his presence here confirmed Dawson's suspicions. There could be any number of legitimate reasons why he was here regarding the investigation into Piper. Though, he did find it unusual that a man of his seniority would be doing routine follow up enquires, he'd grant Dawson that.

Then came the bigger surprise; the passenger door opened and out got Chief Inspector Shirley Lancaster, the acting chief's staff officer; Dawson's old staff officer.

'What in God's name is she doing here, and with him?' Dawson spat.

Daniel didn't answer; it was one hell of a good question. He watched the pair of them cross the cobbled street and head towards the haulage company's main doors.

'You know what this means?' Dawson said.

'Not entirely sure, if I'm honest, but admit that it is strange,' Daniel replied.

'It can only mean that she is in cahoots with Bartholomew. She too must be in his Cabal. No bloody wonder he was always one step ahead of me. And to think I totally trusted her.'

'Time to go,' Daniel said as he started the car engine, and he reversed back a while before negotiating a three-point turn. They had to get out of there before Bartholomew and Lancaster came back out, they would then be in full view.

THE CABAL

Chapter Thirty-two

If he were honest, Bartholomew would have much preferred to come alone, but Lancaster had insisted, she'd argued that she could honestly tell the acting chief that she had been out operationally with him. He'd reluctantly agreed to keep her sweet, but this was hardly operational. Yet she seemed to have the sort of buzz about her that probationary constables or student officers - or whatever they called them nowadays - had on their first day on active patrol. And to think that this promotion hungry zealot was already a chief inspector. He needed her, but despised her. In his view, there would come the day when all senior officers in the police had done jack shit at the sharp end, and then the whole organisation would become a house of cards.

He had demanded that she sack her uniform and had expected her to come dressed as a detective wearing a smart business suit befitting of her rank, but instead she looked like she was going on a photoshoot. And had those annoying high heels on you could hear a mile away. They approached the front and Bartholomew decided to give the reception a miss if he could. And as luck would have it as they crossed the road, the large up-and-over shutter doors started to rattle open as an HGV came into view waiting to leave. He grabbed Lancaster's elbow to swerve her away from the reception and they both snuck under the opening doors. He did notice the receptionist looking out the front windows at them, so she would undoubtedly be on their case unless they were quick. He knew where the office was from the earlier police raid and was keen to get there as quickly as he could to preserve an element of surprise. 'Hurry up, Shirley for God's sake,' he said as he made a beeline for the office door. Behind him he could hear the clackity-clack of Lancaster's heels pick up their tempo as they echoed around the vacuous inner space. He could also hear the receptionist shouting after them. He quickened his pace further; Lancaster could deal with her.

As he approached the inner office, he could see through the closed blinds that the lights were on, and then the door opened and two huge guys wearing matching Crombies stepped out. The door closed quickly behind them so he didn't get a glimpse of the inside. They were in the way. The one with a scarred face said, 'Hey, it's private in here where the f—' but Bartholomew pushed between the men and left Lancaster to cope with them. Maybe bringing her along had helped after all.

He took in the room as the door closed automatically behind him. On his left was the huge desk where Piper had been arrested and the drugs had been discovered. It was currently empty. The whole purpose for the surprise visit was to establish who had taken over from Piper, and therefore identify the real boss of the North End Crew. But although the desk seat was empty, it looked as if its occupant hadn't long gone. A pair of reading glasses was laid out next to some paperwork.

Bartholomew took in the rest of the room. It was spacious but plain. A flat screen TV adorned the wall opposite the desk, and to one side of it was a battered Chesterfield settee and two armchairs which looked even worse for wear. In one, sat a mean looking man in his forties. He looked a handful and his whole demeanour and facial appearance screamed villain. He wouldn't have looked out of place behind the desk. Perhaps the glasses were his. Bartholomew produced his warrant card and badge and flashed them at the man.

Behind him he heard Lancaster screaming at one of the brutes to 'get your hands off me, I'm a police officer.' He smiled to himself as the door reopened and she rushed in looking more bedraggled than she had probably ever looked. The two brutes stood in the doorway, and Bartholomew noticed the man in the armchair shake his head very subtlety. But Bartholomew had seen it. The two brutes withdrew and the door closed.

'You do know this is private property, constable,' Armchair man said.

'It's detective superintendent, and yes, I know, thanks. I've been here before.'

'What do you want?'

'I wanted to know who you are?'

'Sorry?'

THE CABAL

'Don't apologise, but I take it that you are doing Piper's job.'

'I just work here.'

At that stage, the out-of-puff receptionist came blustering in apologising as she had not been able to stop Bartholomew and Lancaster. Armchair man told her not to worry and thanked her. He was in charge.

'I'm just helping, not that it's any of your business. So, unless you have a warrant, please leave. And if you want to come back again without one, request it through our reception and it'll be considered, so long as you clearly state your reasons,' Armchair man said.

Bartholomew could see that he'd rattled the man who had got over the initial shock, and was growing in confidence. He leaned in towards armchair man, 'And who exactly might you be?'

'None of your business, and like I said, I just work here,' he said, his face nearly puce. This bloke was struggling to supress his anger. 'What is it you really want?'

'Just needed to know who to return stuff to from the search, you know, stuff that we don't need to use in evidence.'

'I guess you'll be keeping your drugs, unless you've come here to place some more,' Armchair man said.

'Serious allegations. Good job I can take a joke,' Bartholomew said.

'Joke, joke, you think this is funny. A man is lying in a prison hospital with one eye less than he had when he went in, and you think it's a big laugh, do you?'

Bartholomew ignored the comment, which he was sure would enrage him even further, but said, 'Well, acting boss-man, I want to know who you are, or I'll ask our friends at the Inland Revenue to pay you a surprise visit.'

'I'm not the acting boss, he's just stepped out,' Armchair man said.

'Of course, he has. Just give me your name unless you really do have something to hide, in which case, maybe we do need another search warrant.'

'Look, we don't want any more trouble from your lot. The name is Tommy Johnson; I normally just look after the drivers.

I'm just helping while Mr Piper isn't here - thanks to you - so no big deal. And as I said, I'm not in charge.'

'That's all I wanted; just needed to know who I'm talking to.'

'Well, now you know,' Johnson said.

'So, who *is* in charge?'

'You've got all you're getting.'

Bartholomew noticed that armchair man, or Johnson as he said he was called, looked close to blowing. His complexion was past puce and nearing purple. Time to quit whilst he was ahead. He enjoyed the slack-jawed look on Lancaster's face as he walked past her and out the office. The trademark clatter of her heels struggled to keep up as she followed on behind him.

As soon as they were both in the car, he started the engine and was away as swiftly as he could be, then he relaxed and took a deep breath before turning to face Lancaster. 'You enjoy that?'

'Enjoy it! It was terrifying; I still don't know how we got out of there in one piece.'

Bartholomew patted his chest and felt the shape of his warrant card and badge folder push back from his inside pocket. 'The power of the badge,' he said.

'One day you won't have a badge or it won't actually help, regardless.'

'One day, but not today.'

'I thought that driver/office stand-in guy, Johnson, was going to explode. It's no wonder criminals hate you.'

'We are not supposed to be their friends. That's what's wrong nowadays; police are no longer feared by the criminals as we keep hiring failed social worker types. You've been sat on your cute butt in your plush office for too long.'

Lancaster didn't answer at first, but then said, 'We still don't know for sure who is running the North End Crew.'

Bartholomew had to stifle a laugh. 'Driver? Stand-in? My arse; Tommy Johnson; he's the man running the show.'

THE CABAL

Chapter Thirty-three

Johnson was still marching around the office in circles five minutes after Bartholomew and his tart had left. It took all he had to prevent losing his rag while the cocky detective had been there. But now gone he could vent his anger, which was proving harder to control. If either of the Garys told him to calm down one more time, he'd do them just for sport. No one spoke, and Billy, who had thankfully been taking a dump and had missed the fun, looked like he'd soil himself again on hearing what had happened.

'That bastard is making this very personal,' Johnson said. Everyone just nodded at him. 'If he'd been on his own, I might have been tempted to…but before any of you clowns state the bleeding obvious, I'm not a fool.' No one said anything. Slowly, he stopped his wagon train impression and plonked down on the settee. He needed to think, and he did need to calm down to do so. A couple of minutes passed, then he said, 'We'll deal with that arrogant plod when we can, but he clearly came in here with an agenda. And if he's worked out what I am, then that's even more reason to sort him.'

'Yes, boss. Do you want us to follow him from the nick, see where he lives?' G asked.

'Not yet, he'll be uber cautious now he's rattled our cage, but what we can learn from his visit is that he's not done with us. Fitting Johnny up was just the start.'

'So, we *are* at war?' Gary said.

'We are, but we need to use our smarts. Get our priorities right. Get Johnny's case thrown out and him out of nick first. Then we'll put a stop to everything else.'

'Fair enough,' G said.

'It looks to me that this Bartholomew nutter is doing a Lone Ranger job here. And I've no idea why? But if we stop him, we stop it all, I reckon.'

'Who was the woman he brought with him?' Billy asked.

'No idea, probably just insurance in case it kicked off in here. A witness. She certainly didn't look like a detective.'

'She told us, she was a chief inspector,' G said.

'God knows what's going on then. We'll deal with her too if we must. But for now, we need to smash the prosecution case, and it's time to put that plan into action,' Johnson said. 'Have we got the info yet?'

'Yes, boss, just,' G said, and then glanced at Billy.

Johnson took the hint and said to Billy, 'No offence, but this is not for your ears.'

'I don't want to know, boss. Do you want me to leave?'

'It's OK, enough said for now,' Johnson said and then turned to the two Garys, 'Get what you both need and see me back here at seven tonight and we'll go through it all then.'

Both G and Gary nodded, turned, and left.

***

Daniel sipped his freshly ground coffee while sat in Dawson's rear lounge, which was not dissimilar to his own. But with ornate French Windows rather than patio doors leading to a neatly bordered lawn garden. Dawson was in the front room on the phone to Marty Mathews ACC - Crime, for a friendly chat and a supposed update on the murder enquiry. Dawson told Daniel that he would slip in Lancaster's name; ask how she was managing with the acting chief and see if anything came back the other way. Daniel told him to be as circumspect as he could. Mathews was no fool, and they didn't want to raise any red flags.

Dawson returned five minutes later and looked pleased and surprised at the same time.

'That was illuminating,' he started with.

'How so?' Daniel asked.

'Firstly, the murder investigation is crawling along. Apparently, the witness who saw Merson leave home with two heavies is struggling to add further; like the car details, other than it was a blue saloon. Therefore, the SIO is working through a long list of MO suspects of which Merson's department had reported on where court proceedings are still ongoing.'

THE CABAL

'They're walking through mud, then,' Daniel said.

'Pretty much. And when I causally asked how Shirley Lancaster was getting on with Bernard Darlington, Marty said that she was heading up some initiative to produce a policy to further reduce serious crime, and was linking in with Peter Bartholomew.'

'That explains her presence earlier on, then.' Daniel said.

'I suppose so.'

'She might still be on the level after all?'

'I suppose so,' Dawson said again. 'But when I asked if the idea was his, being ACC - Crime, he had a right moan.'

'Not his idea then?'

'Direct from Darlington completely bypassing him.'

'I bet that upset his senior officer ego,' Daniel said, forgetting for a moment that he was talking to an ex chief constable.

Dawson laughed, 'You're right, everyone from superintendent and above has one. But it encouraged Marty to open up. Apparently, Darlington has got the top job; it's just not been announced yet. The interviews were held yesterday.'

'As expected, so Marty will be chuffed then?'

'He's very *not* chuffed. The new chief has already told him that he does not expect to see an application from him for the now vacant position of deputy chief constable. He's absolutely fuming.'

'We can use that.'

'That's what I thought,' Dawson said. 'I've told him to apply for the first dep's job that comes up anywhere in the UK and I'll help him with it. I've said it will benefit him to serve as a dep in another force.'

Daniel was glad that he had never reached those exalted ranks; the nepotism, backstabbing and brown nosing was off the scale.

'OK, so the jury's out on Lancaster,' Daniel said.

'For now.'

'And Darlington, as the new chief, is not a friendly asset.'

'Arrogant sod.'

'So where do we go next?' he asked, not in a rhetorical way, as he had no idea himself.

'Over to you, Daniel.'

Daniel thought for several minutes as Dawson caught up with his coffee. Then he said, 'I suppose to serve both our purposes, we could do with having a word with Piper. Get a feel for him; see if we believe him. Or is he just another criminal trying to bull his way through things.'

'That'll prove tricky, him in prison and all.'

Daniel knew this, he was just thinking out loud. He also desperately wanted to trace the dealer referred to as Capone. Then he had an idea. 'How friendly do you think Wales really is with you?'

'We get on very well, and it's certainly in our interest to keep a line of communication open with him.'

'Granted, and if he knew we were looking at this independently, he would no doubt be thrilled?'

'I'm sure he would.'

'Thrilled enough to do us a favour?'

'Where are you going with this?'

'The only way we can speak to Piper is via a legal visit.'

'I suppose. Are you suggesting we ask Wales to visit him and ask some questions drafted by us?'

'That was my first thought. But it would be better if one of us could do it. How do you fancy being Wales's assistant?'

'You want me to pretend to be a solicitor?' Dawson said with a look of utter credulity on his face.

'That's the ideal way. You have the relationship with Wales, it's in his interests, and remember, you are no longer a cop.'

'He'll never agree; it must break all their rules.'

'Trust me, breaking rules won't matter if he thinks it will advance his client's defence.'

'I'm sorry, it won't work, he won't do it and I can't do it. It's not going to happen.'

THE CABAL

Chapter Thirty-four

'I have to say, Gerald, I was surprised when you agreed to this,' Dawson said as Wales turned in to the visitor's car park at HMP Preston. He didn't answer right away as he negotiated reversing his car into a parking space. Once he'd completed the move, he turned the engine off and turned to face Dawson in the passenger seat. Dawson was sure that parking the car hadn't required Wales's total concentration; he was obviously choosing his reply with care.

'You sound like you are unsure?' Wales said.

'I was rather hoping that you'd refuse.'

'If you are having second thoughts…?'

'No, no, we are here now.'

'You suggested this to me, remember?'

'I know, I know.'

'Look, I'm just grateful that you and Daniel are having a look at this case, albeit from an independent point of view; which actually makes good sense, by the way.'

'You do realise I am here with a dual agenda, notwithstanding that I personally favour your position.'

'Fully understood and appreciated. Look, I'll do all the talking. I'll introduce you as a paralegal just here to learn procedure.'

'What if he recognises me from the many TV appearances I've done over the years?'

'He won't, these types aren't avid news watchers, and even if he does, solicitors often hire ex-officers as paralegals. It saves us having to get out of bed in the middle of the night when we can send a paralegal to the nick to get the initial run down following an arrest. They brief us later before we attend any of the police interviews. So, no probs.'

'I guess that would work.'

'And I can just say later on if I need to, that you quit when you realised that you'd be needed to provide 24-hour cover.'

Dawson nodded. He was feeling better.

'As I said, you say nothing, but if you see anything which helps you believe in my client's innocence, then it's all in a good cause.'

Dawson nodded again and they both got out the car and he tagged along behind Wales, who was clearly walking a well-trodden path. They queued and booked in. Wales handed over some paperwork and they both handed over their mobile phones. A handheld scanner wand was used to search them. Then they were led away from the reception area. Others were taken towards the main prison building, but they were escorted in the opposite direction, to a standalone annex, which although connected to the rest of the prison, was separate. The prison hospital wing. They were then ushered by a different officer to an interview room located in front of the hospital wing entrance. Inside was a wooden table with three chairs around it. The room had white painted brickwork walls and looked Spartan. Dawson commented so.

'This is plush, we even have a carpet. The legal visit room in the main prison has no carpet, steel chairs and table, and a cacophony of background noise,' Wales said.

Dawson shuddered at the thought. They each took a chair and moments later a prisoner was led in by an officer who closed the door and remained inside the room. The prisoner eyed Dawson with suspicion as he took the third chair. He had an eyepatch over his right eye socket.

'Who is this?' he said to Wales, whilst nodding towards Dawson.

Wales didn't answer him, but turned to face the prison officer and said, 'This is a legal visit. And I am Mr. Piper's solicitor.'

The prison officer grunted in reply and then left the room.

'Why do they always try that on?' Wales said to no one in particular.

'So, the bent screws can blow you out to the other cons if you're up to no good,' Piper said.

Dawson realised that 'up to no good' probably meant doing one's civic and moral duty in normal people's parlance. This place was certainly an experience. He would not admit to Wales or Daniel, or anyone for that matter - that even though he'd been a chief constable and served for over thirty years in the police - he had never been inside a prison before. And he hoped that he would not have to do so again.

Wales quickly answered Piper's initial question introducing Dawson as per their agreed story, and then Wales got stuck into the meat of things, going through the evidence facing Piper and how Wales planned to question it. Piper seemed calm and agreeable to most of what Wales said, but what struck Dawson was his strong reaction whenever the drugs or the drug money was mentioned. He became animated with what appeared to Dawson as a genuine reaction.

'If I am to prepare a brief to try and put doubt in the jury's mind of the validity of the police exhibits, it helps that I can allege that the drug drenched money was also planted along with the drugs found at your office,' Wales said.

'As you know, I'd handed over all my ready cash when I bought the gold bar, which the cops also helped themselves to,' Piper said.

Wales then said that he had a defence forensic expert lined up to re-examine the money and would hopefully be able to say that the drug particles were not in a natural pattern. That they had been submerged in drugs. Plus, they had the witness who will confirm that he had cleaned Piper out of all his ready cash when he dropped the gold bar off. This was not long before the police raid - which incidentally found no other drugs at his home. Wales said that he was confident that he could cast serious doubt on the prosecution case. It was plain to Dawson that this was something Piper already knew about.

'All granted, but what about the drugs themselves, where are we with regard to that?' Piper asked.

'As a matter of course, we can request our own examination of the drugs, not only to confirm that it is a controlled drug, but that the purities are accurate. As you know from our previous chats, it is an expense I would not normally advise as the police labs are very fair and accurate,' Wales said.

Piper nodded and Wales paused a moment.

'But in this case, we can examine a sample of the drug recovered from the money against the recovered drugs. If we can cast doubt that the deposit on the cash is not from, or can't be confirmed as being from, the main drug exhibit, it would be a hole in the police evidence. And with all holes, we just need to create one big enough to put our toe in and then we can start making it bigger.'

'Yeah, I know this, but do you really think it will damage their case that much?'

'Don't forget, all we have to do is create the smallest of reasonable doubt and our job is done.'

Dawson thought that Piper looked less than convinced.

'And as they have fit me up good and proper, then they will have made sure that the deposits on the cash are from the same drugs.'

'Undoubtedly, but even so, if our examination can cast some doubt on the suggestion that the drugs are from the same batch - even if they are - then that will do.'

Dawson was impressed with Wales's determination to have as much of the evidence checked and challenged, as possible, but he could see why Piper was less than convinced of its value.

'It's going to take an age to do, though I guess,' Piper said.

'Well, we have some good news on that front. Our expert was in the middle of another trial when it collapsed yesterday, so he has a few days diary-free. He's going to ring the lab today and set up access to the exhibits for tomorrow, or the day after at the latest.'

Dawson noted the look of surprise on Piper's face.

'But attacking the exhibits aside, make no mistake Johnny, this will get messy in court. It always does when the defence attack the credibility of the police officers involved. Judges will tolerate it, but only when there are grounds to do so. We will have to be careful, we can't just slag them off without good cause,' Wales added.

Dawson was gripped by it all, having never been sat in on such a discussion from the other side's perspective, he found it

THE CABAL

enlightening. It was only after the main stuff had been discussed that Wales eventually asked Piper how he was doing medically.

'They say the operation to remove the ruined eye was a success; some success if you ask me. But once the severed optic nerve has healed over, they will fit a prosthetic eye. I've told them that it is still very painful and they seem to be in no rush.'

'I'm sorry to hear that, are you getting the right pain relief medication?' Wales asked.

'I am, and even though it does still hurt, I'm stretching it out as long as I can. As soon as they have fitted the new eye, the sooner they'll send me back to the main prison.'

'Understood, can't blame you for that.'

Dawson looked at the man and couldn't help but feel a weight of sorrow for him. Not least because of the awful life changing assault he'd suffered, but Dawson was as sure as he'd ever been that Piper was an innocent man dreadfully wronged. And had he not been so in the first place, he would still have both eyes.

'Glad you filed the theft complaint, though it'll probably go nowhere,' Piper said.

'Of course. Have you had some correspondence from them?'

'Better than that. You're my second visitor of the day.'

Dawson sat up, even more attentive as he listened.

'What do you mean?'

'Earlier on I was walked down here for a legal visit, which I assumed was you until I walked in.'

'Who was it?'

'A senior officer from the police internal affairs.'

'You get the name?'

Piper rocked back in his seat as he thought, and then said, 'Carol Win-something-or-other.'

Stanley, Dawson thought, Carol Winstanley. Wales glanced at him and he gave a nod. He would tell him later.

'So, she was here about the stolen gold bar, then?'

'Yep, that's what she said.'

'Well, that's good, isn't it?'

'Like I say, it'll probably go nowhere.'

'What makes you think that?'

'Because, although she said she was here to confirm the details of my complaint, she seemed uninterested as I told her. Distracted almost.'

'Distracted by what?' Wales asked.

'My charges, all she seemed interested in was going over the circumstances of my charges.'

Apart from anything else, Dawson knew that this was highly irregular. Not only was the case nothing to do with her, but after a suspect had been charged there are strict rules in place forbidding any further police interviews. Bar for a couple for rare exceptions, of which, this was not one of them. Wales also picked up on the latter as he continued.

'She didn't *formally interview* you regarding the facts of the case, did she? Because that would be an abuse of process and authority right from the off.'

Piper again leaned back as he appeared to recall the events. Then said, 'No, I wouldn't call it an interview as such - not that I've experienced that many - but just seemed to show a great interest in it. She seemed to listen intently when I said I'd been set up.'

'How did it end?'

'Just thanked me and asked if it could have been another criminal who set me up, rather than a police officer? I reminded her that I'm not a criminal, so it could only have been a cop both times - because everything was as it should have been, both times - just before the police raids went down.'

Wales wrapped things up and they said their goodbyes to Piper. The man looked saddened to see them go. Dawson realised that any visit in these places was a form of recreation; his heart went out to the man.

Neither he nor Wales spoke until they were away from the prison and walking back towards Wales's car.

'What do you think now?' Wales asked.

'I'm convinced more than ever that your client is innocent,' Dawson answered.

'Hallelujah. And what about this Carol Win-something-or-other's visit?'

THE CABAL

'Detective Superintendent Carol Winstanley is head of anti-corruption within professional standards, so maybe his concerns are being looked at,' Dawson said with as much reassurance in his voice as he could muster. He glanced at Wales, who seemed content. But the truth be known, Dawson was far from convinced at the given reason for Winstanley's visit. A week ago, before his impromptu lunchtime meeting with Professor Jason Cummings from the lab, he would have believed what he'd just told Wales. He now knew that much darker reasons lay behind it.

Chapter Thirty-five

Johnson was in the haulage office before the other two and had just come off the phone from Johnny. He was happy that Wales seemed to be all over his case, but that was not why Johnny had rung. Timescales had now changed. He was sat at Johnny's desk and looked up as the two Garys walked in together. 'Can't you two function without each other?'

Gary answered, 'Scarface always needs me to hold his hand.'

G responded with an elbow to Gary's side.

'When you two have finished flirting, we have some serious business to attend to.'

'We know, boss,' G said.

'No, you don't. Things have changed. Tonight's not a recce. Our brief's expert has brought things forward.'

Both Garys then switched on and paid proper attention as Johnson explained what Johnny had just told him. They both nodded and Johnson asked, 'How sure are we about the layout?'

'Proper sure, boss. I followed the cleaner out like you asked, he wasn't hard to clock,' G started.

'He'd be carrying a mop and bucket, no doubt,' Gary threw in.

'Stop it, Gary. We need to get serious,' Johnson said, and Gary threw his hands up in apology. This was not the time to piss about. 'Go on,' he said to G.

'I scooped him up before he hit his home address, and initially he refused to draw a plan of the place. Until I threatened to rape his wife and burn his house down. Then he had a change of mind. I kept my questions neutral so he has no idea what our interest is. Made him describe every room, not just the one we are concerned about.'

Johnson was impressed.

G continued, 'I offered him the two K, which he hesitated over, but when I upped it to five K, his eyes came out like Gary's bottom lip when he loses at cards, and he snatched it. So, I knew I had him in our pocket. He can't go to the filth now he's five K heavier. Plus, I doubt he ever would; too scared.'

THE CABAL

'I'll make you five K lighter when we play cards next,' Gary said.

'Will you two focus, it's like having Ant and Dec in here but without the humour,' Johnson said.

'See, it's infectious,' Gary said, and all three laughed. Johnson had to admit it eased the tension. Then G pulled the handwritten map out and placed it on the desk, Johnson and Gary gathered around as G described its contents. The lab was not a huge place, a modest sized modern industrial unit, part glass, part metal sheeting and part brick wall. Looking at the map, the part they were interested in was behind a brick wall. Which made sense as it would be the most secure from the outside. G explained that the place was a recent build on a newish industrial estate at Risley, a small town near Warrington in Cheshire.

'How sure are we that it's the correct lab?' Johnson asked.

'My contact didn't know, she's only a clerk for the filth. So, I did some digging online and found a post on the filth's main website announcing that they had signed an exclusive contract with this lab for their entire drug related forensic needs.'

'Excellent, it must be the place, then. What about CCTV?' Johnson asked.

'On the outside at the front, especially around the main entrance, but I couldn't see anything at the rear - which is where our room is - but I didn't hang about for long.' G answered and then pointed to a space on the map.

'I know we were only planning a full recce tonight, but have you any idea on bells?' Johnson asked.

'I don't know for definite, but it must be belled up. Probably all the doors, inner and external, and I'd guess passive infrared in the labs and possibly the passageways, too,' G answered.

Johnson stared at the map for a minute, and then started to smile. It was proving to be five grand well spent. The exhibits store was the only one shown on the map. It must act as a central depository for the whole lab. It was on the ground floor at the rear of the building. And as they knew where it was, they wouldn't have to bother breaking in and going through all the high risk alarmed areas. They could go through the Achilles heel of all 'secure buildings', especially one of this design. 'Here,' he said, 'this is where we will go in,' Johnson said, pointing to the rear of the building. 'We can smash through the outer brickwork straight into the storeroom. I'm guessing the inside of the room itself won't be belled-up. Just the locked door and beyond. Should be a piece of piss. Especially as it'll be you two doing the graft.'

'That's a great idea, boss. Do you want me to bring a jack hammer?' G asked.

'Make too much noise, we can chisel the mortar and use sledgehammers on the brickwork, shouldn't take long with two strong lads like you,' Johnson finished with.

Three hours later they met back at the yard, all wearing dark clothing. They were going to use the red Transit van and had all the tools in the back, including a petrol driven jack hammer, just in case. An hour later, they approached the entrance to the site. It was dark now and Gary who was driving turned the van's lights off as they pulled over. There was no traffic around and an eerie silence prevailed. Gary jumped out of the van and covered the registration plates with gaffer tape. Then they slowly trundled on to the site and parked at the rear of the buildings. Although fully dark now, there were several sodium vapour streetlights showering the whole area in a low glow. Fortunately, most of the lighting was on the main access roads, and Johnson was relieved to see far less illumination around the rear of the lab.

Johnson felt obvious noting a couple of CCTV stanchions as they had driven in; he just hoped that they weren't being monitored live. He couldn't see any around the rear of the lab, but told the two Garys they'd all wait in the van a while, and be prepared to do one fast if anyone turned up. After ten long minutes passed, he reckoned they were good to go. They gingerly made their way from the van to the rear wall of the lab. They were wearing boiler suits and now had balaclavas on.

Once at the rear, they paced out the back until they were in the centre of the building's width. That should access them right into the middle of the exhibit's room's outer wall. According to the map, albeit not drawn to scale, the size of the exhibits room was not that large. Johnson reckoned that it was only a temporary store used whilst things were being examined. Once done, the

THE CABAL

stuff would no doubt go back to the police station they came from. Made sense, otherwise the place would soon be overrun.

Once inside, the plan was to find the drugs and the money exhibits, which should have 'Lancashire Police' and 'R - v - Piper' written all over them. He'd also told the two Garys that they needed to nick all the drugs and cash they could find and leave everything else. That way it would look like a junkie's heist, one who also got lucky with some cash. Keep the finger pointed away from Johnny. It would take a bit longer to search, but it would prove a necessary misdirection.

Johnson kept a lookout while the boys went to work and was surprised how quickly they made an impression into the brickwork. The noise was low, too, just the muffled bumps of the sledgehammers, which were only momentary as they struck with each blow. Then their luck got even better. This crappy building only had one layer of bricks which surrounded a timber frame in its centre. The place wouldn't take much to go up. The thought played on Johnson's mind whether they shouldn't just throw a match in. But he shook the thought away, always better to stick to one's original plan, whatever that was.

Then the luck became even sweeter; once inside, the two Gary's turned their pocket torches on and it was as Johnson had surmised. The room was only six metres square, and everything was listed nice and neatly on wall-to-ceiling shelving, each with wipeable labels to the front. Each with a Scientist's name followed by 'R - v - this' and 'R - v - that'. G found the 'R - v - Piper' shelf quickly, more good fortune. The drugs were there followed by the cherry on the cake; the money. The irony was not lost on Johnson; it would give them all the greatest of pleasure to nick the filth's money - evidence destroying aside - it would be recompense for Johnny's missing gold bar. Though Johnson might stick it on a nag instead of keeping it for Johnny, safer to get totally rid of it that way.

As G pocketed Johnny's case exhibits, Gary busied himself grabbing anything else which had the words 'Controlled Drugs' on, and twenty minutes later, both men turned their torches off and started to clamber back through the metre square hole they'd made in the brickwork.

Then their good luck ran out.

G had come through the hole and was on all fours, and Gary was halfway through the gap when Johnson noticed a flashlight stretch along the rear of the building.

He looked up to see a figure silhouetted behind the torch, followed by the words, 'What the hell are you doing?'

Johnson sprinted the few metres between them and launched himself at the man behind the light. He looked sixty, overweight and unfit. The stereotypical low paid security guard. Johnson had no idea if the man was on his own or not and didn't intend to find out. Johnson noticed that he was scrabbling at a radio handset pinned to his shoulder. A look of terror etched across his face. The man managed to pull his handset free but Johnson's speed had won the battle before it started. He grabbed the radio handset from the man's hand before he could depress the red button his thumb was hovering over. He yanked the handset hard which pulled the main radio body with it from the man's waistband, and it also pulled the man forward who seemed to lose his footing.

Johnson threw the device onto the floor and launched a straight arm jab into the stumbling guard. He felt and heard a satisfying crunch as his fist connected with the man's nose. The man went into reverse and flew backwards as blood poured down his face and onto his yellow florescent jacket. He lay on the ground and looked stunned, awake but nullified. Johnson wondered whether he'd done enough damage, as the man looked at him with abstract horror in his eyes. He was no threat.

But awake was still a risk, so Johnson stamped on the man's head and his face turned to its side as he did so. He then felt an arm on his shoulder. He spun around, but it was only G.

'Come on, boss, it's time to go.'

Johnson turned to where the radio lay and stamped on it, but it just sunk down into the soft turf. He'd no way of knowing whether it was still working and he didn't have time to dig it out the ground. He quickly turned back to its user and stamped hard on the side of the man's head, again. He stopped moving; job done. Time to leave.

THE CABAL

Chapter Thirty-six

Daniel was astounded at how well Dawson had done, and the insights he'd been made privy to. And although he'd so wanted to believe that Piper was guilty as hell, he was starting to revisit that in his mind. He was aware that if Piper were guilty, it would verify his old department's intelligence case, which had started the investigation initially. But he knew he had to drop any professional bias he had, and needed to be as objective as he could be. By the time he'd finished talking to Dawson, it was crystal clear that Dawson was more convinced than ever that Bartholomew had set Piper up. Probably with Merson's help and Winstanley covering his back. He had to admit that he shared Dawson's concerns about her visit to see Piper, given what they now suspected after Dawson's chat with the professor from the lab.

But Daniel allowed himself to conclude that Piper wasn't a total innocent; he may not have committed any crimes - that they knew of - but he was happy to be the figurehead at the haulage firm and the North End Crew. And happy not to ask too many questions about what was really going on. Though, that didn't justify fitting him up. And there were proper ways to get at Tommy Johnson and Scarface without the shortcuts. Not that Scarface was on anyone else's radar; but he was on Daniel's. At the end of the call, he openly told Dawson that he may have been right about Piper. And added that working to different agendas would not help their cause. He also suggested that they should bring Jill in to help. He trusted her and she would be much better at keeping observations on the haulage yard. She was unknown. Dawson seemed to buck at the suggestion until Daniel reminded him how close they came the other day to being seen when Bartholomew and Lancaster had turned up unexpectedly. Dawson agreed, and Daniel said he'd ring Jill and ask her to start her obs tomorrow.

'OK,' Dawson said and then asked, 'What do you want me to do tomorrow?'

'Take a break, but be contactable should Jill need to talk.'

'OK, will do, but what have you got planned?'

'I've got a niece to bury tomorrow, so the sooner the day is over the better.'

'Sorry, hadn't realised it was the funeral already.'

'Melanie just wants to get it over and done with as soon as she can.'

'Understandable.'

'Yep. Then I can turn my attentions to finding the scum who is responsible.'

'And I'll be with you every step of the way.'

Daniel thanked Dawson as he ended the call, but couldn't help wondering whether Dawson had a dual agenda; one: to help him find Scarface, and two: to make sure that he didn't let his emotions rule his head. As much as Daniel wanted to punch this monster's face to a pulp, he knew it would make him no better than Bartholomew. He wanted to make sure Scarface faced a lasting and legitimate justice. Probably as well to have Dawson as his guardian angel. He sat back and cracked his neck as he gazed through the open patio window onto the lawn. And as he felt the tension shift from his neck, he realised it was something he had not done since retiring. He looked forward to ending all that he and Dawson had started, and then they could both re-start the next phases of their lives. But back to the here and now, he needed to dust off his black suit to make sure it still fit. It was the one he kept separate for giving evidence at Crown Courts and for funerals. He just wished he was going to Crown Court tomorrow.

***

Johnny Piper had his usual night's sleep; intermittent and routinely interrupted by the sounds of the inside: inmates crying, inmates shouting, inmates being assaulted by their cellmates, and the guards doing their rounds. He wasn't sure how anyone was ever able to get a decent night's sleep in this place, which ultimately left him feeling permanently tired. The days he'd spent in the hospital wing had felt like a holiday, albeit one at a great personal cost. But last night had been his first back on the wing. It was like his very first night all over again. Any ability to

THE CABAL

funnel out the sounds was lost. Back to square one. And he knew as he faced the first full day back on the wing, he'd feel vulnerable again. The screws said he'd be OK as the nutter who'd attacked him had been shipped out and would face charges down the line, plus, his injuries would mean he'd be left alone.

He was grateful of the former, but didn't believe the latter, especially as he'd made a formal complaint about the assault. In the minds of some in here, probably most of them, that made him a grass. What a perverse way of thinking, he'd lost his eye for God's sake. There was no way he could let the nutter get away with that. So, he guessed he would experience a mixed day, one of tacit understanding by some, and disapproval by others. The 'Great Johnny Piper' façade had long lost its currency. Many already knew the truth now; Johnson was the man; he was just his patsy of a half-brother. And in these places, patsies meant bitches.

He hadn't been awake long when his new personal officer, a huge ex-Scots guardsman called Pat, came into his cell.

'Your lucky day, Piper. Pack your kit and be ready to roll in fifteen,' Pat said.

'I'm not being shipped out, am I boss?'

'No, we've received a call from your brief, Mr. Wales. You've got a bail app at 10.30 a.m.'

'Didn't know I could have another one,' Piper said.

'Apparently, there has been a "change of circumstances", but before you ask, I've no idea. You can ask your brief at court,' Pat said, before turning on his heels and leaving without inviting any further discussion.

Fifteen minutes later and Pat returned and led Piper to the prison bus. Thirty minutes after that the bus drove into the secure compound at the rear of Preston Crown Court. The place was less than a mile from the prison; it would have been quicker to walk. By the time he was settled in a holding cell beneath the courts it was 10.00 a.m. At five past, a rushed and harried Gerald Wales was shown into his cell.

'What the hell has happened since I saw you yesterday?' Piper asked.

'CPS rang first thing, duty bound to inform me that key exhibits in your case have been taken during a theft.'

'What?'

'I'll fill you in later, but suffice to say, they may not be able to proceed without them.'

'What?' Piper said for a second time, a surge of hope flooded through him. For the first time since his injury, he didn't notice the pain.

'Don't get your hopes up too high, they still have the documented evidence from their examination of the drugs and cash, but their case is seriously weakened without the actual exhibits. We will of course argue in due course that having been denied the opportunity to have them examined by our own expert, we are severely prejudiced in our ability to conduct a fair defence. They will obviously be hoping that they can get the exhibits back, which could mean that you still face a trial.'

The pain in Piper's eye socket returned.

'But whilst, all these deliberations carry on, we can argue that there is a substantial change of circumstances which should allow a further bail application. Our view being that it is wholly inappropriate to continue to hold you in custody if you are not likely to face prosecution.'

'That's brilliant, Gerald.'

'Thank you. I rang listings first thing and they have squeezed us in "For mention" at Court Number 11 at 10.15 a.m. They are keen to have the question of "change of circumstances" ruled on before that court's normal business resumes at 11.30 a.m. You're in luck that they have a part-heard trial ongoing which can't resume before then due to a witness delay or something. Anyway, the stars are lining up for us, Johnny.'

The pain in Piper's face eased once more. 'Who's the judge?' he asked.

Wales was grinning widely now, 'Our good friend, Judge Carmichael.'

Piper's pain disappeared completely.

THE CABAL

Chapter Thirty-seven

It was nearing midday and Johnson was starting to think about lunch, there was a greasy spoon around the corner run by an avid Preston North End fan. Johnson liked to use it when he was at the haulage yard. The food was greasy, unhealthy, and swimming in oil, just how he liked it. Plus, it was always a safe place to chat; Freddie the Fryer was one of their own. Johnson just wished he'd clean his fingernails occasionally. But before he could feed his belly, he was awaiting the two Garys for a debrief of the previous night's fun. He'd already fired Billy off for an early lunch as it wasn't for his ears.

As usual, the two of them came in together, with three takeaway coffees. Gary put one down in front of Johnson for which he thanked him. Once settled, he asked them to throw in their thoughts.

'According to the news feeds, the filth are running around with their thumbs up their arses,' Gary started with.

'No change there then,' Johnson said.

'And as the lab was in the Cheshire police area, it's a different firm dealing, so it's well away from us,' Gary added.

'And according to the online reports, they are treating it as a general drugs heist, just as we'd hoped,' G said.

'Excellent; and what about the cash?' Johnson asked.

'Like you said, easiest way to clean it is through a bookie's,' G answered.

'How much was there?' Gary asked.

'Twelve grand, so I split it through several bookies so as not to raise any eyebrows. Put it all on Lucky Day, the 3-1 favourite at Aintree this afternoon,' G said.

'Good, it's long gone now, and I'll give Johnny twelve K out of the petty cash, he may as well have it as part payment for his lost gold bar,' Johnson said. He had thought of passing on the twenty grand the Garys recovered from Merson's place, but that would finger them as involved in his death. Best to keep that from Johnny's mind. He'd drip feed the rest to him over time.

That way he'd not be out of pocket. Then he jumped back to their conversation and asked, 'What about the security guard?'

'Critical but stable, got a blood clot on the brain, but expected to pull through,' Gary said.

'He's the clot for sticking his nose in,' Johnson said, and all three laughed. 'But seriously, we don't want the idiot dying; it'll bring too much attention to it. We'll end up with the whole murder squad after us rather than just some local CID.'

'He's expected to make a full recovery, and we were all bally'd up so he can't tell them anything.' G said. 'And the van went through a crusher an hour ago, just to be on the safe side.'

'Great work boys. Let's hope it's enough to sort Johnny out. But we need to get back to normal business. Gary, you go first.'

'All the guns have been moved on as you know, and we have orders for several more.'

'Good stuff. G?'

'As all the H has gone, we can use last night's haul for now. Though we will need to replenish soon. If there's any delay due to the spotlight on us, I can get some on account from Liverpool and keep our local dickheads happy.'

'Good. That brings us to what next? As you know we've stopped *adding* to our legitimate runs as a safety lockdown,' Johnson said.

Both Garys nodded.

'This is just as well, as three wagons full of legit produce have had a tug at Dover in the last few days according to Billy.'

'That tool who marched in here?' G said.

'Bartholomew,' Gary added.

'Must be. So, we need to deter him before the big one,' Johnson said.

Both Garys sat up alert. Johnson hadn't shared this with them yet, as it had all been speculation until the call he took an hour ago. 'There is a firm down south who have their hands on a lot of bullion, and are nervous about smelting it down on home soil as they have their own set of Bartholomews breathing down their necks. Every smelter in the UK, legit or otherwise, has had a visit, so this firm have hired one in Amsterdam to do it for them.

THE CABAL

They just need a way of getting it there with no dramas, which is where we come in.'

'Wow,' Gary said.

'Sweet,' G said.

'The commission alone is out of this world and will put us on a different level. Apart from the potential for spin off jobs, the cash will boost our normal trade,' Johnson said, and turned to face G. 'Your drug network will quadruple across the whole Northwest.'

'That means times four,' Gary said.

'Nob off,' G replied to Gary.

'And for you, Gary,' Johnson said, facing him, 'you can re-arm all of Gunchester and the Scousers at the same time.'

'That means Manchester and Liverpool,' G said to Gary.

'You can nob off, too,' Gary replied to G, then turned to Johnson, 'Nice one boss.'

'We just need a way to conceal the bars, so empty your heads of porn and get thinking. I've already told the client we are good to go.'

'So, no pressure then,' G said.

'At least the goods will be going the other way for a change,' Gary said.

'And not through Dover,' G threw in. 'Hull or Newcastle would do.'

All three nodded.

'What about our little problem?' G asked.

But before Johnson could answer, his mobile rang. It was Wales, he took the call.

'Good news, Mr. Johnson. I'm ringing from Preston Crown Court where we have successfully applied for bail for your brother due to the unexpected events of last night. He'll be on his way home in no time.'

'That is truly excellent news,' Johnson said, and then remembered to ask, 'Oh, what events?'

'I'll let Johnny tell you later, he asked me to let you know that he's having a bit of a shindig at his house at eight tonight.'

'Will you be there?'

'Unfortunately, I have a prior engagement which I can't get out of.'

'Pity, I would have preferred to thank you in person.'

'Just doing my job.'

'Well, thanks anyway,' Johnson said and ended the call, before turning to face the two Garys. 'Looks like it's party time, boys.' He then explained.

Johnson and the two Garys then got stuck into the plan for the gold movement. It was coming to them courtesy of a bullion robbery in London. G said he'd seen mention of it on the TV; they were dubbing it: 'Brinks Max II'. And although, it was nowhere near as big as that job had been decades earlier, the press did love a moniker to add to crimes and criminals. But it was still a considerable amount and a potential step up in the national criminal hierarchy. If they sorted this with no problems, who knew where it might lead. Get it wrong, and it would be heads down and leg it time.

Johnson wanted to speak to Johnny alone, so he made sure he was at the do early. They warmly greeted each other and he asked how his eye socket was. Johnny said he was managing things as best as he could. He then explained how his bail application had come about. Johnson made sure he ooed and arrhed in all the right places, then Johnny asked him straight if he'd had anything to do with it.

'I only wish I'd thought of it, Johnny, but from what the news reports say, it was a drugs heist pure and simple. Just lucky your exhibits were there at the time,' he replied.

Johnny seemed to accept this, and added, 'And as our expert never got the chance to do his own examination, the timing was perfect. Wales reckons it gives him good grounds to say that there is now no case to answer. Let's just hope the police don't find the bloody stuff.'

No chance of that, Johnson didn't say, but it reminded him that the drug money which G had put on a nag had only gone and won. They were all quids in. He pulled twelve grand of it from his pocket and handed it over to a startled Johnny.

THE CABAL

'What's this?' he asked as he took it.

'Let's just say that it's your "lucky day". A little bonus to offset your losses.'

'That's very kind of you, Tommy.'

'There'll be more after the next job I'm planning.'

'On that, I'm glad you've come early as I wanted to tell you on our own that I want out.'

Johnson wasn't totally surprised as Johnny iterated all that had happened, and said it was too much. Even though he never had any detailed knowledge of what went on behind the scenes as the pretend figurehead, he'd paid a heavy price. 'Look, everyone knows I'm in charge now, except the filth, but they are thick, so you'd be in no danger just running the haulage office.'

Johnny thanked Johnson but seemed determined to move on. Said his nerves couldn't take it. Johnson couldn't blame him, and asked him what he would do.

'Probably try and get a job running a fleet elsewhere, but not one that is in direct competition with you.'

'Fair enough,' Johnson said. 'Just one favour?'

'What?' Johnny asked.

'I've got the driver Billy Wellard covering your job, and he's doing OK, but would you stay on for a week or two to skill him up? Show him all your systems, especially all that post-Brexit Customs stuff?'

'No problem, and Billy's a good choice.'

'One last thing?' Johnson asked as he thought about the pending gold movement job.

'What?'

'I know our lorries get the odd pull on their way back into the UK through Dover, but how often do we get a tug on the way out of the UK?'

'Never, it's always on the way back in,' Johnny answered.

'Excellent, I was hoping you'd say that.'

'I don't want to know why.'

'Better you don't bro, now come on, lets grab a beer.'

Chapter Thirty-eight

Daniel Wright could hardly believe what Dawson was telling him. He'd nearly missed the call as he'd been getting changed out of his suit and tie when he'd rang. After he'd explained what Wales had told him about the bail application, and the reasons behind it, he asked how the funeral had gone and apologised for ringing.

'It could have waited until tomorrow, I guess. Just thought you'd want to know now, particularly as there is to be a "Freedom Party" tonight to use Wales's words. Christ, you'd think he was coming home from war or something,' Dawson added.

The last bit made Daniel smile; the more he worked on this with Dawson, the more Dawson dropped down through the ranks - mentally - he'd soon be swearing like a time-served detective. He quickly gave Dawson a run through of his day and how it had gone as well as these things could, but that the need for justice was hampering everyone's grieving process, particularly for Sally's mother, Melanie. It made him more determined to trace Capone.

'What are your thoughts on Piper now?' Dawson asked.

'I'm siding with you, but will keep my mind partially open.'

'And the reason behind the "change of circumstances"?'

'Now that is one huge coincidence, if you believe in such things.'

'Too much of one. Don't forget I was present at the legal visit when Wales told Piper that his expert would ring the lab the day after to arrange their examination of the exhibits.'

'Piper probably told Johnson, who set it all up?' Daniel said.

'Agreed, even if Piper has no idea what his half-brother, then did,' Dawson said,

Daniel didn't argue with Dawson on that point, as they didn't know for sure, but he found it hard to believe that Piper wasn't in the know. If he could prove it, he would. How perverse it would be if Piper got off erroneous charges because of it, but was then

THE CABAL

convicted for conspiring to raid the lab which facilitated it. 'How is the security guard?' he asked.

'According to the news reports, he's serious but stable,' Dawson replied, and then went on to ask his thoughts about the Freedom Party.

'I think we need to cover it. I'll bell Jill and see if she's up for it. She spent the afternoon covering the yard as you know, and saw several faces coming and going, but she's not sure who is who. I might join her for an hour tonight. Just to cover the arrivals so I can identify Johnson to her. Plus, it'll be interesting to see who else arrives. Unless your mate Wales can do that for us?'

'I've already asked if he's going and he is adamant that he is not. He doesn't want to get drawn in socially with them all.'

'Then we'll have to cover it from outside. Just to clock who's who. I won't push my luck; I'll just cover the arrivals and then do one.'

'I'm happy to join you if you wish?' Dawson asked.

Daniel was pleased with Dawson's eagerness, but the less risk they took, the better. He'd not stay long; he'd leave it up to Jill in the main as she was the real professional when it came to observation jobs. He told Dawson this who accepted it. But he offered to keep his mobile handy should things change. Daniel thanked him and then called Jill.

***

Johnson was already merry by the time Gary arrived at Johnny's do. Gary made straight to him after he'd hugged Johnny and exchanged the usual pleasantries. 'Where's your mate?' he asked as he arrived next to him.

'He'll be along shortly, and sorry we are late but we have some pretty exciting news,' Gary said.

'What is it?'

'I should really wait for G to land.'

'Doesn't usually bother you.'

'I know, but it is his graft on this one, and it's the dogs' doodahs.'

'What is? You're killing me here.'

'OK, but let G explain fully when he comes.'

'I promise I'll look all surprised, now give.'

'Did you know that over the last few years there has been a shortage in building supplies?'

Johnson just shook his head; perplexed as to what would come next.

'Bricks, have been short in supply, a lot of factories went to the wall after the financial crisis - if you pardon the expression - and have been slow to re-emerge.'

'And?'

'And in particular, breeze blocks are in big demand. They are becoming a builder's brick of choice as they reduce the costs, and the need for proper bricks by half.'

'Who knew?' Johnson said, trying to stifle a yawn.

'So, a couple of wagons full of breeze blocks going from the UK to the EU would not look out of place.'

'I guess not.'

'And what a good concealment opportunity this would create.'

The feeling of boredom left and Johnson was all ears now.

'It's easy to hollow a letterbox sized slit in them as they are not too dense, unlike G normally, and then one can use normal cement mixed with the hollowed-out debris to make a perfect filler. It should dry the same colour and look untouched. And it is still solid.'

'But with a bar of gold added?' Johnson said.

'Exactly,' Gary finished and took a swig from his lager bottle.

'Boys, you have surpassed yourselves.'

'It's G's idea.'

'How did he know about the breeze block shortage?'

'No idea. Probably read it on the khazi tugging to Builders' Weekly, or summat. You'll have to ask him. He shouldn't be long.'

'Have you tested it?'

'We've just done one and used bars of soap for the gold and refilled the hole, should be dry by tomorrow so we can check it properly then. That's why we are late, and G spilt cement dust all over himself, so has had to nip home to get changed.'

'If it dries as you say, then we are in business. Where is the block now?'

'On Billy's desk at the yard.'

'Make sure you are in before him tomorrow and move it, he doesn't need to know.'

'Sure thing, boss. Drink?'

'I'll go and grab you one. It's my round as Johnny's paying.'

***

Daniel offered to pay for Jill's time, but she wouldn't hear any of it. So, he promised her a slap-up meal and free drinks when things were over, which she readily agreed to. She said she would plot up outside Johnny Piper's gaff at 7 p.m. and he said that he would join her before eight. Which he did. He parked his own motor a five-minute walk away. And as he neared Piper's house, he saw Jill parked up, in a side street facing the house, with her car's rear towards the address. Very covert. As he walked towards it, he could see through the head restraints and the vehicle looked empty. He jumped in the passenger side and saw Jill hunkered down. She was using the door mirrors to watch the front of Piper's place.

'How's it going?' he asked as he too slid down in his seat.

'Good view bar the odd passing traffic, but it's tiring doing it through the mirrors, can't stay like this for too long.'

Daniel understood that. He then filled in the bits he'd left out during their earlier phone call so that she had a good working knowledge of where they were up to. 'Any faces from yesterday?' he asked.

'There were two big brutes in and out the yard yesterday, both wearing Crombies like dicks. Think they are the Northern Krays or something. Didn't get a close look at them, but I reckon one has just gone in. Same coat, build, colour of hair, and the same gait; a knuckle-dragger.'

'What about Johnson?'

'I saw whom I suspect is Johnson several times yesterday, in fact, I dropped lucky when I went for a wander and clocked him in a greasy spoon nearby. Must have slipped out the back of the yard,' Jill said and then grabbed her smart phone from her pocket and fingered the controls for a minute, 'Here,' she said as she turned the phone towards Daniel.

The screen showed a long-distance view of a café as a man was walking out. He took the phone from Jill as she returned her gaze to her door mirror. Daniel used his index finger and thumb to enlarge the digital photograph. 'Yep, that's Tommy Johnson alright. Has he turned up here yet?'

'Nope, just the Crombie guy; unless he's already there. Hang on. Taxi arriving,' she said. 'You keep the obs, I'll try and get in close.'

Daniel nodded and Jill was out the car in a jiffy and waking towards the junction. Daniel concentrated on the door mirror at his side. The taxi had stopped outside Piper's address and one passenger had alighted. The male turned back towards the taxi, presumably to pay him, but Daniel could not get a good view. He blinked and the taxi drove off leaving Daniel with the rear view of a large male as he approached the front door. It was opened almost straight away and the male went in.

A minute later Jill was back in the driver's seat of her car with her phone in her hand. 'From the coat, the walk, and his size, I would say it's the other Crombie man from yesterday.'

Daniel nodded as she manipulated the controls on her phone.

'I tried to get him as he turned to pay the driver,' she said, and then she did the finger and thumb thing before saying, 'Got him,' and then handed her phone to Daniel.

She had indeed 'got him'. Daniel was looking at a grainy side-on photo of the man. He didn't know him, but what was abundantly obvious was a horrible z-shaped scar on his cheek. Bingo. 'Capone,' he shouted.

'Who?'

Daniel told her about his niece and his visit to the drug users' squat.

'My God. That's got to be him. What do you want to do?'

THE CABAL

In truth, Daniel wasn't sure. It had only been a matter of hours since he'd watched Sally being laid to rest. His animal instinct was to kick Piper's door down and then kick Capone's teeth in, and that was just for starters. But he knew of course he couldn't do that. Dawson was right, this needed doing the right way. That way, Capone would stay done. The first thing he needed to do was to 'house' Capone. And to do that, he'd have to stay on this all night, or until Capone left to go home, presumably in another taxi. He explained this to Jill and told her she could stand down; she'd already done enough.

'You kidding?' she started with.

'Plus, we are getting exposed here,' he added. Daniel was starting to get that itching feeling.

'We can do it better with two motors, each covering a different approach. That way we just need a long distance visual of the house front as we have a car that can follow straight away irrespective of which way it goes,' she said.

Daniel knew she was right. He considered using Dawson to relieve Jill, but that would bring a host of other difficulties, no offence to Dawson. That said they could have him parked up around the corner as an emergency back up to cover all bases. He quickly put a call in to Dawson who readily agreed. It sounded like he couldn't wait to turn out and help.

As soon as Daniel was in position on the north side of the main road, he took over the visual and released Jill. Five minutes later she announced that she was in position on the southern side. It would be dark soon so that would give them great cover and as luck would have it; Piper's front door had a street lamp right outside it, together with its own light.

They agreed to alternate the eyeball to give each a chance to rest their eyes. Daniel said he'd take the first thirty minutes. He'd no idea how long they would have to sit here, but he was going nowhere until he knew where Capone lived. It had crossed his mind that Capone might even doss down at Piper's for the night, in which case he'd have to send Jill home and replace her with Dawson. He wondered how enthusiastic Dawson would be if he was still sat in his car at 9 a.m. tomorrow morning.

Chapter Thirty-nine

It was only ten past nine and Bartholomew was already stressed. He'd only learnt about Piper's bail app and the justification for it at the last minute the previous day. A so called 'courtesy call' from some tosser of a CPS lawyer, whose nuts hadn't dropped yet, meant that by the time he'd arrived at court, the proceedings had finished. He'd just come off the phone to the Chief Crown Prosecutor who said it had been thrown at them last minute, too. 'Well, if you'd had got me there in time and put me in the box, I'd have made sure he'd have not got bail,' he'd said.

'Not sure you could have added anything of note,' the Chief CPS lawyer had replied, which was when he'd slammed the phone down. Another tosser who hadn't been shaving much longer than his subordinate.

Bartholomew calmed himself and then called the SIO who was running the enquiry into the lab break and assault. A DI Crompton at Warrington. Bartholomew didn't know her. He quickly outlined the reason for his call and asked if she had any suspects.

'Not yet, sir,' Crompton answered.

'How are you prioritising your lines of enquiry?'

'We've done all the CCTV, got them arriving in a red van with its plates covered up. Three in the front all wearing balaclavas.'

'What about the security guard?'

'Still in an enforced coma, but I'm told he'll pull through.'

'Forensics?'

'Nothing as yet.'

'What are your thoughts?'

'Until we know different, we are treating it as a drugs theft, pure and simple. They obviously knew where to look so we'll have to go through all staff, past and present, and anyone else who would know exactly where the exhibits room was. But it's a long list that is growing so it'll take time. We've also got local ears to the ground to try and pick up any chatter, especially as the press are all over it.'

THE CABAL

'I can save you a lot of time; my target - who was in custody before it happened - will have got his gang to do it. I've got a couple of names to throw at you.'

'With respect sir, my phone has been ringing off the hook from upward of forty SIOs from across the Northwest all claiming that it is their target who has done it.'

'Yeah, but it will have been mine who actually did it,' Bartholomew said, starting to feel tense again.

'With respect, sir, they all say that.'

Bartholomew paused before replying to keep his temper in check, but before he could argue further, Crompton continued.

'We are going through our local MO suspects first, like I said, and in the light of any intelligence to the contrary, we will then move on to the subjects whose exhibits were taken. Starting with those on bail - as they could more easily arrange the job - and I'm afraid, as your target was in custody, he'll be at the back of the queue with the others who were on remand.'

Bartholomew blew. 'Christ, did you paint by numbers as a kid?'

'I'm sorry, I don't know what you mean?'

'What about following a gut reaction, or are you a direct entry DI?'

'Not sure I like your tone. And may I remind you that we are an intelligence driven service, unless we have the evidence, which we do not at this stage. So, unless things change, we will be following the strategy I have outlined to you.'

'May I remind you that I am a detective superintendent, detective inspector?' Bartholomew said, and then instantly regretted saying it.

'And may I remind you that you are not a detective superintendent in Cheshire, and that I'm the SIO. Goodbye.'

'Cheeky bitch,' Bartholomew said to his disconnected phone. He realised he'd have to force the issue somehow, unless he could find any evidence, which he was doubtful about. If this Crompton so worshipped intelligence, he would have to make some up. Pity Merson was dead.

Then his door opened and in walked Shirley Lancaster with a bundle of papers under her arm. She clip-clopped to a chair in front of his desk and plonked the papers in front of him.

'Have you got five?' she asked.

'Do I have a choice?'

'You seem grumpy.'

'Haven't you heard about Piper?'

'I know, bad form, but you shouldn't take it personal.'

Bartholomew's jaw dropped, but before he could berate her, she continued.

'Anyway, here is my draft policy for increasing the force's capability to disrupt serious and organised crime gangs, or OCGs as they're known.'

'I know what an OCG is, what do you think I spend all day doing over here?'

'Sorry, silly me, of course you do. Anyway, I've run it past the acting chief, in principle, and he seems on board. I just need you to sign it off and then I can give it to the senior command team to discuss formally.'

Bartholomew stared at the inch thick bundle of A4 and sighed. What did this career-hungry halfwit really know about serious crime and dealing with real criminals. She had proved an embarrassment the other day when they'd visited the North End Crew's haulage yard. She'd nearly shat on her high heels. But she was wheedling her way into the de facto chief, so he'd have to calm it a bit.

'What's the main suggestion in there?' he asked, pointing at the bundle.

'It suggests that we enhance our system of collecting community intelligence to augment all criminal intelligence with a ground up approach. This is when your excellent teams do their stuff. We can then congratulate the communities involved and give them a real feeling of self-worth when they realise the tree grew from their acorn. They are the main stakeholders and they will feel the main benefit. This will produce more buy-in from the public going forward,' she said and then rocked back in her chair with a self-serving smug look on her face.

THE CABAL

Bartholomew had heard similar rubbish many times over, usually from non-detectives who could only spout about things from within their limited field of experience. Most of whom, had never nicked a decent villain in their lives. 'When is the last time that you arrested, or investigated a level two or three criminal from an OCG?' he asked.

'Well, well, erm—'

'Exactly,' Bartholomew interrupted her with. 'And how do you think any tittle-tattle from Mrs. Blue Perm at number twenty-three - which she picked up at the hairdressers - is going to impact on a team of armed robbers?'

Shirley Lancaster didn't answer; she just stood up and pointed at the bundle. 'As soon as you can, the chief wants to read the draft before it goes to the policy group's next meeting. You've got three days,' she said before clip-clopping out of his office.

Bartholomew was considering grabbing his car keys and just doing one to get out for a mooch and some air to clear his head, when his door opened again. And this time it was Carol Winstanley. Christ didn't anyone knock on doors anymore. He looked up with a weak smile as she took the chair which must have still been warm from his last visitor. 'And to what do I owe the pleasure, Carol?' he said as pleasantly as he could.

'Piper,' she answered.

'Which bit; the lab break or what came as a result?'

'Both.'

'Before you start, I've already been on to the local DI dealing, and that didn't go too well,' he said and then went on to give her a precis of his phone call with the lovely DI Crompton.

'Well, maybe it is a coincidence, a local drug theft?'

'Really?'

'Well, if not then there are forty cases to wade through, I don't envy her.'

All sisters together, Bartholomew didn't say.

'Anyway, I for one am mightily relieved. You knew damn well that Piper was innocent, you only fingered him to flush out the real top dog.'

'Will you keep your damn voice down; these walls are flimsy.'

She lowered her volume and added, 'And we were all sucked in thinking that we were doing some great good. Piper was the root of all evil; according to you and Merson. Or had you manipulated him, too?'

'Look, Piper must have known the craic, and was only too happy to take a healthy wage from it. Anyway, it's a moot point now.'

'Certainly is, and I am massively relieved that the drug money you had me touch has now gone.'

'I didn't *have* you doctor it; you readily agreed to do it.'

'Another moot point,' she said.

'Perhaps you screwed the lab?'

'Typical remark from you.'

'OK sorry, look, I'm just a bit stressed today, I've just had Shirley in here and drop that bag of bollocks on my desk,' he said pointing at the bundle. 'So, what can I do for you?'

'I'm just here to tell you that I'm done. And proper done this time. Piper is out, his case is destined for the bin, and I'm happy that a great injustice has been avoided.'

'Well, what about, Johnson, the real king of the North End throne?'

'I don't know if he is, or if it's just another part of your paranoia. Either way, I'll let you decide that. You don't need me to help you. I'm just ashamed that I let you drag me into all this from the start.'

'You've not gone all "born again" on me, have you?'

'Another typical remark. But no, and don't worry, I can never say anything without dropping myself in it, too. But I can repent going forward in how I conduct myself from here on in.'

'You have gone all "born again".'

Winstanley stood up to leave and then turned back to face Bartholomew, 'I've just passed Shirley on the stairs and I reckon she's out too, once you've signed off that "bag of bollocks on your desk".'

Bartholomew didn't have the strength to argue and just watched her go and his door swing to again. Truth be known he'd only ever needed Winstanley and Lancaster primarily for a specific reason each. He could manage fine now without either of them. The one he did miss was Merson, without him he couldn't access and manipulate the intelligence which gave him free reign. Maybe he could recruit Merson's replacement when he or she was announced. And if he needed others, he'd be more careful next time. Perhaps make sure he had some weapons-grade dirt on them first. Make certain he could keep a tight control that way. It's the way criminals ensnare and bend cops; he could learn that much from them. He could also widen the scope. Sure, he wanted to put the real bad criminals away, but after the little tickle he got from the raid on Piper's house - he didn't see why he shouldn't earn an extra wedge along the way.

As these thoughts crystallised in his mind, he started to feel better. In fact, without having to always handle Winstanley and Lancaster gently to keep them knicker-clad, he'd have total freedom with only himself to consult. The realisation felt liberating. But first things first, he was sure Tommy Johnson was the real head of the North End Crew. He needed sorting. He'd already put his name into the murder enquiry as a suspect, but with nothing to back it up he was under no illusions the Manchester SIO would do anything. It was up to him. He owed Merson that much.

Chapter Forty

Daniel had agreed with Dawson to sleep on things and meet for morning coffee to discuss what to do next. Jill had done a backdoor check on the address and they now had a name that was a known nominal. He'd stopped her pulling in any more favours, as any kind of criminal intelligence check would leave an audit trail, neither he nor Dawson wanted her to put her retirement at risk by pushing her luck. Unauthorised data breaches nowadays were serious business. There was a recent case of a retired officer working freelance, who asked an old colleague to run a Police National Computer check for him. They both ended up inside for their troubles.

It was fortunate last night that they hadn't had to wait long after midnight before Capone left the party and took a cab home. They couldn't get a photo of him in the darkness, but his ugly z-scarred face was an image Daniel would never forget. They had followed the taxi to an address on the Brookfield estate. It was a huge, sixties'-built council estate which housed many of Preston's ne'er-do-wells. Following a car onto the estate would normally be a bit of a no-no in surveillance terms as you'd stick out. But the darkness helped, plus it was always far easier following a taxi as the occupant had no immediate view to the rear. Jill had been the one to follow the cab as a lone female driving looked less suspicious. She'd apparently turned a corner just in time to see which house Capone had entered as the taxi drove off. The three of them then met up for a quick chat on Ribbleton Avenue as it passes over the M6 motorway, before calling it a night.

Daniel hadn't been awake long when Jill's text message had landed. 'C = Gary Lonsdale, 30s, loads of form, mainly GBH'.

Daniel lay back on his bed and rolled the name over in his mind. It was familiar.

Thirty minutes later, showered and dressed, he walked into the kitchen where Sue was finishing a slice of toast.

'You look in a good mood,' Sue said.

THE CABAL

'I am, I feel like we are getting somewhere,' he replied and then filled her in on the previous evening's events and the text from Jill.

'So, what now?'

'There are two ways of going about this,' he started with as he poured himself a glass of orange juice and paused to quench his thirst.

'You mean a right way and a wrong one?'

'I guess.'

'Well, it's head over heart, Daniel; or you'd be no better than Bartholomew.'

'I know.'

'So, what next? Are you going to pass the name on to the cop who is dealing with Sally's death?'

'I'll ring and feel him out and then meet Dawson for coffee to discuss. But please don't mention anything to your sister, yet. I'd hate to get Melanie's hopes up before we know how best to deal with this scumbag.'

'Understood. I've told her nothing so far. In fact, I'll pop around while you are out and see how she's feeling now it's the morning after yesterday.'

Daniel smiled and gave Sue a peck on the cheek as she passed, then he headed towards the front door.

He was soon back at his favourite table at his favourite café in Longton. He'd just sat down as Dawson arrived. They both ordered a full English breakfast; sod the waistline. Then Daniel told Dawson of Jill's update.

'Is she joining us?' Dawson asked.

'No, she's got something to do with her horses, and we've already taken up a lot of her time.'

'What do we do with this new information?'

'Before I came out, I rang the cop who is dealing with the sudden death, but didn't give him the name, I just said I might be able to find it out and asked him what he could do if I did?'

'And?'

'And as suspected; he's just another one of these modern officers recruited for ticking all the right boxes. They only deal with anything that is served up on a plate in front of them.'

'Elaborate, please.'

Daniel immediately regretted his biased, stereotypical, description and held his arms up in an apology.

'I get it that you are frustrated,' Dawson said.

'Sorry, again; he just said that "the information linking the z-scar-faced man was of no value without the supplier of it giving a sworn statement". And even if we could find the addict I spoke to at the squat, we both know that that is not going to happen.'

Dawson nodded, then said, 'So, I guess this modern cop didn't get it too wrong.'

Daniel added, 'I know he is right, though I have to say he didn't show a huge amount of enthusiasm in trying to trace the man, or the other addict that was supposedly with him when Sally was there. But at least we now know who the dealer is.'

'In some ways, our first objective has been completed; i.e., Piper's culpability is known and a vexatious prosecution will be avoided,' Dawson said.

It was Daniel's turn to nod.

'But I still want to prove Bartholomew's guilt, and you want to prove Lonsdale's.'

'Granted.'

'And as Lonsdale would seem to work for Johnson, of whom Bartholomew is so determined to destroy by all means - lawful or otherwise. We can achieve both our aims at once hopefully.'

'And let's not forget Merson's death in all this. He may have been bent, but he didn't deserve to die,' Daniel said as the waiter returned with an over-flowing tray of food and drinks.

They both paused for thought as they ate and Daniel refreshed his thinking along with his belly. He dabbed his mouth on a paper serviette and took a last slug of tea as Dawson also finished his breakfast.

'Don't tell Joan about this calorie-fest,' Dawson said.

'If you don't tell, Sue.'

'Deal.'

'But this food has indeed given me thought,' Daniel added.

'Go on.'

THE CABAL

'If this Lonsdale character is dealing, and obviously dealing on behalf of the North End Crew, then we could kill two dirt bags with one air freshener. That air freshener being a search warrant under Section 23 of the Misuse of Drugs Act, 1971.'

'Do you think he's daft enough to actually keep drugs at his home address?'

'Possibly, possibly not. But it's worth a go don't you think? They might find something else incriminating, and at worst it is a disruption into their business.'

'I'm not sure we have enough to satisfy a cop, let alone a magistrate,' Dawson said.

'Don't forget, the information that the druggie at the squat gave me may not be any good as evidence, but that does not stop it being used as intelligence to justify a warrant.'

Dawson leaned back into his chair for a moment before he spoke, 'And to use a much-maligned term these days, "community intelligence" is to be given extra weight, whether it is corroborated or not.'

'And who knows what else the police have, intel-wise, on Lonsdale and his address?'

'But what if they have nothing, do you think they would react to a single piece of intel; albeit via a retired DI?'

'Only one way to find out,' Daniel said.

'And how do we get Bartholomew to action it, or get involved?'

'Easy, I just mention - honestly - that the drugs are believed to have come from the North End Crew, which is believed to be now run by Johnson.'

'That would hit all his interest markers, that's for sure,' Dawson said.

'Plus, you could ring Crimestoppers saying Lonsdale was seen entering the yard of North End Haulage the other afternoon.'

'Why Crimestoppers?'

'It's an old National Crime Agency trick, to get local police to action something that is too operationally sensitive to admit it has come from them. It might give my intel more weight rather than just coming from me. And it'll protect your involvement. It would raise too many eyebrows that the ex-chief constable was passing information on.'

'Sneaky buggers, you intel-types,' Dawson said with a smile.

'All above board. And if we can pick up when the police intend to do the raid, we can sit off somewhere and watch.'

'That could be trickier.'

'Well, I reckon they would jump on the info by tomorrow and get the warrant by close of play. So, the earliest the raid could happen would be the day after tomorrow. Possibly even the day after that. If we covered the address from 6 a.m. to 8 a.m. over three or four days, it wouldn't be too big of an ask.'

'We'd better start working off all that fried food then,' Dawson said, before reaching for his wallet. 'My treat.'

THE CABAL

Chapter Forty-one

Johnson was impressed with the breeze block which the two Garys had prepared, and as the slit dried out, he was further amazed. It dried perfectly and you couldn't tell that the brick had been touched. G had told him that the UK production of breezeblocks was nearing what it used to be. But the EU were lagging behind, so lorries full of them heading out would fit in brilliantly. Johnson told them both to crack on with it and he would make all the transport and driver arrangements. He'd keep Billy out of it and arrange for him to spend the day at Johnny's where he could be skilled up, as Johnny had promised during the previous evening's party.

The bricks - according to G - were due to arrive early afternoon, and Johnson had arranged for the lorries to travel out via Dover in a few days' time. He decided to stick with their normal port of travel so as not to raise suspicion.

The last call he made before lunch was to his London contact who was supplying the gold bars. An old East End villain called Swiss Bob, though he didn't sound very Swiss.

'Why do they call you Swiss Bob?' he asked.

'Just to remind me I'm not a true East Ender. Born in Swiss Cottage and moved to Bow when I was three,' he answered.

Johnson was none the wiser. Nevertheless, Swiss Bob was incredibly happy about the concealment details. If all went well - and there was no reason to suppose otherwise - he reckoned they could do 'loads of graft' for 'loads of firms' at his end. It was then that Johnson realised Swiss Bob was the arranger and not the owner of the gold, which made it even sweeter for him. He hadn't liked to ask before, bit rude, but was glad to discover it. He'd rather have distance and didn't really want to know whose stuff it was in the first place. That could all stop at Swiss Bob. At the end of the call Swiss Bob said several SUVs would bring the gold up overnight, to split any risk, and would be in Preston before first light. Everything was coming together nicely. He ended the call and decided to grab an early lunch from Freddie the Fryer's café round the back of the yard. The rest of the day would be a busy one. As would the next two or three.

***

It had taken Bartholomew two whole days to calm down from the latest kick in the danglers. He had fully expected the case against Piper to be discontinued; but hadn't expected it all to happen so soon. Wales - the scumbag defence brief of choice for The North End Crew - had put in an early application 'For mention' at court as soon as he had won his bail app. The judge of choice to the scumbags - Carmichael - had granted Wales an audience and even the CPS hadn't anticipated what the defence wanted 'to mention'. But on reflection neither he nor the CPS should have been surprised that Wales was making his play for no case to answer. They just hadn't expected it so quickly. The barrister acting for the prosecution, whose name Bartholomew had already forgotten, said that the defence had brought their play far too early. It wouldn't be a problem. Not that it wouldn't be a problem later, but not yet, it was just too soon.

This time, Bartholomew did get notice, and as senior investigating officer he spent two hours in the witness box in support of the prosecution's claim that it was far too early for such a consideration to take place. The investigation into the break-in at the lab was ongoing and had a clear investigative strategy which Bartholomew said - after speaking to the DI in charge - he was hopeful would lead to an early arrest of those responsible, and the recovery of the exhibits which underpinned their case.

The defence barrister - whose name he had also forgotten - responded by saying that the exhibits *were* the prosecution's case, and that there was nothing further underpinning it. And in any event, the defence were to bring evidence at trial that would discredit both the found drugs and the recovered drug-*drenched* money.

'I actually thought you would be relieved that the exhibits went missing,' the cheeky defence brief had said until even liberal

Judge Carmichael had felt moved to chastise him for that little quip.

'There is no jury to show off to, so don't,' the Judge had said.

The defence barrister apologised and then went for the kill. The CPS man had argued that as Piper was no longer in custody, there was less pressure on the court to rule as to whether there was a case to answer. And that more time should be given to allow Cheshire police to conduct their enquiries and recover the exhibits. Then the defence would have their chance to bring whatever evidence they had in any futile effort to discredit them. Bartholomew was impressed with their man when he'd said that. A good body punch.

But the killer blow came in from the defence barrister when he kept asking Bartholomew about the Cheshire police's investigative strategy. He knew he was being led down a garden path, but hadn't worked out exactly why. Then the defence said that his instructing solicitor, Mr. Wales, had spoken to a DI Crompton. She had confirmed her investigative strategy that if the local thief angle proved inconclusive, she was going to work her way through over forty cases affected. Piper's was at the end of the queue. Bartholomew grimaced on hearing this said out loud in open court; he bet that the bitch of a DI had relished dropping his case to the very end of her to-do-list. And she had added for good measure that the process would take several weeks.

The Judge had thereafter said that to make Piper wait so long with the threat of prosecution hanging over him would be an unfair and inordinate delay. 'Diddums, poor Piper' Bartholomew muttered under his breath. And that was that. The case was dismissed. The judge added if the exhibits were recovered in such a condition that they were able to provenance the expert witness evidence - or indeed if further evidence were to emerge justifying a reconstitution of proceedings - the court would make no bar to further action. The prosecution would be within their rights to seek a fresh indictment. The way the half-wit had said the last bit was as if he was giving the prosecution something;

some sort of balanced judgement to make up for dropping the case. Tosser.

But that was not the worst of it. It wasn't the realisation of what he knew was going to happen which had sent him into a two-day spiral. That little gem was waiting for him in his email inbox when he'd got back from court. Christ, Wales wasn't wasting anytime to twist the knife. He read the email twice before ringing the sender, some jockey called Frodsham in the force's legal department.

'So, you've read my email,' Frodsham said, on answering Bartholomew's call.

'Yes, the pondlife brief must have had it pre-written ready to press send as soon as the hearing was over.'

'Quite,' Frodsham said, 'but it remains a valid claim. If we are not to continue a prosecution, then we would in normal circumstances return the money to its rightful owner, would we not?'

'Rightful owner'. Bartholomew nearly choked on the words and spat them back at Frodsham, but instead replied, 'Yes, of course. But on conviction we would have applied for the money to be forfeited under proceeds of crime legislation.'

'Quite,' Frodsham said again, which irked, Bartholomew. 'But as there is no prosecution to take place, there will be no conviction, so no forfeiture.'

'Give us a chance to at least try and recover the case.'

'I understand your disquiet, superintendent.'

'That's detective superintendent, Mr. Frodsham or shall I call you Mr. Sham?' Bartholomew said, immediately regretting his petulant comment.

'Quite,' Frodsham said again. And then added, 'I will write back to the solicitor representing Mr. Piper, and ask him to defer his proposed action for four weeks. I'm sure any civil court would deem that reasonable. But if no new proceedings are brought in that time, for whatever reason, I will sign off on the repayment of ten thousand pounds from the police contingency account. Without prejudice of course. We can in due course attempt to recover this from the forensic lab's insurers. I trust this sounds reasonable, *detective* superintendent?'

But before he could reply, the line had gone dead.

Not only had Piper beaten Bartholomew's rap, but he'd also lifted ten K which he'd never had in the first place. They were mugging him off. And they'd killed Merson, he shouldn't forget. He'd make them pay. And without Winstanley or Lancaster wittering in his ear, no one was in his way to hold him back.

And he'd do so with as much prejudice as he could.

Chapter Forty-two

Daniel had emailed his intelligence direct to the DI who had taken over his old unit. He asked it to be forwarded to the operational team investigating The North End Crew - after Lonsdale's details had been run through their existing databases. He cc'ed it to John Jones the head of CID. He could get away with the latter as there was no confidential source to protect. He was the originator and classed as an open source. He'd received a swift and polite reply from an analyst named Shelia saying that it would be passed on to the relevant officers. She thanked him and passed on her condolences for the loss of his niece. Neither the new head of his old unit or John Jones bothered to reply. Dawson had already sent in his Crimestoppers report and Daniel was confident that Shelia would crosslink both. It would add an element of urgency, a 'happening now' feel to it all, or so they hoped. Dawson had said that Bartholomew wouldn't be able to pass up any chance of payback against The North End Crew, and would hopefully put a team on it ASAP.

This had been four days ago, and the last two mornings Daniel and Dawson had covered the address in Brookfield with the help of Jill's horse box. As observation vehicles go, it was certainly unusual. And the sprawling council estate that was Brookfield was not the normal place one would expect to see a horse box. Daniel wasn't convinced any of the estate's residents had ever seen a horse, not in the flesh. He was glad that they were only there for a couple of hours, and at a time of day when most of the estate's folk were still tucked up in their beds. The aluminium side panels had several gaps in them which were good for peeping through, and there was a large opening at the front for Neddie to peep through when in transit. There were bundles of hay in the back which were comfortable to sit on, but the air smelled very horsey. A mixture of leather, horse, and something else which was apparently good for roses.

Jill had been good enough to leave her Land Rover attached, which would hopefully take any eyes away from the box itself,

THE CABAL

and as the car was empty it would look innocuous. She'd been a bit concerned that some scrote would nick the lot, so after parking the combo, she'd walked off the estate - which only had two roads accessing it - to a waiting car driven by her husband. They could watch both junctions, just in case. Daniel was hopeful they shouldn't have too much of a problem. Though this being the second day on the trot, he wasn't too sure how long they could keep doing this without a change of OP.

But as luck would have it, two days would be enough. They had only been on plot for ten minutes and Daniel had just poured a hot coffee from his flask, when he received a text from Jill. She'd clocked a convoy of police vehicles headed their way. And although that wasn't an unusual sight on this estate, today's convoy pulled up behind the horse box. Obviously, using it as cover. Daniel and Dawson kept deadly quiet as the search team officers quietly walked down the side of the trailer. For one horrible moment, Daniel thought Dawson was going to cough as he grabbed his throat and put his other hand over his mouth. Daniel passed him his brew and Dawson took it and slurped it down which seemed to calm his reflexes; thankfully. He wasn't too sure how he'd explain to the local officers the presence of an ex-DI and retired chief constable sat in the back of a horse box at 6.15 a.m.

After the footfalls ended, Daniel gave it a couple of minutes and then risked a peak out of Neddie's viewing hole. He watched as the battering ram hit the front door of the target address, just as Dawson's cough came back with a vengeance. He couldn't have timed it better as the splintering of Lonsdale's door echoed all around. The police were quickly in and lights soon came on inside the house. It was nearly fully light outside anyway, but Daniel could still see the upstairs bedroom light go on. He quickly texted Jill as Dawson took a swig of water from a bottle, which seemed to work better than Daniel's coffee as his cough disappeared properly this time.

Dawson wiped his mouth, and said, 'Must be the air in here. Anyway, how long do you reckon the search will take?'

'As it's for drugs, it could take a while. I reckon we'll be here for some time.'

'That water combined with your coffee will no doubt race its way through my system.'

Daniel smiled and pointed at the nearest bale of hay. 'If needs must?'

'How embarrassing.'

'Not at all,' Daniel said. 'You should try being holed up in an OP for days on end. Trust me; number ones are the least of your problems.'

Dawson grimaced and then stood to take a view out of Neddie's portal. 'What the hell is he doing here?' He said a little too loudly for Daniel's liking.

'Who?' Daniel said softly, hoping Dawson would take the hint.

'That rat Bartholomew. What the hell is a superintendent doing at a house search, again? Unless…Oh my God, no, surely not.'

Daniel didn't answer, but shot to his feet and looked out the opening in time to see the back of Bartholomew heading from his parked car towards the splintered front door. He didn't answer Dawson's question as it was largely rhetorical, but kept his eyes on the front of the house. Dawson plonked himself on one of the bales but Daniel kept looking through the portal. Then five minutes later a second none-police saloon pulled up and parked behind Bartholomew's car. Its sole occupant got out and headed towards the front door. This visitor was even more unexpected. 'You'll never guess who else has just pulled up?' he said.

Dawson didn't answer him but was on his feet quickly so Daniel stood back to let him see. He sat down on one of the hay bales and quickly texted Jill an update as he processed what might be going on. He poured himself a coffee and took a sip.

It could only mean one thing.

THE CABAL

Chapter Forty-three

Bartholomew wasn't stupid, he'd let the search team go in first and then give it a couple of minutes; just in case Scarface kicked off; or Lonsdale, as he now knew his name was. Gary Lonsdale: a piece of raw sewerage of this parish. He was certain he would recognise him from his impromptu visit to the haulage yard the other day. He couldn't believe it when the intel report came into his office. The ups and downs of this job were hard to keep up with. But it was an opportunity not to miss. If anyone questioned his presence, he would just say that after the allegations previously made after the Piper premises' searches, he was popping in to quality assure the search team officers.

He wandered in through the front access and smiled at what was left of the front door. The rapid entry team had done a good job, but as it was a council house the damage wouldn't bother scum like Lonsdale. But at least it would be an inconvenience, and by the time the on-call joiner turned out to secure the premises, Lonsdale will had been nicked. And other scum from the estate will have filled their pockets. Not that Lonsdale will have much worth nicking - apart from a ridiculously sized flat screen TV, no doubt - which they all seemed to have nowadays. Irrespective of how poor they all claimed to be.

And he could see that he was correct when he wandered into the front room to see a huge TV on the chimney breast. It was wider than the chimney and overlapped each side by several inches; idiot. There were several officers searching in the front and rear rooms. He then heard footsteps coming down the stairs; he turned to see Lonsdale followed by a sergeant. Bartholomew immediately recognised the man as the same ugly thug from the haulage place, and he could see in his eyes, that the recognition was mutual.

'Sorry sir, I hadn't been briefed that you were attending,' the sergeant said.

'Just thought I'd pop in and see how it was going?'

'You?' Lonsdale said, looking directly at Bartholomew.

He ignored him and kept his attention on the sergeant.

'We've only just started to be fair, but nothing so far. I've just strip-searched Lonsdale and he's clean.'

'Bet you are sorry you missed that,' Lonsdale said.

Again, Bartholomew ignored him and turned back into the front room. 'Have you done the kitchen?' he asked no one in particular.

'Not yet sir, that's next,' a constable replied.

Bartholomew nodded and weaved his way through the bodies and sauntered into the kitchen, which was small but had all the basics. Above the sink was a window with a view into a small rear garden which had a shed in it. Under the sink to one side was a washing machine with its door ajar. Bartholomew checked that no one in the rear lounge was looking, and then slipped his hand into his right-hand side coat pocket towards the ounce bag of heroin he knew was there. He opened the washing machine door a little more with his free hand.

'What are you doing?' Lonsdale said from the doorway.

Bartholomew spun around. 'Just about to look in your washing machine, not that I expect to find any laundry in there.'

'What's in your pocket?' Lonsdale asked.

Bartholomew didn't answer but reached past the bag of drugs and pulled out a surgical glove from his pocket. He then pulled a second one from his other pocket, and quickly put them on.

This seemed to allay any fears Lonsdale had as he then said, 'If you were hoping to do an intimate search of me, you're too late, loser.'

Ignoring Lonsdale, he shouted for the sergeant, who appeared next to Lonsdale moments later. 'Why isn't this man under restraint?'

'Sorry, sir, but he's not under arrest, not unless we find something, so until we do, he is at liberty to do as he pleases whilst we finish the search.'

Bartholomew grunted in reply.

'And I won't be, as you'll find nothing,' Lonsdale said.

This was closely followed by more footsteps coming down the stairs followed by an officer telling the sergeant that the search upstairs, including the loft was negative. He was running out of time. Then Lonsdale's attention was averted as he turned to look towards the chimney. The TV was only loosely fastened to the wall and a constable was trying to peer behind it.

'Hey, watch what are doing. That TV cost more than you get paid in a month,' Lonsdale said to the cop, before walking up to him.

This was Bartholomew's chance and probably his only one, he would have to act quickly, though it should only take seconds. He wrapped his fingers around the bag of heroin but kept his eyes on the back of Lonsdale. All attention seemed to be aimed at the TV.

Then Carol - nosey bitch - Winstanley walked into the kitchen. He let go of the bag and turned to face her. 'What the hell are you doing here?'

'Just thought I'd pop in and keep you company once I realised that you were also attending.'

'And what is that supposed to mean?'

'It means,' she started to reply before lowering her voice to a whisper, 'that I intend to stick to you like glue until this search is over.'

'I don't like your tone.'

'Or should I ask the sergeant to search you?'

'You'd need grounds to do that; grounds which you do not have.'

'True,' she replied, and then grinned; or grimaced. 'But I can still stick to you like glue to make sure we don't have another Piper situation.'

Bartholomew lowered his voice, 'Have you forgotten that you were involved in that as much as I was?'

'I know. And to be honest, I don't think even you are stupid enough to try that trick again. But I'm here just in case. I can't change the past, but I can influence the future,' she said, again with the same false smile on her face.

But before Bartholomew could consider what to say next, the sergeant appeared in the doorway closely followed by Lonsdale,

'Excuse me sir and ma'am, but we've just got the kitchen left to do.'

Bartholomew turned angrily and said, 'Fine, but don't forget to do the bloody garden and shed,' before he marched out into the rear lounge not waiting for a reply. Lonsdale was grinning at him as he passed. How he longed to wipe that smile from his face. And to add to his burden he was closely followed by Winstanley.

'We may as well leave them to finish off, don't you think?' she said from closely behind him. He didn't answer her; he just kept walking until he was at his car door. He then turned to face the house and realised that Winstanley had stopped outside, close to the front door. She wasn't taking any chances; he knew when he was beaten. He may as well go and put the drugs back into the drugs safe at HQ before Winstanley decided to do a stop check there, too.

THE CABAL

Chapter Forty-four

Daniel and Dawson waited until all the police cars had left. And as no prisoner transport van turned up, they concluded that the search was negative. They gave it a further five minutes before calling Jill in, and saw Lonsdale rush out and leave in a blue Vauxhall. He looked in a hurry and wasn't waiting for his door to be secured first. Daniel reckoned he would have a reputation on the estate and only a fool would dare enter in his absence.

They all decamped to Daniel's rear lounge for a debrief and Sue kindly provided bacon butties with three mugs of tea. Daniel had forgotten how good bacon butties tasted when you had been out on an early morning observation job; somehow, they were just the best. Refreshments taken and chins wiped clean of grease, they went through the ramifications of what had happened. 'Pity they found no drugs,' he started with.

'I guess it was always a punt,' Jill said.

Daniel nodded.

'But look on the bright side; had we not been there we would not have seen Bartholomew and Winstanley turning up. Now what do we all make of that?' Dawson asked.

'A strange one; Winstanley particularly; what was the head of anti-corruption doing on a drug warrant?' Jill said.

'I reckon Bartholomew had gone to fit Lonsdale up, just as he did Piper,' Dawson proffered.

'But why would Winstanley show herself, even if she was there to support Bartholomew?' Jill asked.

'If she had been there to support Bartholomew then the drug search would have been positive,' Dawson said.

'Looking that way, Daniel said. 'And as the result was negative, we can assume that she was there to stop him.'

'Which can only mean they have fallen out, or at least parted company,' Dawson added.

'Perhaps Merson's death has had a profound effect on her?' Jill added.

'And if Winstanley is out, then that treacherous rat Lancaster may also be out,' Dawson said, and then added, 'which leaves Bartholomew on his own and vulnerable.'

Daniel was about to speak further when Sue rushed into the room.

'Sorry to interrupt, but you've got a visitor, Daniel, I've put him in the front room.'

'Who is it?'

'Peter Bartholomew.'

'Shit,' Daniel said, a little louder than he'd intended. 'Can you make him a brew and I'll be in in a minute.'

Dawson and Jill said that they would leave via the patio doors and wait behind Daniel's garden shed just to be on the safe side. Daniel nodded and then headed to the front room.

Pleasantries over, Bartholomew said he had just popped round as a courtesy to inform him about the morning's raid on Lonsdale's home, he was aware the information had come from him and the tragic circumstances surrounding it. Daniel thought that this was extraordinarily kind of Bartholomew, and was careful to answer with corresponding expressions. Then Bartholomew asked about the squat. Daniel told him all he knew.

'What about the officer reporting the sudden death for the coroner?' Bartholomew asked.

'He says that without written statements to put the information into an evidential format, there is nothing more he can do.'

'Typical; be nice if he would try a little. Do you want me to lean on him?'

'To be honest all he could do is visit the squat where he would be told zilch. I've had to reconcile the fact that he is right about that.'

'But we now know who the dealer is: Lonsdale. I could lock him up on suspicion of dealing to your niece?'

'Your shout, Peter, you've met him, I haven't. Do you think he would cough dealing to her, and talking her into injecting the stuff rather than smoking it?'

Bartholomew paused in thought for a few seconds and then answered, 'Without any corroborating evidence it *would* be a

THE CABAL

waste of time, and as soon as he was back out, we'd probably end up with two dead addicts fingered for being grasses.'

'That's what I reckoned,' Daniel said. He then watched Bartholomew as he paused in further thought. The man was rubbing his hand through his hair and Daniel could see that his neck had turned slightly pink. He looked under pressure.

'As you managed to get the first addict to open up, how about trying to find him again. Even if he refuses to play ball, he may name the other addict who was present. He may be different,' Bartholomew said, with what Daniel thought had an air of desperation about it. Then he continued, 'If I go anywhere near it, or indeed the sudden death cop, to be honest, I'll probably get my soft bits torn off by Boy Wonder.'

Daniel was about to ask who he was talking about when Bartholomew's phone rang. He looked at the screen, swore and then took the call.

'Yes sir, I was,' he said, followed by a pause. Then, 'Just popped in to make sure—' followed by a further pause. Then, 'He's done what?' A further pause, and then, 'Yes, yes sir, I understand,' and then he ended the call. Daniel could see that the redness in his neck had moved north covering his face and head now.

'Boy Wonder: or ACC Marty Mathews. I mean if you were called Martin, would you choose to be known as Marty?' Bartholomew said.

Daniel didn't answer.

'It tells you all you need to know about the man,' Bartholomew spat.

'Can I ask what he wants?'

'That toe rag Lonsdale hasn't wasted any time. His boss has got onto their brief who has rung the Boy Wonder complaining of police harassment. And that spineless turd has ordered me to back off, in fact, to go nowhere near any of them without fresh evidence. And even then, I must run it past the head of CID first. I mean, I'm a detective superintendent for God's sake.'

Daniel felt sorry for Bartholomew, but only for a second. If he'd gone about things properly from the start, he wouldn't be sat here now in a strait jacket, with complaints and internal investigations hanging over him. 'So, what do you plan to do now?'

'The opposite of what that craven-hearted wimp has said. He couldn't detect his own arse if he shat himself; which must be a daily event,' Bartholomew said, now looking like a heart attack in waiting. He quickly added, 'Please disregard what you've just heard.'

'Don't worry about me, I'm no longer serving.'

'Do me one favour.'

'The squat?'

'Yes, because failing that, I might have to go for a nuclear option.'

'I'll try. Give me twenty-four hours,' Daniel said, and he meant it. And then asked, 'What's the nuclear option?'

'Forget you heard that as well,' Bartholomew said as he stood up. 'And thanks for your time,' he added and then made his way to the door. 'I'll show myself out.'

Five minutes later, Daniel had briefed Jill and Dawson.

'My God, he sounds desperate,' Jill said.

'He certainly did; almost unhinged,' he replied.

'I always knew he was a maverick, but he sounds like he is going off the chart,' Dawson added.

'What's driving him, so?' Jill asked.

'A mixture of pride, arrogance, hatred of failure. Resentment of more senior officers,' Dawson said, and then added, 'He's been paper-sifted the last three years on the trot for the chief supers' promotion board. And each time he has taken it worse than the last. Instead of listening to feedback and formulating an action plan to improve his weaknesses, he just goes off on one and blames everyone else.'

'So, what next?' Jill asked.

'Well, we've started this, so let's finish it if we can. But you can bow out if you wish, Jill. After all, this started off as mine and George's gig.'

'Absolutely, and thanks for everything,' Dawson added.

'Not a chance; I'm in for the duration wherever and whenever you need me,' Jill said.

Daniel and Dawson both thanked her and then Daniel said that he would try the squat, but fully expected to have to go several times. He didn't hold out much hope of success. Dawson cleared his throat and then said he'd put a call in to Marty Mathews to chat and ask how the murder investigation was going. He might pick up some asides about Bartholomew. And Jill offered to keep buzzing past the haulage yard to try and clock any activity. She said it would be too risky to park up outside after this morning's raid, all of Tommy Johnson's crew would be on hyper-alert.

'Brilliant,' Daniel said. And then Dawson added that he'd also put a scoping call into Wales. Daniel nodded and then saw them both off, after first checking that Bartholomew's motor had gone.

He returned to the rear lounge and reflected on his meeting with Bartholomew. He couldn't disagree with Dawson's rationale for the man's apparent dogged determination, and it was interesting to hear of his promotion board failures. Then Daniel had to smile as he re-ran Dawson's remarks through his mind again. He had suddenly stopped being the George Dawson that Daniel had become friends with, he sounded like Chief Constable Dawson again. But Daniel couldn't help wondering if there wasn't another agenda going on. After all, Bartholomew looked like a caged animal in his lounge. Or perhaps, it was just personal for him, plus he probably wanted to stick two fingers where the sun doesn't shine on the ACC.

He grabbed his car keys: it was time to give the squat a try.

Chapter Forty-five

Daniel spent the next twelve hours visiting the drug squat in Ribbleton, and found it empty on each occasion. When he had originally visited after Sally's death, he hadn't taken too much notice of the surroundings, as in, exactly what was there. He hadn't needed to. But when he'd spoken to the young addict in the kitchen, who'd been laid up against the wall in the corner, he had noticed three or four discarded syringes. And each time he visited today there were still only three or four. He couldn't imagine anyone would tidy up much in this place, unless it became overwhelming, so wondered if those who were using it had moved on to a fresh dive. It would make sense after Sally's death, especially if uniform *had* been around asking questions in the days that followed it.

As he left for the last time, he was relieved that he wouldn't have to leave his Jaguar alone in this street again, not that he'd been away from it for long on each visit. But as he approached it, he noticed the youths who had stiffed him to protect it previously. They were stood on the opposite side of the road paying his motor unhealthy attention. 'It's alright, lads, I don't need you this time, and I won't be back.'

'Just providing a service, bro,' the taller of the two said.

Daniel stopped by the driver's door, turned, and said, 'This squat dead, now?'

'As dead as that girl who went over in there,' he replied.

Daniel had to swallow the urge to cross the road and punch his lights out. He wasn't to know who she was to him. But instead said, 'Where have they all moved to?'

'Could be anywhere, bro, they never crank up in one place for too long in case Five-O clock it.'

He just nodded and got in his car and drove away. The current vernacular used to mean the police: 'Five-O' as in Hawaii Five-O, made him smile. The US cop show from the 70's was long before those two, or probably their parents were born. God knows who comes up with these nicknames.

THE CABAL

He was going to ring Dawson to update him, but as his route home took him close to his house, he thought he do a slight detour and speak in person. It was approaching 9 p.m. so not too late. He'd have five minutes with him and then leave him in peace to enjoy his evening.

Joan answered the door and pulled a forced smile across a stony expression. Perhaps, he'd called at a bad time. 'I just wanted a quick word with George, if it's not too late,' he said.

She sighed, but before she could answer, Daniel heard Dawson's voice from within the house, shout, 'Who is it?'

'You'd better come in,' Joan said. 'He's in the back room. But please don't keep him long. She then turned before Daniel could answer and headed for the staircase. He walked into the hall and closed the front door and then quickly walked to the rear lounge.

'It's only me,' he said as he entered. Dawson was sat in an armchair and looked stressed.

'If I've called at a bad time it can wait until tomorrow, I've nothing much to report.'

Dawson coughed and took a sip of water from a bottle by his armchair and looked up. 'Actually, it's good timing, a bit of a break from what Joan and I were discussing is probably a good thing, I'll just make you a brew,' Dawson said, and then rose to his feet and headed out the room.

Daniel took a facing armchair and sat down; he must have interrupted a row he reckoned. He probably had one waiting for him when he got home; he'd told Sue that he wouldn't be out too long. That was hours ago.

Dawson came back with a single mug of tea and Daniel said that he shouldn't have bothered if he wasn't having one.

'It's OK, I'll stick to water.'

Daniel quickly filled him in re his visits to the squat. He had an idea how Dawson could help which was why he'd called in person. But before he could ask, he was only too aware that Dawson seemed distracted, he didn't appear to be listening, and Daniel needed him to listen before he asked his favour. He had drawn blank on his visits to the squat, but it was only when he left the final time and had spoken to the two yobs on the street, that the thought had landed. He guessed they reminded him of his first visit a few days ago. It was then that he remembered recommending that the addict he'd spoken to could get himself in to a drug treatment programme. He'd left the details of whom and where to ring and had later rung the Drug and Alcohol Addiction Team - DAAT - to prime them should the lad call. He'd no way of knowing whether the youth had taken up the offer, and it was an outside chance that he had. But if he had, then his details and address would be on record. The trouble was that if he called them back - as a retired DI - they would not pass on the data.

To be honest, if he were still serving, he'd struggle, so he was going to ask Dawson if he could ask the ACC Crime - his mate Marty - to see if he could access the information. But something else was in play here, and he suddenly felt like he was intruding in whatever was going on between Joan and her husband. 'Look, it'll keep, I'll get out of your way, I'm sorry for interrupting. I'll bell you tomorrow.'

But before Daniel could get to his feet, Dawson suddenly seemed focused, animated even. 'No,' he said sternly.

Daniel was slightly taken aback by Dawson's retort.

'Stay,' he said, more softly. There is something I must tell you, and if I don't do it now, God knows when I will.'

Daniel didn't answer; he just eased himself back into the armchair, and took a sip of his tea.

Dawson lifted his head and looked Daniel straight in the face across the coffee table, and said, 'I've got cancer. And it's inoperable.'

THE CABAL

Chapter Forty-six

Daniel couldn't believe what he was hearing. He sat silently as he absorbed the shock of Dawson's news. His mind fixing on the words 'inoperable'. Wondering what exactly that meant but not daring to ask. Dawson hadn't said terminal, so maybe that was a good sign. Unless it was just an easier word for Dawson to use. He desperately hoped so. He'd known Dawson for years, but had only really known him for little over a week. He liked the Dawson he knew now and felt such sorrow for him. What poor Joan was going through, too, was equally unimaginable.

He wondered where Dawson had the disease, as he knew some areas were far worse than others, but again, dare not ask.

Then he got the answer.

'It's bloody ironic, really, considering how fit I always prided myself in being, and the cruel fact that I have never smoked in my life.'

A further question started to race through Daniel, and as if by telepathy, that answer came, too.

'I'm due to start chemo, and everything will depend on how my body reacts to that as to what happens next.'

Knowing he had to say something so as not to appear uncaring, Daniel swallowed hard and found his voice, 'I'm so desperately sorry to hear this, George. But they can do wonders nowadays; you must keep as positive and upbeat as you can.' As soon as he heard his own words, he cringed at how patronising the latter ones sounded. 'I, I, er…'

Dawson waved his hand in tacit understanding, and said, 'It's a shock when you hear it for the first time, I know. I've had a little while to wrap my head around it.'

Daniel nodded in relief that he had not caused offence. But also wondered what had just taken place between Joan and George. He hoped he hadn't today received more bad news.

'It's why I retired early.'

'You'd done more than your time; you'd earned the right to stand down when you did.'

'That's not what I mean. I wanted to prove my misgivings about Peter Bartholomew before I hung up my handcuffs. But when I received the news, I knew I should leave. Funnily, I *was* considering staying on a while, before I received a letter from the consultant formally informing me of what he had already told me, and, and...' Dawson said before halting to catch himself before continuing, 'And somehow reading it in black and white had an even deeper effect on me, if you can believe that.'

Daniel knew that the brain dealt and reacted to shocking news in a myriad of different unpredictable ways, and just nodded and smiled. He sensed Dawson was off and running and didn't want to interrupt him.

'I let go, I accepted defeat. That was until I bumped into the scientist Professor Cummings over a retirement celebratory lunch with Joan, which you know about. It reawakened the itch to sort Bartholomew out, so I could clear my mind and concentrate on myself.'

Daniel noticed that Dawson was leaning forward now and had his hands entwined resting on top of the glass coffee table between them. He reached forward and put his hand on top of Dawson's, just for a moment; for just long enough. Then he sat back and let Dawson continue.

'Then what Cummings said led me to the solicitor Wales; which incidentally I wouldn't have had to do if arrogant Darlington had taken my concerns seriously. But that said I'm glad now. And do you know why?'

Daniel didn't and said so.

'Because I wouldn't have ended up teamed with you, we would not have got to know each other the way we have. A friendship I could never imagined having, and one I am all the richer for.'

Daniel tried desperately not to let his eyes fill up, but was unable to stop it and had to use a hanky to dab them. But before he did, he had to put his tea mug down on the table. And as he did, Dawson reached forward and touched his hand. My God the man has inoperable cancer and he is consoling him.

Daniel cleared his throat and said, 'As am I. And look how far we have come in such a short space of time.'

THE CABAL

'Exactly.'

'I know this is a stupid question, but how is Joan bearing up?'

'Ah. Well, she has got over the initial shock, somewhat; but that has led to this evening.'

Christ, it did now sound like more bad news. He kept quiet again.

'I'd received a letter two days ago with a date to start my chemo. I didn't tell her straight away because I rang them and delayed the start date. I've only just told her that bit, and as you can imagine she is less than pleased with me.'

'No wonder. Why in God's name did you do that?'

'I just wanted a bit more time to get this thing finished with you. I know once I start my treatment there will be unpleasant side effects. But as for now, I actually feel surprisingly good, bar the odd dry cough.'

'For God's sake, you must start your treatment now. Leave Bartholomew to Jill and me, we'll do our utmost, you know we will. But in the wider scheme of things, a tosser like Bartholomew doesn't matter. Nothing does apart from you getting better.'

'Funnily, that's just what Joan said. The thing is Daniel; I can't clear my mind and concentrate like I know I'm going to have to, until I can get Bartholomew out of it.'

That man had far more to answer for than he could ever know, Daniel thought but didn't say.

'And to be honest, I'm also being a little selfish, as these last few days working operationally again with you and Jill, has been one hell of a boost. It's given me a purpose to get my arse out of bed, and a feeling of still being of use while still conducting a noble cause.'

Daniel started to try and further dissuade Dawson but he again raised his hand, this time to silence him. Then he continued, 'I've never felt more alive, and I've just told Joan that. She is still reeling from the original shock, you see, I only told her about my diagnosis after I retired. I know I should have told her sooner, but I just didn't want to break her heart, even though I knew I had to.'

Daniel could bring no words of comfort to mind that could mitigate Dawson's last comment, so he stayed silent.

'And now I've told her about delaying the start of my treatment. A double whammy with only a couple of days between them. It tears me up seeing the pain on her face, but I've had to dig deep to be forthright. I can't fully commit to my treatment until this thing we are doing is over. She and I can both be quite stubborn, but she'll come around, I'm sure. So, the sooner we can finish this, the sooner I can make my wife happy again; or at least, less sad.'

Daniel opened and then closed his mouth. He wasn't quite sure what he should say, and Dawson was starting to speak with that authoritative chief constable manner he still had in his armoury. But Daniel still needed him to speak to ACC Marty Mathews. A few seconds ago, that was an irrelevance, but if to conclude affairs was the only way to get Dawson to start his treatment, then it now took on a new urgency.

'So, tell me again on how things went at the squat?'

Daniel quickly did.

'Anything else we can do on that?'

Daniel had to smile, and then said, 'Just one favour; it's only a phone call, then you must stand down. Rest, start your treatment and I'll keep you fully briefed.' Last roll of the weighted dice, he knew. But it was weighted the wrong way.

'Stand down; nonsense; so, the sooner we snare this crime gang, the better. Now who do you want me to ring, and why?'

Daniel left for home five minutes later, still in shock and with an enduring sadness aching inside him. He couldn't believe how stoic Dawson was being, and knew that he would have to keep a close eye on his new friend just in case his stiff upper lip faltered. It could leave him vulnerable and unprotected. He'd have to manage what he would ask him to do going forward, but try to do so in a way that was not obvious. He didn't want to hurt his feelings. But there was a balance to be had here. Certainly, no more late night obs jobs, that was for sure.

THE CABAL

Chapter Forty-seven

It had taken Bartholomew until the following evening to calm down after Winstanley's untimely intervention at Lonsdale's house raid. Who the hell did she think she was? She may have joined the 'born again' mob, but she couldn't undo what she had already done. She should be careful she didn't push Bartholomew too far. He suspected she had eventually worked out how he had manipulated and used her. Selling it as some wonderfully noble cause to rid Lancashire of one of its top criminals, where the ends justified the means.

He'd made sure that he was nowhere around the headquarters complex where she might be, to avoid any more grief. He wasn't sure what he would say to her. Best let a bit of time intervene. He was just about to finish for the day when his mobile rang. He checked the screen and was pleasantly surprised. He took the call. 'Didn't expect to hear from you.'

'Aren't you the lucky one,' the caller said.

'In fact, I've rung you several times over the last few days, but you've dicked me.'

'You could never be that lucky.'

'Anyway, what is it? I hope it's good news, I desperately need some.'

'I need to see you.'

'When?'

'Now if you like, I've just got home from work.'

'Be there in thirty mins,' Bartholomew said, and ended the call.

He quickly grabbed his car keys and headed out into the Preston teatime traffic and pondered on what his cousin might have for him as he crawled towards the city centre. His cousin lived on the eastern side of the city in a quiet cul-de-sac near the motorway junctions and it would take thirty or forty minutes to travel the seven or eight-mile journey. They had never really been close but had come together after the accident eighteen months ago, and then again more so in recent months. For a common purpose. Bartholomew still wasn't sure if his cousin liked him, but those with a common enemy become friends and all that.

They were related through their mothers who were sisters. And even though the women were siblings, they in turn had not seen much of each other over the years. Even though both families lived in the greater Preston area. Both were just busy with their respective clans rather than because of any falling out between them. That was until a couple of years ago when the sisters each lost their husbands within six months of each other. His mother and his cousin's mother started to see each other more and more. They provided comfort and solace to each other. This gave Bartholomew pleasure for his mother's sake, and he saw more of his cousin thereafter than he had during their lives to date. But they still hadn't got on too well. They never became any closer.

That was until the accident threw them together in what became a joint need.

Eighteen months ago, the sisters were out together for lunch on a fine spring day. They were walking between a local café and the bus stop when a suspected drunk driver mounted the pavement and mowed them down. They were both killed. It was a quick end for his aunt, but not so for his poor mother who was carried on the car's bonnet for over fifty meters.

He lost an aunt he didn't really know or care about, but lost a mother of whom he loved dearly. Even now he found it painful to recall. What terror had gone through her during those fifty meters before she was dumped onto the tarmac?

The driver was never traced. The nearest the police came was picking up some intel that the driver was a local criminal - he'd already worked that bit out for himself. And that he was 'The Top Man in a local firm'.

Bartholomew shook the unpleasant memories from his mind as he pulled up outside his cousin's house. He really hoped he had good news for him. He was Bartholomew's secret weapon. As far as he was concerned, the scumbag who had killed his mother was part of The North End Crew. He had beaten that much out of a local drug addict soon after the accident, but surprise, surprise, the Traffic Department's enquiries went nowhere. Why on earth the police had not put detectives on the case, he would never know.

Bartholomew walked down the garden path and knocked on the door which was opened straight away. 'How's it going, cuz?' Bartholomew said.

'I haven't got much, but it must mean something,' Billy Wellard said. 'They've kept me out the way for the last two days up at Piper's house, teaching me how to run the haulage fleet properly.'

'And?'

'Something big is definitely going down, I'll tell you inside,' Billy said, and then stood back to let Bartholomew in, and glanced up and down the road as he did. He'd been watching too many cop shows on TV.

Chapter Forty-eight

'Why have you been avoiding my calls?' Bartholomew asked Billy as he slumped down in one of his front room's tatty armchairs.

'Because I'd gone as far as I can.'

'Why is it always two steps forward with you, and then one step back?'

'It's not been you taking all the risks.'

Bartholomew rolled his eyes; Billy had no appreciation of the risks he'd been taking at his end. 'Don't you want the arse wipe that killed our mothers sorting?'

'Of course, I do,' Billy said as he took a seat on the sofa opposite. 'As long as we have the right person. There are more than one decent sized firm in central Lancashire.'

'My intel is good, it's "The Top Man"; and this Toe Jam turd is the top man of the North End Crew.'

'You said Piper was the Top Man?'

'Well, we both got that bit wrong. You thought he was too.'

Billy glanced away from Bartholomew and didn't answer directly. Bartholomew knew he'd got him on that one.

Then Billy turned back to face him, 'You knew it wasn't Piper, didn't you?'

Bartholomew knew he needed to keep Billy onside, but also knew he deserved some truth. 'Suspected, but didn't know. But we now know for sure it's Johnson, so all good, eh?'

'All good, all good, have you forgotten that I was kidnapped and accused of planting the drugs in Piper's desk drawer?'

'Of course not. But you did, didn't you,' he said, immediately regretting how flippant he sounded.

'Yes, but on your bloody instructions as you had convinced me that Piper was *the* Top Man, and therefore killed our mothers. Jesus; and you wonder why our families never got too close.'

'It worked out, OK?'

'No thanks to you. Look, I accept I thought Piper was in charge as he ran the fleet. His brother or half-brother or whatever he is, was often around the yard, but as a driver I took no attention of him.'

'But now you've been promoted to Fleet Manager, you know different.'

'Well, yeah, and they have been good to me, now.'

Bartholomew was becoming exasperated with Billy, 'Yeah, really good to you; kidnapped you and beat the crap out of you.'

'Yeah, and we both know why. Thank God I was able to convince them.'

'You can still make a formal complaint about that, and we can nick them for that, job done. Johnson sorted.'

'Yeah, great idea detective. Look what happened to Piper in prison. Can you imagine what they'd do to me? And don't give me all that witness protection bull. And another thing, what were you thinking when you dropped in to the yard the other day. I could have been in the office; should have been. Nearly shat myself when I found out.'

'Just wanted to see who the Top Man really was.'

'No, you didn't, you already knew; thanks to me. You were showboating; taking unnecessary risks.'

'Just wanted to confirm your intel, no offence. Sus it for myself.'

'Rubbish. You should have stayed away, or at least warned me.'

'Sorry, it was a bit spur of the moment. But I did want to confirm who was in charge for myself; no offence, again.'

'Much taken, again.'

Bartholomew opened his mouth and then closed it. He needed to move this conversation on, so said, 'Anyhow, it sounds like you doubt that Johnson killed our mothers?'

'Well, you did say it was Piper, and now it's his half-brother. Can you blame me? And the Top Man we are after could still be from another firm.'

Bartholomew suspected that as Billy had been promoted and Johnson was treating him well, he was starting to like the dirt ball, and therefore starting to lose faith. He decided to feed a bit more *truth* in to keep him loyal to the cause.

'Look, the firm is definitely The North End Crew,' he started.

'According to the drug addict you beat that tip bit out of. Hardly the most dependable of sources.'

'And my mate Merson had it confirmed from another means,' he lied. 'I brought Merson onside for that very purpose.'

'And look what happened to him?' Billy jumped in with.

'Well, anyway, it's the right firm. But if I'm being totally honest,' - here comes the real truth bit - Bartholomew hoped it worked. 'I pretty much knew that Piper was a screen, but needed to get rid of him to find out who was behind it. And it succeeded.'

'So, you now admit you lied to me at the start, and used me?'

'I wouldn't put it like that, but look where we are now?'

'I nearly got myself beaten to death as a mere pawn in your plan?'

'Look, Billy,' Bartholomew said, and threw his hands in the air. 'I'm sorry. It was a calculated risk. I wasn't to know that they'd suspect you. I'm terribly sorry I put you at risk. But it worked out all fine, and we now know who the Top Man is.'

'That's a first.'

'What is?'

'I've never heard you apologise for anything.'

It was not a word he used very often, that was true, but he genuinely was sorry for putting Billy at such risk. Had he known about the abduction in real time, he'd have raided the yard straight away. But it had probably worked out for the best that he'd been in court, incommunicado, until shortly afterwards. And then he had to get to Piper's to plant the drug money. And as Billy was released shortly afterwards, it had all worked out OK. 'Look, we are where we are and we need to finish it. The help I was getting in-force has gone, and I don't just mean Merson, so it's down to you and me. We it owe it to our mothers. Both cut down when they should have been able to start enjoying life a bit more. Their later years robbed from them,' Bartholomew said, and as he mentioned their mothers, a tinge of real emotion swept through him. It took the tension out of their discussion. Even from beyond the grave she was guiding him.

THE CABAL

He wiped a tear from his eye before taking a grip of himself again. He could see that Billy's face had lost its anger. Maybe Bartholomew's genuine emotion had softened the aura. Maybe he should try that tactic again in the future, he thought, as he regained his normal demeanour.

'OK, but no more bull?'

'Open and honest all the way.'

'And no more maverick, gung-ho, stunts?'

'You got it,' he said, not knowing if he could keep to that.

Billy nodded and then offered him a drink; he was glad for the break. Billy headed to the kitchen and returned with two opened bottles of lager. He took one and asked, 'What's happening at the yard?' Bartholomew then leaned back and sipped his beer as he listened. Billy told him how he'd been kept out of the way at Piper's. But that the real indication that something big was on, came when he'd been told to call all their customers and put them on hold for seven days. And that if they didn't go elsewhere, the next run would be a freebie courtesy of North End Haulage.

'Very interesting? How many wagons do you have?' he asked.

'Seven and this is unprecedented. I know I've only worked for them for a year or so, but I've been driving HGVs for fifteen years and never known it happen before.'

'What do you normally transport?'

'Anything non-perishable; so technically things could wait.'

'But what about your clients' own cash flow and other business issues, and their responsibilities elsewhere?'

'I asked that, and Johnson just said the offer of a free run should keep them sweet, but he didn't sound too bothered.'

'So, whatever your seven wagons are up to must be very lucrative?'

'I guess.'

'Any idea what?'

'They won't tell me.'

'So, it must be illegal,' Bartholomew said as he felt animated again.

'I also get the impression that a lot of activity has been taking place overnight, but no idea what or exactly where.'

'What makes you say that?'

'Just bits and pieces I've picked up. Other drivers ringing me to ask what the job is, and piecing together what little each has been told. Plus, I've had to help sort out the Customs forms.'

Bartholomew had forgotten about all the new regulations in place post-Brexit, so asked Billy for anything he could tell him. All he could say was that all seven lorries would be transporting building products - in convoy - and all would be bound for Amsterdam via Dover. 'That's brilliant. But we could do with knowing a bit more?'

'Like what?'

'Well, are they coming back in convoy, too? Be easier to hit all seven at the same time, assuming that they are bringing drugs back into the country. If they are not in convoy, we may have to pick them off as each one comes through the port, which would be a bit hit and miss.'

'And once you've hit one, the others will find out.'

'Not necessarily, but you leave that with me,' Bartholomew said, and then finished his beer. He told Billy to stay in touch and he'd do the same. They parted a lot friendlier than when he'd arrived.

As he drove away, a plan was forming. If they hit the first lorry and it was negative, they could keep the driver incommunicado until all seven were through the port. Do the same with them all if needed, but only if they were able to arrest them. And if the searches were negative, he'd need other grounds. Conspiracy should do, but he would need to fabricate enough 'evidence' to justify this. He missed Merson, but should be able to pull something believable together himself. Then he had a thought and pulled over while he texted Billy. He needed the names and dates of birth of all seven drivers, Billy rang him straight back to say that that would be no problem. But added that the drivers won't know anything about the potential hidden loads.

'Yeah, I realise that no probs,' Bartholomew said.

'So, you're not going to nick the drivers, are you?'

'Of course not, just need to tie them to the vehicle details, which I'll also need from you.'

'I'll get you the fleet registered numbers tomorrow. But re the drivers, I know them all, they are all solid guys. Decent men with families. I'd hate it if they got wiped up in all this.'

'Of course, Billy, they'll be OK, it's evidence against Johnson we need, not the innocent drivers.'

'So, they won't be arrested for anything?'

'You have my word, cuz, now chill.'

'OK, that's fine then, speak to you tomorrow,' Billy ended the conversation with.

Bartholomew set off again, and headed towards home. At last, it was all coming together nicely. He and Billy would have their revenge with Johnson banged up for many years for importing drugs or guns or whatever the contraband was. The drivers would be nicked, but if they gave evidence against Johnson, he might be able to broker them a deal. But that would depend on the CPS. Billy would be pissed off, but it would be all over so that wouldn't matter. He wouldn't need him again.

And the force would have to take note and at last grant him an audience before a promotion board. He'd make detective chief super yet. And then he could lord it over Carol Winstanley and keep her in line. And make sure that the career hungry limpet, that was Shirley Lancaster, never became a detective super.

Chapter Forty-nine

Daniel didn't sleep well after Dawson's bombshell as he'd replayed their conversation over in his mind. Trying to add context to it. Assess how bad things were. He'd been offered chemotherapy, and although the daft sod had delayed the start of it, the sheer fact that it was on the table had to be a good sign. Or so he hoped. He told Sue over breakfast and she, too, was understandably upset.

'I can't believe he wants to carry on this thing with you and Jill?' she said.

'It's become a crusade with him, and he does say that it gives him a sense of purpose, takes his mind off it, which I sort of get,' Daniel replied.

'Why do you think he's told you now?'

'By the look on Joan's face when she saw me at the door, I reckon she bitterly resents what he's doing, and may have threatened that she would tell me if he didn't.'

'To get him to quit?'

Daniel nodded.

'You'll have to respect his wishes, but do try and minimise what he does.'

'I fully intend to.'

'A difficult balance.'

'Indeed.' Then a loud knock at the door interrupted further discussion. It was a copper's knock. Sue was to her feet before Daniel, and left the kitchen door open as she walked down the hall to the front door. She was only halfway there before she paused and turned to look back at Daniel. He saw what she saw. Their front door was fully glazed with frosted glass and the sun outside accentuated the shape and silhouette of the caller. It matched the knock. It was unmistakably George Dawson. 'How do I treat him?'

'Like nothing has changed. Be normal and don't mention it, unless he does,' Sue said before turning back towards the front door. Sage counsel as always from Sue.

THE CABAL

Sue opened the door and invited Dawson in and Daniel met him mid-hallway and shook his hand before leading him into the rear lounge. Sue hurried off and left them to it. They each took an armchair.

'Always reminds me of my rear lounge,' Dawson said.

'Yours is posher with French windows, but great minds and all that,' Daniel said. He was glad of the trivia to start the conversation with. He offered Dawson a brew, but he shook his head.

'We haven't got time; or to be more accurate, you haven't.'

'Sounds interesting.'

'Your hunch paid off and Marty Mathews came through.'

This was good news, and Daniel couldn't help but notice that Dawson was buzzing. The right decision had been made last night; for now, anyhow.

'Marty rang the lady running the DAAT and phrased it right. Said you were just keen to know if the addict had taken up your advice, but knew not to ask directly so as not to breech their confidentiality protocols.'

Blow smoke up the woman's derrière; great tactic. He knew how arsy she could ironically be.

'And she was thrilled to say that he has joined a treatment programme and was responding well. Then Marty passed on your telephone number asking that he call you if he wanted to. That you just wanted to ask more about your niece, just on the qt.'

Daniel instinctively picked up his phone from the coffee table and looked at the call log; no missed calls.

'No need to wait on that. They've rung Marty back and said that he wants to meet you to thank you in person; he reckons he owes you that. But would prefer to do it sooner. I suggested this morning at your favourite café in Longton.'

'Excellent, you've done a great job brokering that.'

'It was Marty really; he was sorry to hear about your niece. He said he'd have the local DCI link in with the coroner to make sure no evidence gathering opportunities have been missed.'

'That'll please her mum, Melanie no end. Thanks again.'

'Might all lead nowhere, but it's worth a try.'

Daniel nodded.

'I'll drop you off if you like and wait in my motor around the corner?'

'There's no need, you've done enough.'

'There's every need,' Dawson said firmly.

Daniel didn't argue.

***

Daniel was sat at his favourite table in the café's window but had yet to see the youth approach. He hoped he'd smartened himself a bit since last they met, or they would draw a lot of attention. He wouldn't have picked here as a meeting place but the last thing he wanted to do today, was burst Dawson's bubble. He glanced up again on hearing the door chime and saw a smartly dressed man in his twenties walk in. It wasn't the addict, so he went back to pretending to read the menu. He then became aware of someone stood in front of him and looked up to see that it was the lad who had just entered.

'Hi Mr Wright, how's it going?'

Daniel looked into the face of the lad and then shock hit him. 'My God it's you. I'm so sorry, I wasn't ignoring you,' he said as he jumped to his feet and shook the lad's hand. They both sat down. 'Well, man with no name, I'm shocked at how well you look already.'

'I called round to my parents' gaff yesterday. My dad answered the door without his glasses on; it was only when I spoke that he recognised me. So, no offence taken, man. And the name's Jerry Mansfield; names do matter. I know that now.'

Daniel remembered their first conversation. Then they chatted freely and Daniel ordered breakfast for them both. It was a real joy to see this skeleton of a man wolf it down. He still had a sallow complexion but had lost that ghostly shade of nothing. Daniel knew that once an addict had stopped taking heroin the body's repair mechanisms got to work quickly. Blood circulation was immediately improved, as it was with a smoker who kicked tobacco, and that in itself can give a much healthier look, fast. Eating properly adds to it as well. But Daniel also knew that internal problems would take longer to sort out. He lowered his voice and asked, 'How are you managing the withdrawal symptoms?'

'They've got me on those receptive blockers, and I'm taking prescribed methadone daily to substitute the brown.'

'Good to hear. But get off the methadone as soon as you feel you can, that stuff is more addictive than heroin.'

'Yeah, I'd heard that. They are reducing it daily. But I just wanted to thank you for giving me that card and making me think,' Jerry said. And Daniel saw tears well up in his eyes. The young man suddenly looked even younger than his years.

'I thought about what you said and stuff, and thought about Sally. My habit was worse than hers. I always knew I was on borrowed time. I'd made excuses to myself why she'd gone over; you know, her cranking up for the first time and all that. But had to face the fact that it was just a lottery that no one wanted to win, and my turn would come whether I liked it or not.'

'Well, it's a real pleasure to have helped, and I know Sally's mum will find some solace in it when I tell her. But while we are on about Sally, I just wanted to ask you to run through it all again if you don't mind. Now you are recalling things through a sober mind. Anything you can add about the dealer could really help.'

'I still don't know his name.'

'Don't worry, I do; it's Gary Lonsdale, or Capone.'

Jerry looked up, impressed.

'Well, that's the other thing that helped me make the call to the number on the card. Though I'm not sure how it will help you out. And I have to say now, as grateful as I am, if you were after me to set him up in some sting or whatever; I couldn't do it man. I'd end up back on the gear. I hope you understand.'

Daniel now realised why Jerry had wanted to meet face-to-face; it made sense he'd have thought this was what Daniel wanted. 'No worries, Jerry that's not it at all. I wouldn't risk your recovery by putting you through it.'

'OK man,' he said, and looked decidedly relieved. 'But I don't know how else I can help you?'

Daniel wasn't sure either; this had always been an outside chance. Just one line that needed covering, crossing off, and then letting them move on. 'OK no sweat, Jerry. Just seeing you as you are now has made my day,' he said. And he meant it. 'Just tell me about the other thing that pushed you to make the call, the thing about your dealer; Lonsdale?'

'I've been in treatment three days now, and I may look better than the heap of crap you first met, but bath, shave, haircut, and clean clothes can hide a lot. So, I know it's only day three, I have a long way to go.'

'You'll get there; just remember that each day is slightly easier than the last.'

Jerry nodded, and then continued, 'Well, four days ago, I scored a couple of days' worth of gear from Lonsdale, and the pig charged me double. When I asked why he was ripping me, he said some stuff about supply and demand, which I didn't understand. He then said if I didn't want it, I could give it him back. I freaked at the thought and apologised. He nodded.'

Daniel nodded too.

'Then he added that I should make it last, stretch out the dry bits, like he was trying to wean me off it or summat. I still didn't get it, so asked why? Asked if that was why it was costing more?'

Daniel wasn't too sure where this was going.

'That's when he said there would be no more gear for over a week.'

Daniel sat up straight. Now it was making sense.

'Said that he and his firm had to go away on business to Holland in a few days' time, and would be gone for a week. And when he gets back, if I've scored from anywhere else, he'd break my wrists. Said he had a lad working for him so he would know if I had. That's when I thought, it's now or never, and rang the lady at the DAAT.'

Daniel couldn't believe what he was hearing, and he knew Jerry would never understand the value of what he'd just said. It just went to show that the true nuggets of intel could come from the most unlikely of places. He thanked Jerry and told him that his information had been a great help. Jerry nodded but looked nonplussed. He paid the bill and wished Jerry luck. But just

THE CABAL

before he left, he asked, 'What about the other addict who was there when Sally went over?'

'Gone with the wind, man, didn't even know his name.'

Daniel nodded and left.

After he had brought Dawson up to speed, he'd asked what Daniel thought it all meant. 'It's got to be an importation. Think about it: no more gear for a week, they are going to Holland on business, the dealer Lonsdale is going too, and with others, presumably from the North End Crew. I know this doesn't further your aims any, as in Bartholomew, but it could take out several of the North End Crew including the z-faced monster who killed my niece.'

Dawson nodded, and said, 'We are still police, or were until recently. This is too good an opportunity, I agree.'

'I belled Jill as I was walking from the café and have asked her to keep the haulage yard warm and report any unusual activity.'

'The next question is what do we do with the info?' Dawson asked.

'The trouble is, if we give it to the real police—'

'Like we should,' Dawson interrupted with.

'Granted, but if we do, it is nothing more than supposition at this stage, and we still don't have any specifics as to who exactly - apart from Lonsdale - when, or what. It's too vague to get the police excited. But my gut is going overboard. And in over thirty years it has served me well.'

'What do you suggest?'

'Let's just keep a watching brief for now and if we see anything to put any corroboration on this, then we can discuss further what we should do. But for now, we just don't know enough.'

'Also agreed.'

'But it must be big and bad; I've never ever heard of a prolific dealer shutting up shop for over a week like this, so whatever it is, it must be worth their while.'

It was Dawson's turn to nod, though he looked less convinced that Daniel felt. And who knows, he might be right. But it was worth a punt.

Chapter Fifty

Johnson was knackered but excited. He'd managed to grab a couple of hours' kip while the two Garys finished off. All the breeze blocks were done and looked great. He'd sent a series of close-up photos of a converted one to Swiss Bob - via WhatsApp - and had then asked, 'Which side?' Swiss Bob couldn't tell which had been touched, he was extremely impressed. It didn't do any harm to keep him happy. After this gig was over the sky would be the limit.

All the wagons were fully prepped, and the drivers briefed, though none of them knew what was happening, just that they were all going to Amsterdam via Dover, and in convoy. He'd impressed on them that all seven lorries were to stay in procession and must travel through the port together. But without telling the drivers why. He also told two of them that the two Garys would be riding shotgun with the middle two vehicles. Rumour, according to Elaine on the front desk, was that management suspected someone was either skimming off some of their goods or taking extra things on board. This was why they all had to go as one, and have two chaperones with them.

It was a good cover story, so he'd let them believe it. He was even tempted to join the party, but G said that might appear a bit over the top. He had a point, plus he had to find time to sit down and think what to do about their thorn in the arse; Bartholomew. Corrupt or kill, were the two obvious options; they couldn't go to the next level of business with him continually getting in the way.

He'd also told Piper to keep Billy with him, and to stick to him like glue. Even take his phone off him and keep him at Piper's place. Not that he didn't trust Billy, he did, now; but he wouldn't be able to talk to anyone without a phone, about what he didn't know. Piper was cool and made a point of telling him, 'Whatever it is, I don't want to know, either,' which was fine by him. Billy had taken the incommunicado news a little worse and had rung Johnson as soon as Piper had told him. But Johnson just said it was safer that way, for him. He didn't want to end up on the wrong end of a hook again. He went quiet when Johnson said that, and he regretted the comment. But added, 'Look, you've no family, and you'll have a ball at Johnny's, and I'll pay you five grand extra this month to cover the inconvenience.'

'OK, boss, no probs and thank you,' he replied.

So that was that loose end tied. He'd sent the two Garys home to get some sleep, and they were due back soon. Then it would be game on when the drivers landed. Things were looking up following their recent hiccups.

****

Daniel offered to join Jill but she said that two people in a car, even a man and a woman would start to look iffy around the haulage yard. Even she was feeling the heat and had to keep moving. She said she had settled at the far end of the street with a very long-distance eyeball, but even that had its shelf life. There was no way anyone at the haulage place would connect her with them at that distance, but others where she was parked could notice her and wrongly assume she was interested in them. That was the trouble with an area so full of villains. If any of them saw anything sus, then it was always Old Bill, and it was always them that the Old Bill was interested in. A mixture of criminal arrogance and paranoia. Daniel and Dawson had returned to their respective homes and awaited developments.

The last call of the day from Jill was at 10 p.m., it was just going dark so she was going to quit soon. Plus, she was running out of places to go to keep a long-distance eyeball, and without night vision goggles it would be useless. But she did report a lot of comings and goings during the day and the last thing she saw was a succession of HGVs all arriving at different times of the afternoon and evening. But none had left. Most of the lights had been turned off as of ten minutes ago, and Daniel agreed that it was time to call it a day. He thanked her again, and said that he would take the early shift from first light, just so they didn't miss anything. Though Daniel wasn't sure what *anything* would look like. He just hoped they would know it when they saw it.

The only real trigger they had was Lonsdale; where he went, they would too. And according to Jill, she saw him and his brutish double leave a couple of hours ago and neither had been back. When Daniel filled Dawson in, he volunteered to keep an early watch on Lonsdale's home address, or the access roads on and off the estate at the very least. Initially, Daniel tried to dissuade him, but he said it made sense, and as Jill had put in such a long shift today, it was only fair. The logic was hard to disagree with, so Daniel relented. They agreed to be on plot for five a.m.

'One last thing,' Daniel said.

'Yep.'

'Bring a holdall with some clothes with you; we don't know where we'll end up if it's suddenly, game on.'

'Right you are,' Dawson said before they ended the call.

Joan will really hate me for that, Daniel thought as he headed upstairs. Time to get his own head down; he'd have to be up at four.

THE CABAL

Chapter Fifty-one

Daniel had only been on plot for ten minutes when the first activity started at the yard. He saw several guys turn up in taxis, separately, but all had a holdall or a backpack with them. They must be the drivers. He rang Dawson to prompt extra vigilance in case Lonsdale was on an early start too. He next woke Jill and apologised for disturbing her lie-in. He'd managed to get a look through his binoculars at two of the 'drivers' and fed their descriptions to Jill. She said that they matched the look of two she had seen the evening before arriving with the wagons. 'It's looking good for today then?' he said.

'But to be honest,' she added, 'they all look like extras from a Yorkie chocolate bar ad.'

'These two certainly hadn't been on a treadmill in like, ever.'

'I'll be with you as soon as I can, I'll pick a spot at the other end of the street to you.'

Daniel ended the call, and as soon as he did, Dawson rang all excited.

'Looks like a bed wetter at this end, he's in a taxi headed your way,' he said.

Daniel loved it when Dawson spoke more and more like that, he'd lose all his chief constable-ness soon at this rate. 'Excellent, stay back and keep the follow loose. If he comes straight here, can you join me at the east end of the road?'

'Will do and will do,' Dawson said and then cut the connection.

Daniel was only too aware that Dawson was not surveillance trained, and they didn't want to risk a compromise at this late stage. Following a taxi at distance for the short journey to the yard should be OK, but once the game was on, he wanted Dawson with him.

Ten minutes passed and then Daniel saw the taxi drop Lonsdale off at the yard, also with a bag in tow. Two minutes after that, Dawson drove past and then pulled in behind him. He threw his own bag in the boot of Daniel's motor before joining him in the car. He was bustling.

'This is exciting,' he said, as he closed the passenger door.

'Let's hope so.'

A further ten minutes passed as the pre-dawn light stretched its glow and the sun eventually breached the horizon. It was going to be another lovely day. It would make their job that much easier. Not that following a wagon should be too difficult, even with just two motors. Then Daniel received a text from Jill to say that she was on plot at the far end of the street. They had it boxed now and could sit back and relax a little.

The lull didn't last long. Daniel, although some distance away, was parked at a slight angle and could see when the large up-and-over corrugated entrance door to the main yard went up and stayed up. The stretching rays of the morning sun reflected off the shutters confirmed what he was seeing. He put in a quick call to Jill and she reckoned she could do one walk past without causing suspicion. She said she'd deploy the dog leash. Always a good prop.

'What's with the dog lead?' Dawson asked.

'Gives you a reason for being there. You can walk almost anywhere with an empty dog lead, shouting "Here Rover, who's a naughty boy then" and no one pays you any attention.'

Dawson roared with laughter and said, 'I'm loving this surveillance malarkey; signed many an authority over the years, but never had the pleasure of doing it before now. On that, do we not need some kind of authorisation?'

'No George, we are no longer police, or even acting as agents for them; so, all good.' Then Daniel's phone rang through the car's Bluetooth. Jill.

'Hi darling, can't find the blessed dog, but you know what he's like, he'll probably run straight home, so I'm going to carry on. Keep your eyes peeled for him; I reckon he'll be there any minute.'

'Will do, Jill,' Daniel said and started the car's engine. And sure enough, a minute later, if that, the first wagon edged its way out of the yard and then pulled up a hundred metres further down

THE CABAL

the road. Then came the second one, and then the third. Once all seven were lined up, they all started to drive off like some Australian outback road train.

Dawson was lively again, and said, 'Why aren't we going after them?'

'Because we had the eyeball, so just in case they clocked us, which I'm sure they didn't, Jill will take up the follow, and we'll drop in at an appropriate distance behind her.

Dawson nodded and Daniel stayed put until he heard from Jill via the Bluetooth.

'Jill with the eyeball, it's a right, right, right onto Blackpool Road, all seven through the lights heading towards Ribbleton, keeping the football ground to my offside.'

'In convoy, Jill,' Daniel said.

'I'll call you when I need you to make ground,' Jill said, and then the line went dead.

'They are headed in the general direction of the M6 Motorway junctions,' Dawson said.

'Looking that way,' Daniel said, as he accelerated hard towards the major traffic light-controlled crossroads between Deepdale Road and Blackpool Road, both major thoroughfares. He was determined to make the right turn onto Blackpool Road before the lights changed.

He had to brake hard to get the speed off before making the turn as the lights turned to amber. Then he was able to slow down to 25 m.p.h. Up ahead in the distance, he could see the rearmost wagon and Jill's car two vehicles down from it. If they were headed to the motorway, then Daniel knew that Jill would feel comfortable keeping the eyeball. Blackpool Road was a major road, and the route they were on was a natural one for anyone headed to the M6. Daniel expected that she would want to change places once they were on the motorway. Normally, it would be nigh on impossible to conduct a mobile surveillance with just two cars, but a follow down the motorway would be the easiest option open to them. He explained this to Dawson.

'Presuming they do go onto the motorway, what do we do then? We still don't know what is going on?'

'That is the million-dollar question, George, and I have no idea what the answer is?'

'Shall we ring Jill to discuss it?'

'She's on her own and will be concentrating on her surveillance tradecraft. We are double-crewed, so let's leave it until we have the eyeball and then you can ring her.'

'Fair enough,' Dawson said.

Plus, it would give them some more thinking time, Daniel thought. As of now, he'd no real idea what was going on, but his gut was shouting at him. That much was plain.

***

Peter Bartholomew hated it when people didn't return phone calls. He found it the height of ignorance, especially when it's obviously important, such as a work-related thing, and especially when he'd left a voicemail. And yesterday he had left his cousin Billy Wellard seven voicemails after each unanswered call. No one spent all day charging their phone if that was what he was doing. He was up at six and tried again, he desperately needed an update from Billy, and it was essential he was given the details of the seven drivers so he could pass them on to the Border Force.

The phone went straight to voicemail again. He didn't leave a message this time but looked at his watch. Ten past six; Billy would still be in his pit with his hands wrapped around his only real friend. Time for a rude awaking. Bartholomew smiled at his own unintended pun. He drove straight across town to Billy's gaff, but could not get an answer at the door. Was the maggot dissing him now, had he had a change of heart; wanting to protect all his driver mates? Or had he just lost his bottle? Either way he'd have to answer the door before Bartholomew woke the street up.

After a further pounding on the front door, he stood back to catch his breath and then noticed that there was no motor in the drive. He also saw that the curtains, upstairs and down, were open. Where was he? Perhaps he had got lucky for the first time in his life. Or had he gone in to work incredibly early, which might mean something. Either way, he wasn't here.

THE CABAL

Bartholomew mused whether he should keep obs on the yard, or at Piper's, to see if he could see Billy. But he was bothered that the scumbag Tommy Johnson would clock him. He didn't want to give the worm further ammunition to feed his complaints against him. He'd head to his own office and consider his next move.

Chapter Fifty-two

All seven wagons snaked their way onto the M6 southbound and stayed together in the inside lane. Daniel had taken over the eyeball and Dawson had called Jill via the car's Bluetooth and all three were trying to work out what to do. But before that, they had to consider what was happening. All seven wagons had left together for a reason, but as Jill argued, it would be impossible for them all to travel to Dover, or Harwich or whichever port they were headed for and stay in convoy. They were bound to be split up by traffic.

'Perhaps they will regroup near the port and then go through as one?' Dawson suggested. It made sense, and if it was their intention to travel through as one, it was probably an anti-pull strategy, Daniel had added. If one was carrying money, drugs, guns or whatever, then they would obviously feel safer in numbers. The chances of all seven getting a random tug were incalculable.

'That would only happen if the Border Force were acting on firm intel, which they are not. Well, as far as we know,' Jill said.

The next question was what are they hiding going out? They quickly discounted drugs; they would be going out to bring that in if that was the game. But they may be hiding large amounts of cash with which to pay for them. Money laundering legislation would ensure undeclared large amounts of cash was stopped leaving the country, and seized. An investigation would then follow. Plus, it would seriously hurt and disrupt the gang's activities and effectiveness going forward if nothing else.

The other feasible option was guns, but as with drugs, it was far more likely that they would bring those back into the country, rather than be taking them out. But whatever their game; drugs or guns, they would need a lot of money to pay for it.

'But they could pay for the drugs or guns by another means?' Dawson pointed out.

'So why this wagon train, then? If that was the case, then all seven wagons would just travel out normally, independently, and save the cowboy act for the return journey when they had the hot goods on board,' Daniel said.

'I agree,' Jill said. 'They are definitely hiding something, and money seems to be the most likely.'

The next question was what they should do? Try and organise a pull by the real police while the wagons were still together, or have them all pulled at the port. Normally, Daniel would have favoured the port option, but they didn't know which one. They'd have to stay with it until they found out, and as they were no longer real police that could prove tricky. They would have to be prepared to keep with it all the way, and Daniel was worried about over-tiring Dawson. If the port was Dover, that was the best part of eight hours' drive away.

Then things happened to direct events; Dawson had a coughing fit, the worse by a long way that Daniel had witnessed to date. After five minutes, the poor man eventually calmed and drank a full bottle of mineral water to ease his throat. He said he was OK afterwards, but Daniel knew he was far from OK. To save him any embarrassment, Daniel had hit the end call button when Dawson had started coughing. Jill didn't know, and it wasn't Daniel's secret to share.

Then the rearmost wagon activated its nearside indicator as it neared the half mile marker board for Charnock Richard services. They were still in Lancashire, so a bit early for a comfort break; but they were stopping for a reason.

Charnock Richard services south of Chorley is a large motorway service area, which had a sizable wagon park separate to the main car parks. This could prove tricky; a car would stand out a mile in the lorry part. Beyond the lorry park en route back onto the motorway was a petrol station. Thank God the designers always put the fuel stop as the last thing before re-joining the motorway. Daniel reconnected the Bluetooth and shouted, 'We'll take the car park and deploy on foot.'

'I'll take the straight on by the pumps, try and get a reverse eyeball, too,' Jill replied with.

The car park was half empty, so Daniel quickly parked up and jumped out with his phone to his ear as Dawson followed. Jill reported that she had a good spot by the water and air and it was taking the wagons a little while to park up. Daniel said that they'd hang back in case the drivers headed towards to service station main building. A minute later, she was back in Daniel's ear, 'All seven are parked in a line, and all the drivers are out and talking in a huddle.'

Obviously receiving new instructions.

'But you won't believe who's just joined them from the middle two wagons; numbers 3 and 4?'

'Who?'

'Lonsdale and his ugly twin lookalike, and they are leading the discussions.'

'This confirms that it's game on. And it's significant that Lonsdale and his mate are not travelling together.'

'I agree, and if they leave separately in wagons 3 and 4, then I suggest that they should be our focus. I'll get their reg numbers when they pass me.'

'Also agreed,' Daniel said and quickly briefed Dawson who nodded.

'Standby, standby, standby, all subjects are back to their vehicles, and Lonsdale is towards vehicle 4 and the second target towards vehicle 3.'

Daniel knew it was decision time regarding Dawson and quickly tried to persuade him to bow out now. He could easily get a taxi home from here.

'Are you insane?' was his answer.

'But we don't know when you'll get another chance to bail out.'

'I'm guessing they are back on the move?' was his reply.

Daniel nodded, at least he'd tried.

'Confirming all subjects have retaken their original places and ignition, ignition; all vehicles are manoeuvring. I'll keep the eyeball,' Jill said.

Daniel and Dawson retook their seats and Daniel started the engine.

Jill came back on through the car's speakers, *'Wagons 3 and 4 are off towards the exit road. The others seem to be waiting with their engines running.'*

They'd split; for whatever reason they'd decided to continue separately.

'We going with 3 and 4?' Jill asked.

'Dead right we are,' Daniel replied.

Daniel risked a sideways glance as he passed the lorry park and could see the diesel exhaust fumes coming from the remaining five wagons. It didn't look like they would be there long. As they re-joined the motorway a few hundred metres behind Jill, Daniel turned to face Dawson. 'Decision time; do we try and get these two pulled en route, or do we wait until they regroup and hit them all at the port?'

'It's only our presumption they will regroup at the port. What if the other five aren't really needed until the return journey?' he replied.

A fair point in line with Daniel's thoughts. 'There is a reason Lonsdale and his mate are in different wagons, so my money is on their money being split between them.'

Dawson nodded.

'So, let's hit these two.'

'Agreed and organising a hit on two will be much easier than on seven,' Dawson said.

It was Daniel's turn to nod.

'And therefore, easier to sell to the real police,' Dawson added. 'But how the hell do we get the police to do it? Your Crimestoppers gag won't work in real time.'

'I know; this is where you come in?'

Dawson turned to face Daniel. 'I thought you might say that.' He then picked up his phone, dialled a number and said, 'Marty, is that you?' He then paused and whispered to Daniel, 'His secretary's picked it up.' A further pause followed and he continued, 'It's George Dawson here, your ex-chief constable, I'm afraid you'll have to disturb his meeting. It's particularly important and time critical that I speak with him.'

Chapter Fifty-three

Bartholomew put his desk phone back in its cradle and wondered what that tosser of a Boy Wonder, dressed up as an assistant chief constable, wanted now. He was forever on Bartholomew's case. He sighed as he stood up and made his way as slowly as he could across the headquarters complex to the main building. And then up to the top floor which was the rarefied space reserved for assistant chiefs and above. He wondered if it was to do with Shirley Lancaster's hilarious draft policy on serious crime reduction. He couldn't have been more wrong. It was an actual operational matter.

Bartholomew sat slack jawed as ACC Marty Mathews quickly gave him an intelligence briefing regarding Bartholomew's investigation into The North End Crew. How seven wagons had left in convoy and that two were now on their own with a Gary Lonsdale - a career criminal - watching over one, and his accomplice, the other. Bartholomew was truly astounded, but also irritated that Billy hadn't already told him. He must have really bottled it. But he was even more bemused as to how the hell Mathews had come by the information. He was about to ask when Mathews waved his hand to silence him as he carried on. Ignorant creep.

He continued to opine several hypotheses as to what the two wagons may be carrying, and how he favoured that they may be loaded with large amounts of money. They might be, and it was an educated guess, but not by Matthews's. That, Bartholomew was sure of. But he felt obliged to not simply agree, and said, 'Or they may be carrying tins of baked beans for all we know.'

'So, you think we should just let them get on with it and hope they don't bring loads of guns or drugs into the country?'

'Or we could wait and pull them on their way back in?'

'But we both know how many things can go wrong if we do that, at least this way we can seriously hurt them. And give you and your team substantial conspiracy evidence, not to mention a money laundering prosecution potential.'

THE CABAL

He was suddenly the SIO now was he, but instead of saying that Bartholomew said, 'Can I ask where you have come by this information?'

'Come, come Superintendent, you should know better than that. Suffice to say it's from a live source and the reporting is in real time.'

If Bartholomew had ever wanted to head butt someone, it was now with this condescending prick, but he knew he had to swallow his aggression and play along. 'And it is detective superintendent' he wanted to say, but instead said, 'OK, sir, give me the details and I'll arrange a motorway pull. We'll say it's some random post Brexit goods check, or suchlike; just in case it's a false call. That way we can prevent a compromise and keep our operation a secret from the criminals if it all goes to rat shit.'

'That sounds like a feasible plan. I've actually already tasked two motorway patrols to catch them up. They just need their final instructions.'

'Where are the wagons now?'

'Last I knew, M6 south just past the Skelmersdale turn off.'

Bartholomew jumped to his feet.

'Where are you going?'

'To cover it from the ground, of course.'

'No superintendent, you'll stay in here with me. I will operate as Gold Commander and pass on any further intel updates I get to you. And you - as Silver Commander - can organise the tactical response from here,' Mathews said, and then slid a piece of paper across his vast desk to Bartholomew. 'Here are the details of the two motorway units. I've already told the sergeant in the lead one that he is Bronze Commander on the ground. And you will need to turn out a search team. There should be one at Skelmersdale nick. I'll also ring my secretary to organise some coffee.'

The head butt option was creeping back onto the table. Bartholomew closed his eyes and counted to five, before picking up his phone and reading the details on the piece of paper, whilst Mathews bored the life out of his secretary.

Chapter Fifty-four

The two wagons kept to a steady fifty miles per hour in the inside lane as they made their way southwards through Lancashire into Greater Manchester. Jill kept the eyeball from two or three cars back, and Daniel maintained a view of Jill from several cars further back still. Dawson came off the phone from his third call to Marty Mathews.

'Right, it's all set up, two motorway units will fall in behind the wagons and then pull them over onto the hard shoulder, they will then escort them to the next services which are at Lymn in Cheshire; at the M6 and M56 interchange.'

Daniel knew the place, it used to be just a truck stop, but welcomed cars now, too. And it was not too big so should prove easier to watch the searches.

'Marty has agreed to keep Bartholomew in his office, but will need a fuller explanation from me after it's over.'

'That's good; stop him interfering in a negative way.'

'I just hope we can still get him,' Dawson said, and then coughed, but far less violently than before. Almost accentuating the fact that Dawson's involvement would become time limited.

'We'll sort this first, and then concentrate on Bartholomew. I take it that no one knows of our involvement here today?'

'Only Marty, and I've promised that we will keep in the shadows once his officers take control.'

Daniel nodded and then accelerated to slip in behind Jill as Dawson rang her and gave her the update. Daniel noted that they had crossed over the East Lancs Road at Haydock; they were now only ten minutes away from the Lymn Interchange. Then flashing blue lights caught Daniel's eye in his mirrors. Two motorway patrol units were making ground fast in the outside lane. They were nearly on them before he heard their air horns. Instinctively, Jill and Daniel pulled back even further allowing several vehicles to now fill the void between them and the rearmost lorry.

THE CABAL

One patrol car pulled in abruptly behind the two wagons and the other chopped them off at the front. Seconds later, the procession of vehicles pulled onto the hard shoulder and Jill and Daniel's cars slid by. As soon as they were past, Jill put her foot down and Daniel matched her. They made as much headway as they could, intent on getting to the services in plenty of time to plot up from where they could watch the search go down. Daniel hadn't arranged this with Jill, he didn't have to; it was instinctive. Any surveillance team would do the same as the real police did the stop and search. A tactic they both had been involved in many times.

As soon as they had both indicated to leave the motorway and head to the service area, Dawson said, 'I promised Marty that we would disappear and leave them to it.'

'What he doesn't know won't hurt him.'

Dawson grinned his agreement.

Daniel followed Jill onto the main parking area and started to look around for a suitable spot to pull over. Then he saw two large vans with the Lancashire Constabulary crest on their sides: the search team. He rang Jill, but before he could speak, she said, 'Clocked them. You plot to their south; I'll cover the north.'

'Agreed,' Daniel said, and then looked around for a suitable place that would give them a good view. But allow them to stay hidden.

A short time later, the two wagons bookended by the two patrol cars, snaked their way onto the service's car park. They headed to the outer edge of it where the two police search vans were waiting. Daniel called Jill so that they could keep an open line of communication. He then took a pair of binoculars out of the glove box and focused in on the scene.

He could see the scumbag Lonsdale and his mate leading the conversations with the police, whilst the two drivers stood back in an obvious subliminal deference to them. God, he hoped they found something, and not just for the obvious reasons, but for Sally. He so wanted to see Lonsdale in handcuffs. How his wife and Melanie would love to see that, too. On the last thought he realised he was too far away to get a decent photo with his smart phone, but he did have a proper camera in the boot, one with a zoom lens. If it looked like good news, he'd get a shot with that. He knew that any arrested person would need transporting in official prisoner vans and that would give him time to set his camera up.

He could see Lonsdale beckon over one of the drivers who proceeded to unlock the rear of the trailer of one wagon and swing open the double doors to reveal the contents. 'Bricks,' he said.

'What?' Dawson asked.

But before he could answer, Jill came over the Bluetooth, *'Pallets full of bleeding breeze blocks.'*

'They must have the cash hidden in there somewhere,' Daniel said; as he watched one of the officers inspect the end pallet, while the sergeant went back to his vehicle and picked up his radio handset. Two minutes later as the sergeant was stood next to his vehicle, Dawson's phone rang.

'It's Marty; I'll put the loudspeaker on,' he said and then took the call.

'I could do with an intel update, George if you have one?' Marty said. *'The first vehicle seems to be full of bricks.'*

Daniel listened as he watched the second trailer's doors being opened to show a similar view as the first one.

'Wait one,' Marty said, and then the line went quiet.

Daniel could see that the was sergeant back on his radio. Then Marty came back via Dawson's phone, *'As apparently is the second vehicle.'*

'The money is in there somewhere, and it's a substantial amount. You've gone this far, Marty, you need to have the search done thoroughly,' Dawson said.

'Yes, but breeze blocks! It's not like lifting a few boxes out and checking the contents. We can see the contents, and they are heavy.'

'Which makes the commodity a perfect one to hide the cash in amongst,' Dawson replied. The line went back on mute and Daniel took the opportunity, 'Nice one, George, good play,' he said. Then a crackle came back on the line.

THE CABAL

'OK, I've just liaised with Silver and he agrees, we may as well be sure. We'll get a forklift truck down there and get the lot out, but I hope you are right; Darlington will have me for breakfast if it's a false shout,' Marty said, and then the line went dead.

'Good of that bent worm Bartholomew to agree with me,' Dawson said.

'If he only knew, it would drive him insane,' Daniel said, and they both burst out laughing. It lifted the tension a little. He then gave Jill a quick update and told her to take a break if she needed it; they were going to be here for some time.

Hoping for the best possible outcome and thinking about Sue, and particularly Melanie again, he got out and went to the boot of the car. In it he had an SLR camera and zoom, but he also had a tripod. He set it all up behind his car which provided line of sight cover. He angled the camera past the edge of the car's rear windscreen and focused in on the scene. It was all set up so he could quickly take a few snaps when it came to handcuffs time. Or so he hoped and prayed it would.

Chapter Fifty-five

A long two hours later, and all was not looking good. The police had brought a fork lift truck in on the back of a low-loader, from God knows where, and painstakingly lifted every pallet from both the wagons. A police dog had been and gone with no tail wagging. And the search team then examined each pallet and Daniel could see them lifting one or two breeze blocks off the top of each pallet which looked to be about 2 metres square in size. He could see them shining torches in between the cracks and down from above, and after each pallet had been looked at, he could see head shakes aimed at the sergeant supervising things. Daniel would have preferred a more thorough search with every breeze block being lifted off, but he knew that this was as good as they could hope for.

Dawson received the occasional call from Marty who was becoming increasingly agitated by the updates he was getting. They were all feeling the pressure build, and Daniel was becoming more worried about Dawson as his coughing fits were coming thick and fast. 'Try and relax, George; if you can. A tight chest is the last thing you need.'

He nodded a reply until his throat cleared and then added, 'Easier said than done.'

The police refilled the first wagon before they started on the second, and although called as a negative search - Daniel was relieved the sergeant refused to let that wagon go until the second lorry had been done. By the look of Lonsdale flaying his arms about, and marching up and down, he was becoming more and more aggravated. Jill had commented that she had noticed one of the PCs taking a backward stance with his hand on his yellow holstered Taser.

As each pallet search resulted in more head shakes, and the number of pallets yet to be checked became fewer, the mood between the three of them crashed deeper and deeper. It was this side of the job which Daniel didn't miss. The number of downers against the number of uppers was always an unfair fraction. And then soon enough, the forklift picked up the last remaining pallet and started to trundle towards the rear of the second wagon. Daniel could see that Lonsdale was in the sergeant's face now, no doubt enjoying his moment of glory.

'The money must have gone across separately, after all,' Dawson said.

'I guess, but what was all that messing about earlier for, and why didn't Lonsdale and his mate travel in the same wagon?' Daniel asked.

'We'll never, know, but it was worth a go. I've just got to try and appease Marty now; which won't be easy. Plus, that bridge going forward is well and truly burned,' Dawson added.

But Daniel stopped listening and concentrated on what he was seeing. All hell seemed to be breaking out in the huddle behind the two wagons. Jill shouted that she would deploy on foot and try to get in closer. The forklift had somehow dropped the last pallet and there were now breeze blocks all over the tarmac, some broken. Lonsdale looked as if he was going nuts about it. The two drivers helped pick them up and were starting to rebuild the pallet like some giant puzzle.

'Christ, the police will get sued for damages now, too. That'll send Marty over the edge,' Dawson said.

Then Daniel saw Jill sneaking down the gap between the wagons with her phone arm outstretched. The little beauty. In all the mayhem no one was looking her way.

Jill's phone rang through the car's Bluetooth, and Daniel could hear - whom he took to be Lonsdale - shouting, swearing, and threatening this and that legal recourse. The sergeant was telling him to calm down or he'd be nicked for breach of the peace. That seemed to make him worse as the volume went up.

Then another voice could be heard above the others, 'What the hell is this?' it said, and everything went quiet as everyone turned to face a search team officer among the broken breeze blocks. He held an oblong object up above his head. Daniel couldn't see what it was but it looked yellow and shiny. The sun bounced off it.

Then Jill came over her open phone line, whispering, *'It's a frigging gold bar.'*

Daniel and Dawson shared a look of incredulity.

Then it all went to mental as the meaning of it sunk in.

The police made a grab for the men. Both drivers were jumped on by the search team and two patrol officers grabbed Lonsdale's mate. The sergeant and the remaining PC were wrestling with Lonsdale. Dawson was straight on the phone to Marty requesting urgent assistance. Daniel concentrated on the battle Lonsdale was having. He witnessed him give the PC a vicious butt to the head which floored the poor officer. He saw Jill break cover and go to his aid. 'You stay here, George, and man the phone,' Daniel said as he started to get out of the car intending to run the hundred metres or so, to help the sergeant who was struggling to get Lonsdale under control.

But as Daniel slammed his car door shut, he could see Lonsdale break away from the sergeant and take flight across the relatively empty car park. Straight towards their car. The sergeant was soon on his heels and was the fitter and faster of the two. Lonsdale was carrying all the gym and steroid enhanced weight that boneheads like him seemed to value, but it was slowing him down.

Daniel realised he could take him out with a side swipe, but needed to surprise him. He quickly ran to the rear of his vehicle and opened the boot lid to give himself cover. He was preparing to launch himself as Lonsdale reached the front of their car. But the sergeant beat him to it and landed on Lonsdale's back, bringing them both down close to the front passenger door.

Then Lonsdale flipped the sergeant onto his back and produced a knife in his right hand. He thrust it into the sergeant's right thigh, and said, 'See if you can run after me now, you filthy pig.'

Daniel knew this was bad as the knife seemed to go in a couple of inches at least, and if it hit the officer's femoral artery it could be fatal. In the next millisecond, Daniel had to decide whether to attack Lonsdale or go to the sergeant's aid. He saw that the blood flow from the wound wasn't firing everywhere. Lonsdale it was then. As the man stood up and arrogantly took a second to

THE CABAL

admire his handiwork, Daniel grabbed a wheel brace from the boot of his car and ran at the back of Lonsdale, still unseen.

Lonsdale spun around and Daniel could see the look of surprise on his face as he flew at him. He could also see that Lonsdale still had the blood-soaked knife in his hand, which he was quickly starting to raise.

Daniel's police training told him that he should not aim a blow at a suspect's head, but at his right shoulder to incapacitate the right arm and therefore the knife hand. But in the split-second that followed, Lonsdale must have moved. Opps. Too late, his swing was on its way.

The wheel brace struck the right-hand side of Lonsdale forehead and his knife clattered to the ground just before he did. He was out cold with a decent looking wound to his head.

Dawson was now out of the car and tending to the injured sergeant. He quickly identified who he and Daniel were.

Daniel stood over Lonsdale and slowly raised the wheel brace once more. Dawson must have seen him as he shouted, 'Don't Daniel, you'd be no better than him.'

He looked at his new friend as the sergeant threw his quick-cuff handcuffs across the ground towards Daniel. They were both right. Daniel shook the moment from his mind and tossed the wheel brace back into the boot of his car. He then set about putting Lonsdale onto his side and into the recovery position, but with his hands suitably handcuffed behind him.

Then Lonsdale stirred, opened his eyes, and said, 'I don't who you are, or what you just hit me with? But you have made a big mistake.'

Daniel leaned towards Lonsdale, but not too close. Just enough to be out of earshot of the sergeant. 'The only mistake I made was not hitting you harder. Oh, and just so you know, that was for Sally.' He then stood up and moved back as Lonsdale looked at Daniel perplexed.

Chapter Fifty-six

As soon as they were able to leave the scene, they did, promising Bartholomew's detectives that they would write and forward their own witness statements as soon as feasible. A detective sergeant who had arrived asked what they were doing there in the first place.

'That's a little tricky to explain right now, and I'm not sure we can incorporate that in our statements,' Daniel had said.

'Well, it's a question that I'll still need an answer to at some stage,' the detective sergeant added.

Daniel nodded and then asked, 'Where's your boss, I'd have thought he'd be here?'

'He's leading a team to this firm's haulage yard to nick the main player,' the detective sergeant answered.

'Toe Jam?'

'Who?' the detective sergeant said, and then a second later laughed.

'Yeah, that's right, Tommy Johnson is now up to his armpits in it,' he answered before he was called away by one of his team.

As soon as he was out of earshot, Daniel said, 'Just as I worried would happen.'

'What,' asked Jill, who had now joined them.

'Bar-bastard-tholomew will now be trouncing around as the hero he isn't. Lording himself over anyone and everyone.'

'Yeah, but he can't claim this success; we are the ones who brought down the North End Crew. Three retired cops with no resources and no equipment. Not Bartholomew and his entire serious crime dept. Fact. And that can't be airbrushed out as our evidence here on this car park is crucial,' she said.

And she was right.

'But it still means that the bent snake gets away with all his sharp practices and wrongdoing, and it makes me sick,' Dawson said.

'Look, we've done good here today. Incredibly good; and Bartholomew will come. Mark my words,' Daniel said.

THE CABAL

'How?' Dawson asked.

'No idea. But we'll find a way,' Daniel said, but he wasn't overly convinced by his own words.

Then to change the subject, he suggested that they sit down and write up some jointly agreed notes which would act as a surveillance log; a joint pocketbook from which they could draw their statements. And thereafter use the notes to refresh their memories in the witness box. All agreed and they elected to do it from the comfort of the service area café, with some much-needed sustenance to accompany them.

By the time they had finished, all the prisoners had been taken away in vans and the wagons were being driven off the car park by HGV trained motorway cops. They would be taken to police headquarters where every breeze block would be broken and searched properly. Daniel was hopeful it would provide a healthy return on the effort. No one would go to all this trouble to hide one solitary bar of gold. The three agreed to meet up the following day at Daniel's where they could finish the admin. Jill shot off and Daniel said he would take Dawson back to the yard to reclaim his motor.

En route back Dawson worked the phone taking several calls from a mightily relieved Marty Mathews; things were getting better and better. Johnson had been nicked at the yard in possession of his mobile phone, with which he'd had several calls to and from Lonsdale during the day. And then the cherry on the cake came in. The security guard at the forensic lab raid had earlier recovered consciousness. He reported that his attacker - and the man that pulled him away - had left him for dead and made their escape in a red van. He had still, just, been conscious as they fled, and had risked opening his eyes as they reached the van. The third man must have already been in the driver's seat as the engine cracked up as they arrived.

Both his attacker and the second guy pulled off their masks before jumping in the front of the vehicle. It was parked next to a sodium vapour streetlamp so the guard had got a clear, if only brief, glimpse of both men. He was confident he would pick them out in any line up. Any identification would face a host of challenges by defence lawyers down the road, but he said he was prepared for that. He had already given the Cheshire detectives a detailed description of them both. He described seeing the z-shaped scar on the face of the man who had pulled his attacker away. And he also heard the z-scarred man refer to his attacker as 'boss' and 'Tommy'.

When Marty told Dawson this over the car's Bluetooth, a joint cheer went up in the motor.

But Dawson was still a little bitter-sweet, as when the call ended, he said, 'Bartholomew will be loving the glory of this, too.'

And Daniel had no doubt that he would.

Then Marty rang back to say that he would need to see Dawson face-to-face when the dust settled to discuss his sensitive concerns. They agreed to arrange something in a few days' time and then ended the call. This seemed to lift Dawson's mood.

'At least he will listen to me in a way the new chief - Darlington - won't.'

'That's a start,' Daniel answered, but wondered if it would lead to anything concrete.

They soon neared the area where the haulage yard is, and Daniel drove past the road he should have taken. He kept driving northwards.

'You've missed the turning,' Dawson said.

'I know. We'll get your car in a bit. We have an errand to run first.'

Dawson looked strangely at Daniel, who kept his gaze fixed on the road in front.

'What errand?'

'We are going via the Royal Preston Hospital, where I'm going to take you to the Oncology Unit, where you can make an appointment to start your treatment.'

'Honestly, Daniel, there's no need. I'll ring tomorrow.'

'There's every need, as no you won't.'

'We're not finished here.'

'I think we are; for now. Bartholomew's time will come.'

'But how? Now the whole North End Crew are locked up, our opportunities to catch him bending the rules are gone.'

'What about Marty's offer to sit down and hear you out?'

'Politeness, I've nothing firm to give him.'

'But it might lead to something.'

'No, it won't.'

Daniel suspected that he was right, but before he could answer, Dawson had a further coughing session which was excellently timed in support of Daniel's detour. He waited until the poor man recovered before he added, 'Men like Bartholomew don't quit while they are ahead; they are too arrogant. His time will come. Now let's try and put a smile back on your wife's face.'

Dawson put his hands up in surrender as Daniel indicated to turn into the hospital grounds.

Chapter Fifty-seven

Bartholomew was frustrated; angry even at Boy Wonder's refusal to say from whom he was getting his intelligence. But by virtue of the many hushed telephone conversations he was having, it clearly was a live feed. But he soon forgot about all that when the job went well. Initially, he was waiting to give it to the ACC large when it appeared that the wagons were empty. And he could see the tension in the man rise until the last pallet dropped its load. What were the chances of that. And as chuffed as he was by the outcome, he was furious that he would not be able to claim all the credit for it. Exacerbated that it was Boy Wonder's intel which had led to it. He must be getting it from one of the drivers, he mused. By how the hell was an ACC in receipt of a live intel feed? It didn't make sense. God, he missed Merson, as head of intelligence he would have had all the answers.

But forgetting his ego for a moment, he had to take the gift that had been given. He could hopefully wrap up all the North End Crew, and would have the ultimate pleasure in nicking Tommy Johnson. He left the Boy Wonder during a further clandestine phone call, and quickly gathered a team to hit the haulage yard.

En route he took a call from his main office, that bitch of a DI in Cheshire had been on, the injured guard from the lab raid had described his attackers. It was Johnson, Lonsdale, and the other goon. He'd keep that up his sleeve for now. Cheshire could wait their turn to have them. As good as the news was, he'd waited too long to wipe the smile from Johnson's face to let anyone else have first dibs. But it was a success which he could claim, as and when the Cheshire lot got to put their case to them. It riled him that the DI hadn't rung him directly with the news. Cheeky bitch. He'd told her at the outset that his targets were the top suspects, but she'd known better of course. Known better: known nowt.

Johnson was sat at what had been Piper's desk in the transport office at the yard. And the thick scumbag still had his own mobile phone on him. The one he'd used to ring Lonsdale all day

THE CABAL

with. Bartholomew let his junior detectives make the arrest, he just stood back and watched, all regal-like. Enjoying the scene. Johnson just glared at him with the utmost hatred, and as he was walked past Bartholomew, he resisted his escort to pause by him. Bartholomew nodded at the escorting officer to give him a second.

Johnson leaned in and spoke softly, 'Why? Why such determination?'

'Because you are a top criminal at the head of Lancashire's worst organised crime group.'

'No, it's more than that. Almost personal.'

'OK, it is personal,' Bartholomew said, and added, 'you remember mowing down two harmless old ladies a couple of years ago?'

'I remember the incident, but I mowed no one down.'

'Yes, you did; one was my aunt and the other was my mother.'

Johnson didn't answer straight away, he clearly didn't know this; why would he. But then a smile spread across his face. Bartholomew so wanted to punch him, but knew that too many eyes were on them, so instead said, 'We'll see who is smiling when you are banged up for ten or twenty years.'

'Prove what you can against me regarding my business, but you'll never pin that one on me, as I didn't do it.'

Bartholomew knew it was useless engaging with the man further and nodded to the escorting detective to lead him away, which he did. But before Johnson was out of earshot, he turned to look back at Bartholomew, still wearing that sickening smile and shouted, 'I heard that the driver of that job was the "Top Man" of a local firm. And that wasn't me. I know who it was though, and you'll never ever find out, let alone prove it.'

The escort pulled Johnson's arm and he was soon out of view as he was led towards a waiting police van outside. Bartholomew stood in the office and mused over what had just been said. Then it hit him.

Piper.

It had been Piper all along. He'd fit up the right man without realising it. How could he have been so stupid? Piper had not been the 'Top Man', but everyone had thought it. They were supposed to think it. Johnson had engineered it that way. The addict he had beaten the information from had told the truth, or what he believed the truth to be. Bartholomew had fitted up Piper to identify the 'Top Man'; not to get to the head of the North End Crew, but to get the animal who killed his mother. And now Piper was running free and he could do nothing about it. He erupted into a fit of white-hot rage and started kicking the desk and smashing what was on it with his fists until one of his detectives rushed in with a bemused look on his face and stopped him.

THE CABAL

Chapter Fifty-eight

The arrests were all over the news channels for the next few days, the job could not have gone any sweeter. According to Marty - via Dawson - the bar of gold was worth forty grand, and when all the breeze blocks had been smashed open, they had recovered two hundred of them. Total value, eight million. Enquires were ongoing as to where it had all come from.

The security guard had done a video identification parade and picked out both Tommy Johnson and Gary Lonsdale. So, charges were awaiting them for the raid on the lab, assault, and conspiracy charges here. Daniel had asked Dawson how they had found another eleven stooges on the system with a z-shaped scar on their faces for the ID parade.

'They couldn't,' he told him over the phone, 'so they superimposed the scar on them, including overwriting the real z-shaped scar on Lonsdale so they all looked the same.'

'That'll be a feast for the defence lawyers to chew on in court,' he'd replied.

'No doubt, but that will be the least of their troubles,' Dawson added.

'How come?'

'Apparently, the witness who saw the two men tightly walking Merson from his home on the night of his death, have also picked out Lonsdale and his mate; so further charges await them too. Marty says the SIO is confident that Johnson is behind that as head of the crew, so hopefully, loyalty will fly out of the widow when they get hit with that.'

'All good then?' Daniel had said, which prompted Dawson to complain about Bartholomew - and his assistants - still roaming scot-free. Then he came to the real reason for the call; he was meeting Marty to discuss his Bartholomew issues tomorrow and wanted Daniel to accompany him. Daniel agreed but said he had an errand to run first.

He went to see Melanie first thing the next day to give her the update on Lonsdale, and show her the photos he'd managed to take. Lonsdale may not be facing charges relating to Sally's overdose, but justice was to be done. Especially, if he was convicted for Merson's manslaughter, or for any part in it; he'd get an exceedingly long sentence. There had been a lot of tears, many of relief as well as sadness, and Melanie said she felt a huge weight start to ease from her shoulders. They'd got Capone, Scarface, the z-scarred dealer; or Lonsdale as they now knew him as, which was always their mission.

Then he drove to police headquarters and was now sat in an anteroom with Dawson. He hadn't been there long before Marty's secretary appeared and invited them both in.

Once seated, Marty opened with, 'Firstly, can I thank you for all you have done, and please pass on my gratitude to Jill, too.'

Daniel and Dawson nodded.

'I understand where your interest came from, Daniel, and please pass on my condolences to your sister-in-law,' Marty started, before pausing to take a sip of coffee. Daniel nodded again. 'But your involvement is more of a mystery,' he said, turning to face Dawson.

'I'm guessing Darlington never shared in detail my concerns with you?'

It was time for Marty to shake his head, and Dawson then opened up about his fears re the true depth of Bartholomew's corruption. And that he had coerced Merson, Winstanley and Lancaster, too. But he had no real evidence.

When he'd finished, Marty sat back in his chair and whistled before he said, 'Winstanley, Merson, and Lancaster?'

'Yes, it's a bloody Cabal, I tell you,' Dawson said. 'A bloody Cabal.'

But Daniel picked up that Marty had not mentioned Bartholomew in his reply. Perhaps the others were a greater surprise. Then it hit him. He leaned forward and said, 'You knew about the depths of Bartholomew's corruption, didn't you?'

Marty grinned, and said, 'Let me first tell you about the gold.'

'I was going to ask you about that.'

THE CABAL

'Do you remember a huge heist of gold bullion in London a few months ago, the press nicknamed it "Brinks Mat II" after the gold robbery at Heathrow in 1983 when 26 million pounds worth of bullion and gems were nicked?'

Both nodded.

'Well, this job was eight and a half mill and all the bars had a marking which identified them. The two hundred bars we recovered from the breeze blocks are from that job. It just leaves twelve bars outstanding. The Met are on cloud nine and a team are on their way up here to interview our targets.'

'My God, you don't think Johnson and his crew did that job, do you?' Dawson asked.

'Not at all. The Met have suspects, but little evidence. Their take is that our villains were assisting in fencing it for them, probably for a healthy commission. Once they face being charged with the initial robbery, the Met are confident they'll soon take a handling charge, but will have to name names first.'

'That explains why all seven wagons tried to travel in convoy; so, they could give cover to the middle two carrying the goodies,' Daniel said.

'Exactly. But I have even better news,' Marty said.

Both Daniel and Dawson leaned in even closer.

'Five of the missing twelve bars have turned up with gold dealers all around the country.'

'How come?' Daniel asked.

'Not sure, maybe the robbers paid someone off with them and they have been trying to launder them, or perhaps they intended to try and launder the lot this way, a bit at a time, until our targets became involved. The current hypothesis is that the two hundred were being taken abroad to be smelted, and could be done in several countries across several jurisdictions once on mainland Europe,' Marty added.

It made sense.

'The robbers must not have been aware of the identifying marks on the bars,' Dawson added.

'Possibly not. Apparently, they are subtle and you have to know where to look. But it is vital as it has turned out,' Marty said. 'But the really good news is that since the post arrest publicity we have been contacted by a dealer in Blackpool who says she bought one of the bars.'

'How very interesting?' Daniel said.

'Has she been spoken to?' Dawson asked.

'Yes. And she has provided details of who sold it to her.'

Toe Jam, it must be, Daniel thought, probably his payment, or part payment for shifting the main load of gold.

'Johnson?' Dawson asked.

Marty ignored the question and said, 'The bar has also been identified as having come through a dealer's hands in Preston first. We are still trying to ascertain how he came by it. But it could have come from anywhere. These people buy and sell nationally.'

Dawson and Daniel exchanged looks. Daniel had no idea what this meant.

'The Preston dealer sold the bar to a customer, and the Blackpool dealer bought the bar, but from a different person,' Marty added, and then started grinning again. Then he said, 'The customer at Preston was a certain Johnny Piper.'

Daniel exchanged a further look with Dawson, but one of incredulity, as the words sank in.

Dawson shouted, 'Please tell me that the seller at Blackpool is the person I'm willing it to be?'

'Peter Bartholomew. He signed for the cash, and is on the shop's CCTV handing over the bar, which was also photographed in close-up showing the identifying marks with Bartholomew next to it, though he would have been unaware.'

'That means we've got him, at last I've been proved right,' Dawson said as tears welled up in his eyes.

They all sat in silence for a moment until Marty broke it. 'He's being arrested as we speak; I wanted you to hear it from me first. But I didn't know about the others. We'll get Winstanley and Lancaster in and play them off against Bartholomew. But can you give me anything to pass on to the team dealing, regarding them?'

THE CABAL

Dawson then filled Marty in with what Professor Cummings had told him about the money exhibit and Winstanley's attempts to cover the facts up. About her investigations into Bartholomew which all led to nothing, all of which would require going back over. Dawson said he was in no doubt now, that hidden and ignored evidence would abound there. He also mentioned how Lancaster could have only been the one who leaked information he had shared with her, to Bartholomew. There was clearly much to do.

Marty said that Bartholomew was absolutely knackered - evidentially. And he felt confident they would amass enough against Winstanley and Lancaster for misconduct in public office offences at the very least. As misguided instruments of Bartholomew, Marty said he expected them to open up pretty quickly. Both Daniel and Dawson agreed.

'I wonder why he was so driven to nick Piper, and then Johnson, by whatever means he could, most of it corruptly?' Dawson asked as they stood to leave.

'I guess we may never know,' Marty answered.

Both men left the ACC's office as if they were walking on air. They remained silent until they were outside the main entrance.

'I guess we've both achieved our objectives,' Daniel said.

'I guess we have,' Dawson replied, and then added, 'but just think: if it hadn't been for that gold bar, Bartholomew would not have been brought down.'

'And had we not brought down the wagon train, there would have been no publicity, and therefore no dealers would have double-checked their stock,' Daniel added.

Dawson nodded.

'And you know what else it means?' Daniel said.

'What?'

'It means that now you can concentrate on beating this cancer. You've beaten corruption at the very highest level, so you can beat this. And I'll be with you all the way,' Daniel said, as he felt tears joining those that Dawson had shown earlier, which were also making a reappearance once more.

He put his arm on his former chief constable's - and new friend's - shoulder. 'But first, I think we've earned a dinnertime pint.' Daniel felt good as he saw a warm smile break out on Dawson's face.

'Let's invite Jill, too. Plus, it's time I levelled with her.'

Daniel nodded and both men headed towards their cars.

The End.

Printed in Great Britain
by Amazon